What readers are saying about previous books by

PEGGY STOKS:

"Heart-wrenching, heartwarming, honest and pure."
—Johanna Asmi, Washington

"Ministered much to my soul. So encouraging, so real."
—Twila Simonson, Minnesota

"Oh, how I wished it had been longer! I don't ever recall reading another book that has held my attention like this one."
—Edna L. Bell Winland, Ohio

"Written from the heart, written beautifully. Captivating and real, and I believed every moment."
—Terri Gross, Minnesota

"I laughed, I cried, I rejoiced. It was wonderful."
—Sattie Jo-Ann Trusiak, Pennsylvania

"Couldn't wait to get to the end—then I was disappointed it was over."
—Ruth Bennett, Minnesota

"You can't stop now—you must write another book!"
—Pat Doocy, Minnesota

"Thank you so much for the great entertainment you have given me this week!"
—Lee Ann Cline, Missouri

HEART QUEST®

HeartQuest brings you romantic fiction
with a foundation of biblical truth.
Adventure, mystery, intrigue, and suspense
mingle in these heartwarming stories of
men and women of faith striving to build
a love that will last a lifetime.

May HeartQuest books sweep you
into the arms of God, who longs for you
and pursues you always.

Olivia's Touch

PEGGY STOKS

HEART
QUEST®

Romance fiction from
Tyndale House Publishers, Inc.
WHEATON, ILLINOIS

Visit Tyndale's exciting Web site at www.tyndale.com

Check out the latest about HeartQuest Books at www.heartquest-romances.com

Heart Quest is a registered trademark of Tyndale House Publishers, Inc.

Designed by Jackie Noe

Unless otherwise indicated, Scripture quotations are taken from the *Holy Bible*, King James Version.

Library of Congress Cataloging-in-Publication Data

Stoks, Peggy.
  Olivia's touch / Peggy Stoks.
    p. cm. — (Abounding love ; bk. 1)
    ISBN 0-8423-1942-5 (sc)
    1. Women healers—Colorado—Fiction. 2. Colorado—Fiction. I. Title.

PS3569.T62237 O45 2000
813′.54—dc21   99-089359

Printed in the United States of America

05   04   03   02   01   00
9   8   7   6   5   4   3   2   1

For Paula McGrew
A friend with faith
A friend who loves at all times

Acknowledgments

The idea for *Olivia's Touch* was born about six years ago. However, our youngest daughter was born not long afterward, and Miss Olivia Plummer took a backseat to Miss Rachel Stoks for quite some time.

First and foremost, I would like to thank God for the innumerable blessings he has rained down upon our family. I consider Jeff and the girls, my parents and brother, my extended family, each one of my friends, and the wonderful faith community at the Church of Saint Paul among the best of those blessings.

Once again, Elaine Challacombe and Stacie Traill of the University of Minnesota's Wangensteen Historical Library lent invaluable assistance as they dug up old medical books, answered questions, and ran off copy after copy for me. My heartfelt thanks to you both. I'm sure I must owe you another few loaves of banana bread.

To the mother hens at the Centennial Branch of the Anoka County Library goes my gratitude, as well. Your smiles and friendliness and support keep me going through every project, and I am amazed I haven't burned you out with my endless book requests and ILLs.

I am also in debt to Dr. Garry Peterson, Hennepin County Medical Examiner, for the information and suggestions he provided. With all your plotting ideas, Dr. Peterson, I think you need to write a series of your own! My gratitude goes, too, to Dr. Douglas Drake for his patience in answering my questions about hand injuries and nerve damage.

Special thanks to Fr. Bob Bedard and Fr. Sean Wenger of the Companions of the Cross in Ottawa, Ontario, for their teachings on wisdom and the Lord's will. May your community and your mission be blessed beyond your wildest dreams. In addition, I am obliged to Jeff Cavins and his excellent Bible Timeline workshop which, for me, shed a great deal of light on the covenantal structure of salvation history.

I would like to acknowledge the Colorado Historical Society, the Colorado Railroad Museum, the Colorado Medical Society, and the Colorado Board of Medical Examiners for assistance rendered. A special thanks goes to Ms. Shannel Lorance for her willingness to share her knowledge and love of pioneer women.

Without the proofreading of Paula McGrew and Mary Epps, I would no doubt turn in manuscripts in much worse shape. And if not for Char Swanson's translation, I would have been up a creek, because the information about Auguste Tardieu's findings in *Manuel Complet de Médecine Légal* was recorded solely in French. *No hablo Francés. Ni Español tampoco.*

Finally, to my agent, Claudia Cross, and to the entire HeartQuest team at Tyndale House Publishers: my deepest thanks. Me, an author?

Sometimes I think I must be in the middle of a dream.

Chapter 1

Tristan, Colorado ❧ *Autumn 1880*

"Miss Olivia! Miss Olivia! It's the new doctor, ma'am, he needs you!"

Blacksmith Haskell Jarvis was winded from his breakneck ride from town. Both he and his Percheron sent great clouds of steam billowing into the chilly morning, while the neighboring Connally dog continued to bark at the disturbance.

"He needs me? For what?" Any and all charitable thoughts Olivia Plummer had tried to muster toward Tristan's new medical doctor vanished in an instant. Dressed in his Boston finery, Harvard-educated Dr. Ethan Gray had caused nothing but trouble since his arrival earlier in the week, challenging her healing practice with a vehemence that made her head spin. Why, within minutes of his arrival, Dr. Gray had insisted on seeing her credentials, when all she'd done was set poor Claude Harker's broken leg. And then, in front of a large number of her townspeople, he'd ordered Marshal Irvin Briggs to arrest her—for practicing medicine without a license. *The nerve of the man*, she thought angrily.

Olivia—and her granny, Adeline Esmond, before her—had always taken her long hours and exhausting workload seriously. Delivering babies, mixing concoctions, nursing the sick, and laying out the dead were as much a part of Olivia's life as the simple act of breathing.

Now this stranger had come and threatened all that.

"He don't . . . *want* your help, ma'am," the plainspoken blacksmith emphasized sympathetically, as if he had been following her train of thought, "but he *needs* it real bad. His hand's cut wide open, and he's makin' quite a puddle."

"The wound is that severe?"

"Yes, ma'am."

At the news, her aggravation cooled. Her agitated feelings toward the tall, arrogant newcomer would have to wait. Mentally, she ran through the supplies in her bag, making a note to take extra rolls of the linen sponges she and young Susan Connally had boiled clean last week. She carried a supply of needles and silk thread wherever she went, for sewing people's cuts and wounds was something she did with frequency.

"Give me a few moments to get what I need, Mr. Jarvis. Would you saddle Pete for me?"

"Eh," he said, shaking his head, "I think you'd better just ride with me, Miss Olivia. The doctor . . . he wasn't lookin' too good."

"I'll hurry," she called over her shoulder, already reaching for what she needed.

It seemed like no time at all before Haskell Jarvis's powerful horse whisked them the three-quarter mile from Olivia's snug cabin to the main street of their little northeastern Colorado prairie town. Over the years, Olivia had been transported in more precarious and uncomfortable positions than the one in which she now rode, but even so, she held tightly to the blacksmith's coat. Her saddlebag had been secured by the man intent on delivering her in record time.

As they rounded the corner of Walnut Street, Olivia saw that outside the doctor's building—formerly Elmer Beverly's insurance agency—a group of townsmen engaged in hushed, intent conversation. A lone wagon, half loaded with boxes and tarp-covered items, sat in the street, ignored.

"Miss Olivia!" The serious-minded attorney, Warren Hawley, broke away from the group of men and hailed her arrival. His movements were hasty, his manner nervous. "The tailgate . . . it just gave way and almost lopped off Dr. Gray's hand. I told him we'd unload his things for him, but he insisted on helping . . . and now . . ."

No doubt the attorney's pride at having engaged such a finely educated physician to care for the people of their town had been dealt a serious blow by this turn of events. That he felt responsible for the accident was plain to see, and in his haste to help her dismount from the giant beast, he nearly caused her injury as well.

"Sorry, ma'am," he apologized in misery after she'd caught her balance. "This morning has not been good at all." Taking a deep breath, he looked down at his feet. "And after what happened in town the other day, I didn't know if you'd come."

"I've never chosen those I'll tend and those I won't, Mr. Hawley," she replied with some effort, thinking of the unpleasant interchange she'd had with the new physician upon his arrival. "You should know by now that if someone needs help, they'll get my best efforts. The question is, will Dr. Gray accept my care?"

The attorney's words, already rapid, accelerated, as did his nervousness. His voice dropped, meant for her ears alone. "You're every bit as good a healer as your Granny Esmond was, Olivia, and everyone in Tristan is mighty grateful for the hard work you do for us. I've been running advertisements for doctors in Eastern papers for years—you know that. No one ever expected we'd actually get a taker."

Olivia nodded while the blacksmith handed her the saddlebag. Hawley's words were true enough, she knew, yet the warm greeting she had anticipated giving Dr. Gray had been thrown back in her face in the midst of his welcoming ceremony . . . before the population of the entire town. Deep in her heart, she had been naive enough to hope for a peaceful coexistence, perhaps even some type of partnership, with the new physician.

"That you, Livvie?" Marshal Briggs's voice boomed from inside the open door of Dr. Gray's office. "Bring your stitchin' and get on in here!"

Hurrying up the blood-splattered stairs into the building, she noticed that counters and shelves lined walls that had previously been bare, but there was no time to investigate the boxes and fascinating items covering their surfaces.

"Back here," Briggs said, motioning from the hallway at the rear wall of the large front room. "We got him up on the table for you."

The marshal—a man in his early thirties with the bluster of a bear but who, in truth, reminded Olivia of an overgrown bear cub—led her to what she guessed was a modern examination room. Momentarily, she marveled at its refinement and the amount of equipment. Had she known the doctor was so well stocked, she needn't have bothered bringing her bag.

Her patient lay upon a grand and most complicated-looking table of padded leather. With the turn of a wheel or twist of a lever, it appeared, adjustments could be made to raise or lower any part of a person's body. Olivia had never seen such a piece of engineering and couldn't fathom how much coin it must have taken to purchase.

Dr. Ethan Gray's face was bleached of color, but his dark eyes remained sharp. Dermot Johnson, Tristan's deputy marshal, held a makeshift tourniquet over the affected wrist with one hand and a wad of clean cotton cloth over the doctor's hand with the other.

"Thank goodness you're here, Miss Olivia." The deputy's expression of relief was profound. Beneath his stylish forelock, his face was nearly as pale as the wounded man's.

"Thank you, Mr. Johnson. You have done the doctor a great service, indeed," she praised the quiet deputy, not eager to reenter conversation with the physician. The bleeding was well controlled at present, a good sign.

"I didn't . . . well, he told me what to do, ma'am."

"And you did well. Would you be so kind as to fetch me

some boiled water? I'll take over for you." Setting down her bag, she slipped into the seat vacated by the young lawman. Without glancing up, she knew Dr. Gray's brown eyes took in her every movement.

"You must know I don't want you here," the physician said, but with less vigor than at their first meeting.

"I'm sure not," she agreed mildly, determined to do her job and get back home as quickly as possible. After delivering Cora Skeever of her first baby during the wee hours, she hadn't returned home until nearly first light. Gently she removed the bloodstained cloth from his palm and loosened the tourniquet a small bit.

"What are you—ow! What . . . do you think . . . you're . . . doing?" The weak but supercilious demand came as she studied the injury. Blood welled up from the end of the wound over his thumb; the cut appeared to be much deeper and more jagged than the remainder of the slice running diagonally across the back of his hand.

"Merely seeing to your injury," she replied, periodically blotting the flow of blood while she assessed how she might best repair the splayed edges of flesh.

"God help me." He closed his eyes, looking as though he was restraining himself from saying more.

"He will if you ask. And if you don't, I'll ask him for you." She looked full into the doctor's face, but his eyes remained closed and he shook his head.

Taking the opportunity to study his countenance, she grudgingly decided he was nice-looking enough . . . and much less threatening without that crackling, intelligent gaze trained upon her. A neat, trimmed blond mustache complemented a slightly crooked nose, arched brows, and thick blond hair. Her gaze dipped, and she took in a strong-looking set of shoulders. A few golden strands of hair escaped from the loosened collar of his white shirt.

"She heals. She prays. She walks on water."

Glancing up, she saw Dr. Gray's gaze upon her and she flushed.

"I . . . beg your pardon?" In addition to belittling her practice, he now mocked her faith? Granny Esmond had taught her that not praying for those she tended was doing only half a job.

"I have to admit, you've pulled the wool over everyone's eyes. I've heard nothing but your praises sung since I arrived."

"Why are you so hostile toward me?" Renewed anger tightened her voice.

"Because I've spent my entire career fighting people like you—" His body strained upward as he tried to make his point.

"People like me? You don't even know me!"

"I knew dozens like you in Boston. Poorly trained. Illiterate. Incompetent. The sick and wounded deserve better than to—"

"Shall we just call it a day then?" she interrupted, fury churning in the base of her stomach. Locking her gaze with his, she fought a childish desire to shout that she could too read. Never before had she met anyone who had spoken to her in such a way.

"That's about enough, you two," Briggs barked from the doorway, bearing a steaming pot of water. "Gray, as I see it, you ain't got much of a choice about matters. Either Miss Olivia sews you up or I do."

Olivia remained silent, waiting for the doctor's reply, the thrumming of her pulse loud in her ears.

Breaking eye contact with her, Dr. Gray stared at the ceiling. "As I seem to be left with no choice, you may as well go ahead."

"I was hopin' all that book learnin' translated to good sense." Briggs poured water from the heavy pot into a basin. "I'll keep the hot water comin', Livvie," he added on his way out the door. "I know how much you like." A moment later, she heard the clatter of the stove being stoked.

"Dr. Gray," Olivia said, addressing her patient, "are you able to hold the dressing over your hand while I prepare my things?"

"For what purpose do you use so much boiled water?" came the challenging response. "And just what 'things' do you intend to use?" In one motion, he pushed himself upright. With his left hand, he took hold of the cloth over his right, flinching at the movement. "Slide that table over here in front of me."

It shouldn't surprise her that he hadn't said please. Without a word, Olivia did as he asked, incredulous that he'd asked her for what purpose she used boiled water. Did the man know nothing of cleanliness? Granny Esmond had taught her to boil everything she used. She scanned his general appearance. Other than the mess the blood had made, he didn't seem ill kempt or carry a bad odor.

Working quickly, she rolled up her sleeves. No sense in prolonging this experience; the sooner it was over, the better. Spreading out the contents of her saddlebag on the table her patient had just vacated, she selected the items she would use, at the same time sensing Dr. Gray's hawklike vigilance.

"What are you doing now?"

She bit back an exasperated sigh. "Washing my hands. See?" As she moved toward the basin of water, she held aloft the bar of strong soap that was always found with her belongings. Dirt and blood might have their place in Boston sickrooms, but not here in Tristan. Granny Esmond had insisted on cleanliness at all times, especially with respect to open wounds and child-bearing.

"Oh." He sounded disgruntled. "Well, you'll need carbolic acid solution. In that cupboard over there—"

"I brought my own."

"You . . . brought your own?"

"Isn't that what I just said?" There was only so much provocation she could bear. Whirling to face him, she intended to give him a piece of her mind. But when her gaze lit upon the blond-haired stranger, her words of criticism died upon her lips. She saw a manly, determined face, but behind the features she read both pain and fear.

Shame on you, Olivia, she berated herself, turning back to her hand-washing. *As obnoxious as he's been, he's still a man the Lord has placed in your hands for healing. There will be another day for having words with him. Today is a day to hold your tongue . . . and your temper.*

"Sewing flesh isn't the same as stitching a sampler, you know." Choosing not to follow up on his previous offensive, he attacked from a new direction.

Nor is it a whole lot different, Doctor. "Do you mind if I use this small basin here?" she asked, not waiting for an answer. She dipped it into the steaming water and moistened one of her clean linens. "I prefer quilting," she remarked, stepping over to her patient. After letting the cloth cool slightly, she began washing blood from his arm.

"Same difference."

What would he know? Suppressing another sigh, she worked in silence, determined not to let his jibes get to her. Having had the last word, the physician was also content to remain quiet. Once his arm was cleansed, she liberally applied carbolic acid solution from his elbow to his fingertips. Needle, silk, forceps, and scissors followed in carbolic as well. Placing a clean towel beneath his hand, she sat down opposite her patient and prepared to work.

"Wait," he commanded, studying the wound. He pointed with his left index finger. "Start on the deep end, right here."

She nodded, taking heart from the fact that she had already decided to begin at that same place. It also had not escaped her attention that he had moved from the opinion that she would not lay a finger on him to accepting that she would be the one repairing his injury. Sponging the blood continuing to well up from the area, she glanced at him before making the first stitch.

"Just suture, Miss Plummer. If anything for pain needs to be administered, it will be of my choosing and my prescription."

Obedient to a fault, Olivia sent the curved needle on its course. Down, in, across, up. She heard his sharp intake of air as the instrument exited his flesh, trailing its runner of silk thread. In a deft set of movements, she tied the knot, cut the stitch, and blotted the wound. Repeating the process twice more, she effected good control over the worst of the oozing.

"Time to loosen the tourniquet a bit more. How are you holding up, Dr. Gray?" she inquired, taking a moment to check his expression. She couldn't have been more surprised at his last several seconds of silence.

"I'm . . . I'm fine." His voice sounded hoarse, as though it were stuck in his throat, and a sheen of perspiration coated his face. Despite this, he had the vigor to complain. "You tie your sutures all wrong. I'll be lucky if they hold. If you were my student, I'd make you do them over."

"Why, I'd be happy to do them over." Picking up the scissors, she called his bluff. "It'll take me just a moment to cut these out."

"No . . . no! Those first three will do, I suppose, but I want you to follow my instructions for the next."

Though the motions weren't second nature, Olivia was surprised at how easily she was able to tie the next several sutures using Dr. Gray's technique. His instructions were distinct and simple to follow, which was remarkable given that the stitchery was being performed upon his person.

"Why did you come to Tristan?" she asked, once the greater portion of the wound was closed.

"Right this minute, I couldn't give you one good reason."

"Not even one?" Her lips curved ruefully at his assertion. "You realize that, for weeks now, people have been wondering why a highfalutin Boston medical doctor would want to come to our town. Denver and Leadville have been drawing all kinds, understandably, but not small towns. Most wagers were that you were putting out to pasture."

His eyes widened at her candor; then he sighed. "I can assure you I have no intentions of grazing, Miss Plummer. I came here because I wanted to. . . . What was your bet?"

"My bet?"

"About me. Did you think me deaf, blind, and toothless, as well?"

"I . . . didn't give your age much thought. I was more concerned with how we would—"

"Well, well, well. If it ain't some morning. Mortal enemies cozied right up together," announced Marshal Briggs, who also doubled as Tristan's newspaper publisher. As he stood in the doorway, running his fingers over his chin, Olivia knew he was thinking up cover lines. His use of the English language, as common as the everyday man's when he was upset or agitated, could at other times be a schoolmarm's delight. "It's been a strange few days. To my way of thinking, you two have raised the biggest uproar in this little town ever since . . . ever since I don't know when. But you know what?"

"What's that, Marshal?" Olivia asked, not comfortable with the speculative look on the lawman's face. He strode over to the table and studied Dr. Gray's hand.

"Folks are all up in arms about 'Miss Olivia and Dr. Gray,' and I'm going to have an extra page of newsprint this week to prove it. Now correct me if I'm wrong: you aren't going to be doing much of anything with that hand out of commission, are you, Doc?"

"I'm sure I can—"

"And you've been wanting to see more of the townspeople . . . get yourself established?"

"Yes, but—"

"Now, pretend you're the marshal, and one day, out of the blue, your peaceful town has been turned on its ear. It's gotten so bad that a man can't even step foot out his door without someone spouting one opinion or another. Dr. Gray this. Miss Olivia that. Then one morning you walk into a room and see the answer to all your problems sitting right in front of your face."

"What are you getting at?" Wary, the physician straightened in his seat.

"Yessir, it warms the very cockles of my heart to see you two working together so harmonious, and I'm thinking we're just going to make this a permanent state of affairs . . . for the time being, anyway."

"But we aren't—," Olivia began, aghast.

"Oh yes you are," Briggs stated with a decisive nod, "and you're going to continue to do so till this cut is healed. I'll make it plain: your hands will be the doc's hands, Livvie, for as long as I say. You will see patients together, make calls together, and above all, you will learn to get along."

Olivia thought she'd stopped breathing upon hearing the marshal's pronouncement. She was to serve as Dr. Gray's assistant? Just like that? What about her own patients? These problems in town were not her fault; she had been willing to work with the man from the get-go. He was the one who had started all the trouble!

There was no way she was going to submit to such a ridiculous set of circumstances—no way at all. She opened her mouth to speak, but her patient was the first to recover his tongue. As sparks snapped in his eyes, she was relieved to see they actually agreed about something.

Chapter 2

"By what authority do you make such a decree?"

Only Dr. Ethan Gray's low tone of voice belied the white-hot anger surging inside him. Ever since his arrival in Tristan earlier in the week, his temper had simmered until his emotions had reached a slow boil. The interruption of the mayor's welcoming speech by a cantankerous farmer with a broken ankle had been one thing, but the farmer's surly refusal to allow the doctor's care—in front of the assembled townspeople—had been quite another. *Get me Miss Olivia!* the man had bellowed like a bull in a rage. *I want Miss Olivia to fix my leg!*

Ethan had learned of Tristan's resident healer, as well as her grandmother before her, in his initial correspondence with Attorney Warren Hawley. In his ignorance, Hawley had referred to the prairie midwife in glowing terms, apparently not realizing that every city had an abundance of poorly trained persons claiming healing and curative powers.

Always strongly supporting the movement of restricting medicine to those with proper training and experience, Ethan had "Miss Olivia" pegged long before his arrival. He could not understand why otherwise intelligent people were so blinded to her type. She was no different from any of the other "wifies" or quacks or incompetent medical practitioners with whom he'd crossed paths in Boston.

"All the authority I need is right here," Briggs proudly boomed, tapping the silver badge on his leather vest. "Things in the West are no doubt a bit different than they are back East . . . less formal, if you will. We make do with what we have. And as you no doubt noticed, we don't have doctors runnin' thick as antelope in the corn. Miss Olivia is a fine healer, and we've been mighty fortunate to have her."

The instinctive tightening of Ethan's body drove a spike of pain down his right arm and hand. "You mean Miss Olivia practices medicine without a license, and everyone's been lucky so far." His eyes zeroed in on the woman before him like an arrow finding its target. Though she had withdrawn her hands from his, the needle and silk looked as comfortable in her forceps as they might have with any of his Boston interns—and the realization made his anger churn all the more. He had not traveled some sixteen hundred miles to practice medicine in a doctorless community only to be upstaged by an unschooled lay healer.

The happenings of this short morning—no, this whole week—were beyond belief. Nothing but trouble had plagued him since his arrival in this dusty little town in the middle of nowhere. Had he made a dreadful mistake by leaving Boston? Was he ever going to get the chance to practice medicine for the right reasons?

Heaven knew he'd spent too much time chasing the wrong ones. Once he'd made the long and difficult climb from a childhood of poverty to an adulthood of learned plenty, he'd been accepted into a prosperous Boston medical practice. But the past several years of tending to society's upper crust had not satisfied him as he always envisioned it would. Over time he'd become increasingly aware that his partners—and many of his colleagues— were in the business of healing not out of altruism but out of avarice.

One afternoon, after tending to a particularly trying and hypochondriacal society matron, he had taken a long walk, disillusionment weighing on his heart like a millstone. How had it happened that, with all his training, his passion and zest for healing, he now catered to sedentary rich women who seldom took his advice? To this he knew Aldous Jackson, one of his colleagues, would only laugh and say, "The richer and more sedentary, the better, my boy. Who else could line our pockets so easily?"

But Ethan knew his love of medicine would soon die if he continued on his present course. The intricacies of the human body had always fascinated him, even in the body's normal, healthy, functioning state. Add to that illness, disease, accident, or injury, and there was an even more fascinating puzzle to solve. Somehow, though, he had realized over the past eight years of caring for the Mrs. Prescotts of the city that he'd become as short-sighted and self-serving as the rest of his partners.

The self-revelation had shamed him deeply.

The reason he'd striven to become a doctor was to help people who were truly in need. Later that day, while reading the paper, he'd seen the advertisement for Tristan, and some sort of inner prompting had made him reply. The little northeastern Colorado town was about as far from big-city society as he could hope to get. A scant two months later, here he was, hoping to reaffirm his reasons for practicing medicine: doing work that was greatly needed and, undoubtedly, greatly appreciated.

But a simple country woman challenged all that.

Or maybe not so simple. How had she come by her skills? Though he wanted to fault her performance, the other day in town she'd reduced the farmer's fracture and immobilized the man's ankle in a very serviceable splint. And now she'd sat this morning—in *his* office—stitching together his hand as efficiently as any of his peers might have. Helpless, powerless, angry, in pain, he wanted to do damage to this drab-looking woman and her bag of tricks.

He noticed that her jaw had tightened at his words, and an answering glint of anger had kindled in her clear gray eyes. "I wouldn't get to feeling too smug," he warned, seeing her features tense even further. Recalling their clash over Claude Harker's broken ankle, he added, "Your days in this town may be numbered."

"Oh? Do you plan to call for my arrest again?" Setting down her suturing, Olivia pushed back the chair. Despite her ire, her voice was well modulated. "Marshal Briggs already told you I wasn't breaking any laws."

"No, Briggs said he wasn't *certain* you were breaking any laws. The Colorado Medical Society may have a different opinion. And when that glad day comes, I'll send you—and your roots and herbs—packing."

"What do you mean?" Olivia's voice crackled with outrage. She stood so rapidly that her chair tottered and nearly fell.

"Hold on, you two," Briggs interjected, displeasure evident in the flush that stole upward from his collar. "He means he followed through on his threat the day you met and posted them a letter."

"How would you know?" Ethan felt his face grow hot.

"Welcome to small-town living, Doc. Ain't much that goes on that's a secret."

"I do not need a medical license to heal people," Olivia interjected before Ethan could speak, her words abounding with the depth of her emotion. "And that's all I am—a *healer*. I don't pretend to be a doctor, nor have I ever represented myself as such. My desire and calling have always been to help people, and quite simply, that's all I do."

Pink flags appeared on her pale cheeks, and her stormy eyes flashed with feeling. "My grandmother was born with the healing touch, and so was I. When we care for folk, we're doing nothing more than using that God-given ability. Granny always said she wasn't about to stand before the Judgment Seat without telling the Almighty that she did the best with what he gave her, and I hold with that line of reasoning completely."

Ethan snorted. "What would you say if I told you God sent me here to heal the people of this town? Maybe he means for you to step down and stand aside while I do his work. Perhaps you might pray on that while you go back to stitching your sampler."

"Not before she finishes stitching the other half of your hand," Briggs cut in, forestalling Olivia's riposte. "Or did you forget about that while you went off and vented your spleen?"

Glancing down at his hand, Ethan felt fresh nausea wash over him. What was he going to do? He had nothing or no one but himself to fall back upon, yet he couldn't very well suture his own hand.

"That's right," Briggs went on. "You're about as helpless as a worm in a bed of ants. You'd be loathe to admit it, but I'd say Miss Olivia's done a more-than-fair job of putting you back together. Like I already said, this *ain't* Boston, and I *do* have the final say on things. If you hear back something different from the Colorado Medical Society, you can let me know, but for the time being, Miss Olivia will work by your side. Save your breath, 'cause there ain't no one to appeal to except me." His lips twisted wryly as he retrieved his hat and placed it on his head. "And I already made up my mind."

"Marshal, I don't think—" Olivia's appeal was arrested by Briggs's enormous, work-roughened right hand raised in a manner that brooked no argument.

"Sorry, Livvie, but I expect you to rise to the challenge. If you have all you need to finish your handiwork here, I'll leave you two to sort out the particulars of your new partnership." Reaching into his vest pocket, he checked his timepiece. "Wanda Neff's making ham hash today, and I aim to get it fresh. I imagine you don't feel much like eating right now, Doc, but as soon as you're on the mend, I'll treat you for lunch at Neff's Café. Finest food this side of Denver."

Once his heavy stride had carried him out the front door, Irvin Briggs allowed a long sigh to escape his lips. What on God's green earth was he going to do with the pair he'd left inside the

old insurance building to battle out their differences? He'd
sensed trouble a-coming since Hawley had told him of Gray's
credentials. What he couldn't figure, along with everyone else,
was why the fellow had settled in Tristan. The cut of his suit and
fine manner of speech put him in far higher circles than were
found in these parts.

When he wasn't all riled up about Miss Olivia, Gray
seemed to be a pleasant enough gent. Briggs had dropped in to
chew the fat a few times while the fair-haired man was setting up
his office. They'd talked superficially about such topics as the
town and the weather, and of Gray's plans for his medical practice. Briggs didn't understand some of the medical vernacular
used by the educated man, but he saw, plain as day, that Ethan
Gray had a burr in his britches as far as Miss Olivia was
concerned. Even from those short visits, he realized the doctor
took his business very seriously.

That the physician had actually posted the Colorado Medical
Society worried Briggs. He didn't know if he had it in him to tell
such a fine, hardworking person as Miss Olivia that she couldn't
treat folks anymore. He'd worked by her side many a time and
found her to be a competent, able practitioner. Hitching up his
trousers, he wished Ethan Gray might come to the same conclusion.

The wagon containing the last of Dr. Gray's gear remained
in front of the building, the crowd of helpful townsmen having
dispersed after Miss Olivia's arrival. He had no doubt he'd find
Mayor Weeks and the rest at Neff's, savoring forkfuls of ham
hash while they awaited word on the doctor's condition.

A lonely wind blew from the north, carrying the chill
promise of a freeze. Beyond the landscape of modest buildings,
the flat countryside was painted in tones of sienna. Times had
been hard the past few years with the way rainfall had dried up.
More than a few farmers had pulled up stakes and moved on,
deciding that the plentiful rains of the years past were gone
forever.

A glance up and down the street confirmed all was peaceful

outdoors, at least, for the present time. What was happening inside the walls of Dr. Gray's office was no doubt another matter. Miss Olivia appeared to be the gentle, unassuming sort, but Briggs knew she had plenty of sand. The gal could be as strong as a steel bar when she had to, commanding respect from even the most ill tempered and surly. If he hadn't already realized it, Dr. Ethan Gray would soon learn he wasn't dealing with the lowly sort he assumed he was.

In the midst of Briggs's worries, his stomach growled. A delicious aroma carried on the air, spurring him on to his usual blue-and-white-checked oilcloth-covered table near the eatery's front window. He'd give the pair an hour to iron out their differences. He didn't count on any type of friendship springing up between them, but he expected cooperation.

A taut silence stretched between Ethan and Olivia after Marshal Briggs's departure. Fierce pain engulfed Ethan's entire arm, but he'd be accursed if he'd take so much as a grain of morphine while Olivia Plummer remained in his presence. However, he also knew he must remain seated on the table and allow her to finish suturing his wound.

Looking everywhere but at him, the prairie healer studied each and every piece of equipment in the treatment room. In turn, he scrutinized her appearance. She was of average height, her hair a mousy brown color. The quality of her clothing contrasted sharply with his, the blue skirt and cream-colored blouse she wore stamped with homespun, homemade character. Though their fit was unremarkable, he noticed her shoulders were square, her carriage erect. Taken alone, her posture was a welcome sight when he recalled the droop-shouldered, hump-necked women previously in his care.

He had noticed Olivia Plummer's hands his first day in town. They were at once delicate and capable, the movements of her fingers filled with uncommon aptitude and grace. To his private astonishment, she had followed his suturing instructions better than any second-year intern, nor could he fault her aseptic precautions in any way.

What are you thinking? She's nothing but a midwife, his anger countered, *with no legal right to dispense the treatment she does. As a physician, you have a moral obligation to uphold the practice and standards of modern medicine.*

Ethan grimaced, his pain growing worse with each passing moment. Settling heavily in his seat, he lifted the cloth away from the wound and nearly cursed with frustration. To have any chance of full recovery, he had no other option but to ask the woman to finish what she'd begun.

That acknowledgment grated at his very core.

"Are you ready?" Though she had not turned, her voice was quiet and even.

"Yes."

She nodded, repeating the thorough hand-washing she had carried out upon her arrival. Once again, the strong odor of carbolic filled the air. Without speaking, she took her place and set to work.

For some reason, the needle's bite was even more excruciating than it had been earlier. Never before had he experienced such a degree of physical pain, and he found it took every ounce of his willpower to disguise that fact from the woman before him.

Though a faint furrow creased her brow, an even pulse beat beneath her jaw. As she focused on her task, he wanted to shout at her to hurry, to speed up her pace, yet he knew it wasn't in his best interest. Without the use of his right hand, his doctoring days would be over . . . which brought him back to Marshal Briggs's mandate that he practice his profession with Olivia Plummer's assistance.

Every ounce of self-respect recoiled at that concept, but he also knew that, one-armed, he would be of little use to his patients. How had Briggs summarized his situation? Helpless as a worm in a bed of ants? That was about the size of things. It appeared he had no choice save to obey the lawman's decree—and will himself a speedy recovery.

One fact he hadn't yet allowed his thoughts to linger upon was the possibility of permanent nerve damage to his hand. Since the accident, all attempts to move his thumb and index finger had been in vain. Even now, with the gash nearly sewn, he could not make them stir. While Olivia paused between stitches, he tried again to move the digits even a fraction of an inch.

Nothing happened.

When the wagon's tailgate had slammed down on his hand, he'd assessed the damage and told himself that things could have been much worse. But now, faced with the proposition of going through life with a useless hand, he decided that he couldn't, after all, think of anything more grievous for a physician to suffer.

"Miss Olivia, you've got a letter," John Young called from behind the counter of the mercantile bearing his surname. "How's the new doctor? I heard—"

"His arm was hangin' by a thread! Ain't that a sorry turn of events for the poor devil?" Harvey Pease said, his gray beard wagging with his excited words as he sat with Abner Girard over their never-ending game of checkers. "Mayor Weeks was in and told us all about it."

"What *I* heard was that his hand was sliced open by Nathan Baker's tailgate," Girard spoke in his reasonable manner. "I don't know why you need to pile it on higher than a January snow, Pease. If you was a boy tending the sheep, ain't no one I know would come if you decided to holler wolf."

"You're just sore cuz I'm whippin' your tail, you old—"

"Hellooo!" The bell over the door tinkled at the same time Delores Wimbers's bulk filled the frame. "O-*livia!* I just heard!" Swathed in pale pink gingham, which only emphasized her girth, the matron swept into the store. "You must tell me about

Dr. Gray! I was down at Ella Farwell's this morning—she's making me two new dresses, you know. One is out of that green print that used to sit right on the end of that shelf over there. See? Look right where that blue plaid is now—and we saw you bumping around on the back of Haskell Jarvis's beast of a horse."

Olivia could not disguise her weary sigh. After the events of this tension-filled morning on top of a few hours' sleep, she longed for the comfort of her bed. If only she hadn't stopped to see if a letter from her friend Romy Schmitt had arrived. Being cornered by Delores Wimbers often proved to be an exercise in endurance. Olivia noticed that Pease and Girard had wisely given their attention back to the checkerboard, where no doubt their ears strained to hear every detail of the doctor's injury.

"I felt it was my duty to pay a call to our fine new doctor the day after he arrived," the matron prattled. "It wouldn't do to have him thinking everyone in Tristan had the manners of Claude Harker. I don't know why the old fool had to go and break his leg the day he did, anyway. It's a pity you and Dr. Gray started off on the wrong foot, Olivia, but I've always been more than a little concerned about the things you do in your unmarried state. Gracious! I didn't mean that to come out the way it did. I just meant that most women your age are settled down, raising their families, while you're traipsing around the countryside tending to people's such . . . physical matters."

"It is unfortunate that people get sick, isn't it, Mrs. Wimbers?" Thanks to Granny Esmond's wise counsel, Olivia had stopped chafing at the matron's remarks years before.

"Don't I know that! My dyspepsia's been acting up something fierce." The older woman rubbed a fist along her breastbone, then glanced about the room before dropping her voice. Her eyebrows lifted with meaning. "As well as those other matters. But when I spoke to Dr. Gray the other day—what a gentleman!—I was overjoyed to learn he knows so much about women's diseases. I'm seeing him first thing next week. I hope you understand." Mrs. Wimbers studied her closely while inwardly Olivia sighed.

She didn't like the idea of giving up any of the people she treated, but the thought of Delores Wimbers taking her many complaints and ailments to Dr. Gray was not unpleasant. If only the woman wouldn't eat so many rich foods . . .

Since the townspeople had learned of Dr. Gray's coming, speculation had run rampant about the new physician and what Olivia's reaction to him might be. Initially, her feelings had been mixed when Hawley had announced the Harvard graduate's reply to his long-standing advertisement. But as worn-out as she'd felt of late, she had begun looking forward to his arrival. In her naiveté, she'd hoped they might work out an amicable arrangement.

But ten minutes after his arrival he had drawn a line in the sand, making no disguise of his disapproval of her and her practice. And now, this newest turn of events had occurred, forcing the two of them to work together. How could she possibly join with someone who detested the very sight of her? Over and over she'd replayed the events of that first day, of Claude Harker's blaring insistence that she be the one to tend him. She'd been more than willing to allow Dr. Gray to treat the farmer, but Harker had rained down such verbal abuse on the physician and his kind that she'd had no choice but to set the ankle. She didn't know what else she could have done.

No doubt that unfortunate episode would be grand gossip fodder for years hence. Since then, her thoughts ran hot and turbulent every time she recalled the way the doctor had challenged her, asked for her credentials, then called for her arrest. If his manner with the sick was anything like it had been with her, he'd doubtlessly run out of patients to treat back East. A more pompous, arrogant, conceited human being she'd never met.

And now, temporarily, he was her partner. After she had dressed his hand, he muttered that she might as well come by the office Monday morning. She suspected Delores Wimbers wasn't going to like hearing that any more than Olivia liked the idea of working side by side with the man.

"My goodness gracious!" The older woman expressed impatience at Olivia's silence. "You mustn't keep us in suspense a moment longer! Tell us about Dr. Gray."

"I'm sure you heard he cut his hand. . . . I merely tended to his injury."

"But how bad *was* it? My stars, after what happened between the two of you out on Main Street the other day . . . I mean, how did he—"

"Why, Mrs. Wimbers, you've never known Miss Olivia to stand in the middle of the mercantile and talk about people's private matters." John Young came to Olivia's rescue with a surreptitious wink. Stepping from behind his counter, he put the long-awaited letter in her hands. "Is that Briggs out there waiting for you? You'd best get a move on, my dear. You must be exhausted after spending all night with the Skeevers."

Olivia smiled her relief toward the kindly store owner and made a speedy departure to spare herself the worst of Delores Wimbers's sputtering protestations. "I'm ready," she called to Briggs, who was farther down the boarded walk, deep in conversation with Warren Hawley.

Looking up from Hawley, he waved. "Be right there."

The cool air felt good against her face but did little to stave off the fatigue that burned throughout her body. Hunger knotted inside her belly, and she realized she hadn't eaten since the previous evening. Sleep was more pressing, however; food could wait.

She was sorely tempted to open the letter at once but knew waiting until she was home would be more pleasurable than trying to read pages flapping in the wind. At the very least she could take comfort in Romy's neat handwriting addressing the envelope. No matter what else had transpired, she knew her gentle-hearted, dark-haired friend was alive.

But what had caused the long silence? Romy had always been a faithful correspondent, but Olivia hadn't received mail from Washington Territory since the beginning of summer. She and Romy and their friend Elena Breen had been as close as puppies during their growing years in St. Louis. Olivia and her grandmother had left during Olivia's adolescence, settling in Colorado. After Romy had received her teaching certificate, she had traveled to the burgeoning town of Pitman, Washington Territory, to start a school.

Of Elena, to their great sadness, she and Romy knew little. Raised in an unhappy home, their honey-haired friend had run away at the age of sixteen to pursue her dream of performing in the theater. Sporadic, vague letters had arrived from time to time, then stopped coming altogether. For years Olivia had scoured every major newspaper she laid her hands on, hoping to find a theater headline mentioning her name. It was a slim hope, she knew, but still she looked . . . and hoped.

"You about ready? I got your bag loaded."

Lost in her thoughts, she hadn't noticed Briggs's approach. Nodding, she tucked the letter inside her cloak and walked with him to the wagon.

"Some cold weather coming, I think." The marshal helped her into her seat and went around to his. "Feel that wind?"

"It'll freeze one of these nights." After sharing years of camaraderie—and friendship, she thought—with Irvin Briggs, Olivia was at a loss for what to say to him regarding what had transpired in Dr. Gray's office.

"I spoke to the doctor after you left," Briggs opened, sounding strained as well, "and he said you'd be starting with him Monday morning."

"That's what he told me."

"Aw . . . Livvie, I hope you're not too sore. You did a fine job with your needle and thread. I know it couldn't have been easy to walk in there after what happened the other day. I'm sorry about what I had to do, but this situation has gotten so out of hand that I had no choice."

"Well, it appears none of us has a choice, so we'll just have to make the best of it." Olivia sighed, watching the countryside roll past. "I give you my word that I'll do my part . . . if he'll do his."

"And you'll meet in the middle," the marshal quipped, his expression lightening.

"If you say so," she responded in kind, knowing it was the last thing on earth that would ever possibly happen.

Chapter 3

Arriving home, Olivia was touched to find her cabin neat and her morning dishes washed and put away. Protective sadness rose within her when she thought of her young neighbor, Susan Connally. The twelve-year-old girl had lost her mother to the wasting sickness two years ago, and now she and her fourteen-year-old brother Seamus lived—nay, merely existed, in Olivia's opinion—with their father on the Connallys' increasingly ramshackle farm.

When his wife, Deborah, became ill, Donal Connally had turned to the bottle. After her passing, he'd tried pulling himself together and courting Ella Farwell, Tristan's milliner and dress-maker, but the rather homely, long-in-the-tooth Miss Farwell had no intention of giving up her modestly successful business to live in the country and replace the recently departed Mrs. Connally as farmwife, laundress, and substitute mother.

After his failed bid for Ella's hand in marriage, Donal had taken to drink in earnest. It was a rare day when he couldn't be found at Kelly's Saloon, polishing a stool with his backside. Susan and Seamus had been forced to quit school and work the farm. And now, as a result of Donal's perpetual inebriated state, the Connallys barely eked out a living. Outraged at the conditions under which the children were forced to live, Olivia had made an arrangement with Susan, whereby in exchange for the young girl's making sure Olivia's cow was milked and her stove was kept going while Olivia was out, the midwife generously passed along to Susan what food and goods she could as payment.

Susan must have left not long ago, for the cabin was warm. What a luxury it was to come home to a hot fire . . . and the kettle ready for tea. She smiled at the table setting her young friend had laid out: plate, teacup, saucer, spoon, and napkin. Pouring the steaming water into her cup, Olivia found the worst of her weariness had slipped off. She was still tired, but perhaps not too tired to eat. She cut a slice of bread from the loaf, layered it with butter and jam, and sat down to offer thanks.

She added prayers for Susan, as well as for Romy and Elena. Cora Skeever and her new baby came next. Petitioning the Lord for Dr. Gray's healing came harder, but she knew it wasn't right to exclude him just because she didn't like him. Granny Esmond had been emphatic that she and Olivia were to pray for *everyone* they healed, even those whose situations seemed hopeless.

Pray especially for those, Livvie, the older woman had admonished, *for you never know what miracles the Father has in mind to perform. To the same end, pray for your enemies, no matter what the offense.*

Olivia wondered if her grandmother had ever come up against such prejudice and contempt as Dr. Gray had shown her. The man had established himself as her enemy at once; surely it would take a miracle for that to change. Reasoning that the sooner Dr. Gray was healed, the sooner she wouldn't have to work with him anymore helped her utter the request and conclude with a satisfied "Amen."

She took a bite of bread and chewed, trying to make sense of the events of the past week. For a town Tristan's size to acquire a physician was a celebrated event, indeed, but what she would never understand was how Dr. Gray's welcoming celebration had turned into a matter of such controversy and upheaval in a matter of minutes . . . with her in the center of it.

Gone were any hopes of having a peaceful working relationship with the man. But she knew the Testament well enough to realize there wasn't any dickering with the Lord on the issue of forgiveness—this set of circumstances being no exception. Why was it that setting her will with God's had always proven easier said than done? Was it really his plan for her to endure the new physician's censure and criticism for days on end?

She swallowed and took a sip of the steaming tea. Romy's letter! How could she have forgotten? Quickly she retrieved the envelope from her cloak, slit open the top, and withdrew the folded pages. Taking her seat, she began reading.

Dear Olivia,

I apologize for the amount of time that has passed. No doubt you are wondering if I received your increasingly anxious letters.

The answer is yes. However, I have had a bit of trouble throughout the summer. Actually "a bit of trouble" may well be an understatement, for you see, I have had an accident and have been separated from the lower part of my leg.

For a time I did not know if I should live or die, but it now appears I shall remain in this life. The surgeon caring for me has done a fine job, I suppose, but how I have longed for our girlhood days back in Missouri and the loving care of your granny. I realize that her mantle has now passed to you, but in my mind you are still fourteen years old and one of my two very best friends.

Do you remember the time Elena dared me to climb that tree? I'll never forget how gently Granny tended to my sprain and soothed my distress. Poor Elena. She was filled with such remorse at the outcome of her challenge that she wrote me a song.

Dearest Olivia, I have yet another shock for you. I hope you can make your way to a chair before you read further. (Are you safely seated?)

I am married.

Married! What the news of the amputation failed to do, Romy's wedding announcement accomplished. Romy was *married?* Olivia studied those three words to be sure she'd read them correctly. Whom had she wed? As far as Olivia knew, Romy hadn't even had a beau, just a case for a businessman in her town. Anxious for details, she continued down the page.

Most days I can scarcely believe it myself. You do remember Jeremiah Landis, the store owner of whom I wrote? Within the space of an hour, Mr. Landis saved my life and took me as his bride.

I would tell you more, but I tire. There is no one else in this town willing or able to teach my students, so I must continue gathering my strength. Please forgive any distress I have caused you, and remember me always in your prayers. I will write again soon.

With my deepest apologies and my love,

Romy

Olivia reread the pages twice before setting the letter aside. There were so many questions she wanted to ask. What kind of accident had Romy had? How had Jeremiah Landis saved her life *and* married her in such a short space of time? How had the wound healed? Had an artificial leg been made? Did Romy now reside at her husband's home, wherever that might be? Would her next letter coyly hint of feeling poorly in the morning?

Romy—in love and married. How romantic that sounded! Briefly, Olivia allowed herself to wonder if love and motherhood stood in her future. Her own parents had died when she was young, and Granny Esmond had been a widow when she'd taken Olivia in. So what Olivia knew of love and marriage firsthand was little, garnered by observing others.

You'll never be wed, Livvie, she told herself as a deep yawn overtook her. *Just when do you think you'd have time for a husband and children?* Exhaustion and lack of sleep caught up with her once more, and she plodded toward the cheerful, quilt-clad bed across the room, anticipating its soft comfort.

Granny Esmond would have chided her for not undressing

and slipping beneath the covers properly, but Olivia was so tired she lay atop the bed and unfolded the patchwork prize gracing the foot of the bed. The quilt, done in blue and red calico, was similar to the Star in the Window pattern but of original design. So grateful for Olivia's care of her ill sons two winters past, Emily Marlow, a hardworking ranch wife, had presented her with the warm, colorful work of art the following summer. "Thank you," she'd said without elaboration. "Remember us."

Tucked in from toes to chin, Olivia bent her lips in a sleepy smile as she pictured the Marlow boys, running and tumbling and bursting with health the last time she'd seen them, showing no ill effects from the whooping cough that had nearly claimed their young lives. Yes, she remembered them often, as well as many others.

Praise God for his mercy, she thought, yawning. She was asleep almost immediately.

"I was hoping Dr. Gray would be in church this morning." Janet Winter, Olivia's friend and Tristan's schoolteacher, hooked her arm through Olivia's as they made their way down the church steps. "His injury must be causing him a great deal of pain." Amused, she added, "Even so, it's my prediction that the women of this town are going to take to ailing in droves. My goodness, he's a handsome one, and a single newcomer, to boot."

"I'm certain I'll be able to resist his charms."

Despite much prayer, Olivia's feelings continued to run hot whenever she thought of the man. How many more slurs and insults would the next morning bring? she wondered. How could she withstand such treatment, day after day . . . and for how many days?

Janet's voice was gentle. "It doesn't sound as though he's shown you his most charming side. But you have such a way with people, Livvie. I'm sure he'll come around. And what do you always tell *me* about worrying?"

"Mornin', ladies," Marshal Briggs greeted, tipping his hat. Instead of his usual trousers and leather vest, he wore his Sunday finest, a charcoal gray suit. His face creased with a wide smile, and he gestured toward the blue sky. "Fine day, isn't it?"

Olivia noticed that whenever he was in Miss Janet's company, he strove to make his grammar his very finest.

"Why, yes it is," Janet responded with more color in her cheeks than was warranted by the wind.

For the past few years, Janet had confided to Olivia her interest in the burly marshal. And it was plain to Olivia that Briggs was equally enamored with her fair-complected friend. She had always found it coincidental—and amusing—that Janet and Romy, both schoolteachers, each held a secret attraction for a man in their town.

Now that Romy had married her businessman, Olivia watched the not-quite-yet budding courtship before her with new eyes. Would Janet one day walk down the aisle to join with Irvin Briggs? At the rate they were going, however, it might take another decade. Perhaps giving them some time alone might shave a year or two from their wooing.

"I'd best be off," she announced, disentangling her arm from Janet's. "I promised the Skeevers I'd stop by on my way home from church."

"Oh, Olivia," Janet said with a sigh, clearly torn, "I was so hoping we'd have time to talk. I've barely seen you all week . . . and then there's the news about your friend Romy. I must hear more about that."

Briggs cleared his throat and looked at the ground. "I . . . ah, could drive you out for a visit later this afternoon, Miss Janet. If you have no objections," he rushed to add.

Pleased beyond measure, Olivia bit back a grin at the sight of the self-confident marshal looking unsure of himself. It served him right after his dictatorial decree the other day.

"That's most kind of you," Janet replied, her blush deepening. "I should like that very much."

Olivia made her farewells, allowing herself a smile as she

walked toward her horse and small buggy. It was high time those two commenced with things. Who said nothing ever happened in Tristan? Plenty had happened during the past week.

Olivia found she had much to think about while she made the drive to the Skeevers' meager farm. Uppermost in her mind was Dr. Ethan Gray and her apprehension of what explosions might occur as they tried to see patients together.

Take therefore no thought for the morrow: for the morrow shall take thought for the things of itself.

Olivia could almost hear Granny Esmond's distinctive voice break in on her worries. The older woman had known the Scriptures backward and forward and had been uncommonly perceptive about applying them at just the right time, in just the right way. *You'd best take to your knees, Livvie,* would be her next piece of advice.

Adeline Esmond had administered such counsel frequently, certain that prayer, Scripture, and the tincture of time were the cure-alls for any of life's problems. Languishing in anger, bitterness, or self-pity was something for which Granny'd had no time. One had her compassion and concern, certainly, but one was also given a stiff talking-to about "getting on with things."

Well, perhaps it was indeed time to get on with things. Dr. Gray's hand had been cut—badly. There was no help for that but time and healing. Marshal Briggs had been uncompromising in his orders: she was to assist the physician until he had recuperated. She could change nothing . . . except her attitude.

How many hours had she wasted fretting about Dr. Gray and his disagreeable temperament? What had that done to her own? Once stirred, her anger was not quick to subside: a sinful state of affairs.

Surely the physician's threats would come to nothing. Even Marshal Briggs said she hadn't broken any laws. Why would the Colorado Medical Society care if she treated gout, stitched up cuts, or delivered babies? If they were so all-fired concerned, why hadn't they sent one of their kind to Tristan years ago?

As she directed her horse onto the Skeevers' drive, the reality of tomorrow struck her. She would be paired with Dr. Ethan Gray, her tether jerked short. Would he even permit her to make such basic calls such as this, she wondered, or would he insist on overseeing her every move? Did he even realize how much traveling he would have to do to see his patients? Some would come to his fine, modern office, but many rural folk either would not or could not.

Her bravado wavered while doubt shadowed each good intention. *Oh, Lord,* she prayed, *I don't want to work with Dr. Gray. Only you can help me make the best of this situation until I'm on my own again. Please heal his hand swiftly, and lend me your grace in the meantime.*

Parking her buggy outside the Skeevers' lowly soddy, Olivia put a smile on her face, determined to enjoy to the fullest her last bit of independence.

All too soon, Monday morning arrived. With leaden limbs, Olivia milked her cow and hitched old Pete to the buggy. A low ridge behind the animals' shelter protected the sod-and-wood structure from the worst of the Colorado winds. Upon arrival from St. Louis, Granny Esmond had studied their plot of land, taking into account the terrain as well as the direction of the prevailing winds. She had been very particular about how the buildings and gardens were to be situated.

"Morning, Miss Olivia." Susan Connally slipped around the corner, winded. "I didn't know if you'd still be here."

"I'm leaving now. Did you have breakfast?" For the past two years Olivia had tried in vain to round out the neighbor girl's rawboned form. A short, too-thin coat covered her threadbare dress.

"No, ma'am."

Olivia knew that the girl and her brother lived in fear of disturbing their father's slumber. From the midwife's carefully worded questions and her frequent observations, she discerned, at the very least, that Donal Connally did not use his fists on his children. He did, however, neglect to provide for their material and emotional needs.

"I made plenty of eggs and toast, hoping you'd be over in time to join me," she said, fastening the last buckle on Pete's cinch. Turning from Pete, she laid her hand on the girl's thin shoulder. "Come inside while I get my things. You'll take the rest to Seamus, won't you?"

The dark-haired girl nodded. "He's already in the corn, but I'll bring it straight out to him. We're shocking today . . . he'll be glad for a good breakfast."

Olivia's heart twisted at the thought of Seamus and Susan endeavoring to bring in their meager crop while their father slept off his liquor. What kind of man could let himself slide into such ruin? Not only were his children impoverished physically, but their moral and spiritual upbringing had ground to a halt because of his intemperate behavior.

The pair entered the cabin, its warmth welcome after the chill of the autumn morning. With sudden eagerness, the girl sat at the table and reached for a slice of toast. Had she eaten anything the day before? Olivia wondered, dispatching a silent prayer for her young friend while she loaded Susan's plate with fluffy, yellow eggs.

"Who are you seeing this morning?" Susan asked, finishing her first piece of toast. She reached for a second. "Someone far off?"

"No . . . actually, I'm spending the day in town."

"The whole day? How can you know that already? Will there be a new baby?"

"No, no babies."

Seeing the girl's quizzical expression, she went on. "The new doctor hurt his hand a few days ago, and the marshal says I am to assist him until the wound is healed."

"You don't seem too happy about that."

"I'm not . . . but I'm trying to be. You see, Dr. Gray is a man of high education and believes anyone who heals should be schooled the same way he was."

"Oh. Does that mean you're going to get high education too?"

Despite her glum spirits, Olivia smiled at the far-fetched notion of attending medical college. "I've heard tell of a lady doctor down in Leadville, but I don't know if she really exists. No, Susan, more schooling isn't the answer for me. What Granny Esmond taught me about healing and childbearing has served me well enough through the years."

Her confident attitude faltered, however, once she shook Pete's reins and began her trip toward town. Just what did a Harvard medical doctor learn during his years of study? Would he be better equipped than she at handling accident and injury, affliction and disease? He certainly had more equipment at his disposal. If she'd thought Ethan Gray's office well supplied when she'd rushed in to treat his wound, what would it be like when the remaining half-wagonful of items was unloaded and put away?

Too soon she reached her destination. In the early morning light, Tristan was just stirring to life. The shades of Wilmington's Bank were still down. John Young swept the walk in front of his mercantile while a sole man entered Jay Payne's barbershop. At this hour, the majority of the town's activity was taking place at Neff's, where many locals breakfasted regularly.

"Ready for your first day with the doctor, Miss Olivia? Briggs told me you'd be coming about now," Deputy Marshal Dermot Johnson said, greeting her outside the doctor's building.

The deputy was as quiet a man as Briggs was loud. Whereas the marshal's appearance could, on occasion, tend toward disorderliness, Dermot Johnson's shirts were always clean and well pressed, his appearance dapper, his neck and jaws clean shaven, his mustache freshly waxed. For whom he maintained his appearance, no one knew. It was rumored he saw a woman in the next county, but Olivia had no idea if there was any truth to that hearsay.

"He was that sure of me?" she inquired.

"Yes indeed, ma'am. He's setting type this morning, but he asked me to watch for you."

Thinking of the many difficulties and woes Briggs had encountered over the past few years while attempting to publish his small weekly, she smiled. "Do you suppose the *Tribune* will be out tomorrow on schedule?"

Johnson shrugged and dismounted from his horse. "I reckon only the Lord above can know that. Marshal was grumbling something fierce about all the letters to the editor this week. You and the new medical doctor have gotten to be quite a hot topic."

Up the few steps they walked, continuing their conversation. Rapping twice on the doctor's door, the deputy turned the knob and bade her to enter at the same time a bell tinkled their arrival. To her surprise, the fair-haired man was already seated at his desk, engaged in conversation with Ella Farwell.

Though a white dressing covered his right hand, his appearance was spruce—as was his office. A large square of colorful oilcloth covered the majority of the floor, giving the room a warmth it had never known with Mr. Beverly's occupation. Against the back wall, on either side of the door leading to the structure's center hallway, was a pair of glass-fronted bookshelves that had not been there the other morning. The countertops along the sides of the room still supported many boxes of items yet unpacked.

Three chairs sat vacant before the window, ready to hold sufferers and victims. Upon their entrance, the dressmaker rose quickly from her seat opposite Dr. Gray's desk. The physician rose as well, his manner businesslike but cordial. "I thank you for your welcome, Miss Farwell," he spoke, a brief smile lighting his features.

Seeming ill at ease, the tall woman turned and explained her presence. "I was just on my way out of town to deliver some things and thought I'd introduce myself to the new doctor." Ella Farwell was somewhere near thirty years of age, with big bones and big features. Though her marital status was the same as Olivia's and Janet's, she had never responded to their overtures of friendship, preferring instead to keep to herself.

Olivia studied the other woman, finding only her fidgety appearance and pink-flushed cheeks out of the ordinary. A dark-colored cloak covered her full figure. "Are you well, Ella?" she inquired, wondering if there might be another reason for her visit. "The deputy and I can go back outside, if you like."

"Oh, no. Please. I was just on my way," she replied quickly, with a glance toward the trim lawman at Olivia's side. A nervous laugh escaping her, she moved toward the door. "I told the doctor I'd be honored to be his patient, only there isn't anything the matter with me."

The door opened and closed. Johnson let himself out on the dressmaker's heels, leaving Olivia and Ethan facing one another. The low, steady ticking of a clock was the only sound heard in the physician's front office. His affable manner had vanished with the visitors' departures, and he regarded her with wary eyes. The strained, apprehensive feeling inside her grew.

"How are you feeling today?" she asked simply, removing her bonnet and cloak, wanting instead to question him about the appearance and odor of his wound. Had there been any suppuration? Of what quantity and color? She longed to examine his hand, but a single glance at his face told her it was better not to ask. She prayed that her next words would sound more gracious than the grudging emotion behind them. "Have you thought of how I may best assist you this morning?"

"My hand hurts like the devil." His reply was curt. "And yes, I have laid out several tasks for you. To begin, you will unpack the remainder of these boxes—under my direction, of course."

Unpack boxes? As if she had nothing better to do with her time than serve as his flunky? She had come to help him tend folks who needed care. Before she could find her tongue, he went on.

"I'll be seeing a few patients this morning. During that time

you'll continue your assigned duties. You may have thirty
minutes for lunch."

"How very generous of you." Though her words were as
brisk as a mountain wind, Olivia felt her face grow hot. "Is there
anything you *haven't* thought of, Dr. Gray—like following
Marshal Briggs's orders? I assure you, I don't want to be here any
more than you'd like to see me long gone, but out of respect for
the marshal, I came to 'be your hands.'"

He walked to the nearest box, retrieved a heavy-looking
book with his left hand, and set it on the counter. Pulling
another from the box, he stacked it on the first. A third followed.
Leveling a glance at her as he reached for yet another, he said,
"Well, Miss Plummer, my hands would have been busy unpacking this morning . . . as yours will now be."

"But what about the—"

Olivia's protest was cut short by the sound of the door
opening. Outfitted in a cloak and matching hat of robin's-egg
blue, Delores Wimbers made an affair of her entrance.

"Good morning, Dr. Gray," she trilled. "We missed you at
church yesterday. Deacon Carlisle gave a most inspiring sermon
on the virtues of—" As she stopped short at the sight of the
midwife, the pitch of her voice tumbled a full octave. "What are
you doing here? I was certain *I* had the first appointment of the
day. Do you have need of the doctor, as well?" Mrs. Wimbers's
manner was both rankled and inquisitorial, her narrowed eyes
and cocked ears at the ready, Olivia was certain, to absorb any
scrap of titillating information for later dissemination throughout the town.

Dr. Gray intervened smoothly, holding up his bandaged
hand. "Why, you do indeed have the first appointment of the
day, Mrs. Wimbers. Because of my injury, the marshal was
thoughtful enough to provide Miss Olivia's services around the
office."

"Well, why didn't Marshal Briggs tell anyone that she was—"
Understanding dawned across the matron's face, and she
beamed at the physician, ignoring Olivia. "Oh, I see! She'll be a

clerk . . . or your errand girl, am I right? Being from Boston, you're probably accustomed to having dozens of domestics about. I grew up much the same, but in Philadelphia. Have you ever been there?"

Delores seldom allowed anyone time to reply to such questions. On she prattled, removing her hat, suddenly at ease. "Did you know, Dr. Gray, that when I was a child, we had more servants around our home than I could ever manage to count? My daddy was a *very* wealthy man. . . ."

Olivia waited in vain for the physician to clear up Delores Wimbers's misunderstanding. When five minutes had passed and yet the older woman talked on, covering a wide variety of topics having to do with herself, the midwife turned her interest to the contents of the box nearest her. More books. Had the physician used an entire freight car to transport his library?

With a sigh, she pulled a volume entitled *Illustrated Manual of Operative Surgery and Surgical Anatomy* from the crate. Published in 1861, the book appeared to have seen much better days. Why would a man with such exacting standards as Ethan Gray keep a nearly twenty-year-old book, its cover and binding both in such sad shape? Expecting a series of dry, monotonous chapters, Olivia flipped through the pages, immediately spellbound by the division titles and accompanying plates of exquisite detail.

"Operation for Cataracts." "Ligatures of Arteries." "Repair of Uterine Prolapse." She read greedily, drinking in the wondrous information as delightedly as a parched man might swallow gulps of sweet water. Her pulse quickened when she discovered the chapter entitled "Union of Wounds," and she forced herself to slow down, absorbing every word of the text: "The different methods of promoting the union of wounds vary according to the nature and condition of the solution of continuity, and the ultimate object to which the surgeon has in view. When a wound has commenced to—"

"Miss Plummer?" The physician's voice broke in on her concentration. "I said Mrs. Wimbers and I will be in the examination room. In the meanwhile, I want the manuals and journals put neatly into the glass bookshelves."

"Oh, I am just certain, Dr. Gray," the matron gushed, "that you can do something once for all with my dyspepsia." The glance she shot Olivia was pithy. "*Nothing* has ever worked. The same goes for my—" she cleared her throat and failed, in Olivia's opinion, at affecting a coy expression—"female problems. I wouldn't dream of bending your ear for so long, but I could go on all day about my difficulties with the change of life."

Olivia hadn't expected to be fighting laughter during the course of this dreaded day, but that was exactly the case when she saw a wearied expression cross Dr. Gray's face. With Delores Wimbers wound up at the prospect of relating each and every detail of her physical woes to a real live doctor, the fair-haired man might not escape her clutches until noon.

Somehow, the idea of putting away books while he saw to the matron's maladies had become very appealing. How many hours had she spent in the past year alone engaged in such conversations with his new patient? She would have ample time to finish reading the chapter on wounds, and perhaps one or two more, before getting Dr. Gray's books into order.

Nodding her assent, Olivia hoped her smile stopped short of expressing her good fortune and conveyed only pleasant agreement.

Chapter 4

A ripple went through town as word got out about Olivia's practicing with Dr. Gray. The two who had taken such an immediate
dislike to one another were now working together? A small article
in Tuesday's *Tristan Tribune* confirmed the rumor for its thirty-
seven paying customers. Making good on his promise, Briggs had
also devoted more space than usual to the many letters to the
editor generated by the subject of medical doctoring.

Conversation at Neff's this noon was lively, the hot topic of
Kansas's temperance movement completely forgotten for the
time being.

"I'm tryin' to think up an ailment that might not be too
costly, just so's I can see what's goin' on down there." Charlie
Ingersoll shifted his toothpick and spoke from his table at the
back of the café. Guffaws broke amongst a dozen men, and just
as many ridiculous suggestions flew into the air.

"Now, hold on, gentlemen. Dr. Gray brings just the refinement this town has long needed." To make his point over the
lingering boisterousness, Warren Hawley raised both arms. "Our
persistence in soliciting our very own physician has paid off
handsomely."

"Hawley's right," short, portly Mayor Weeks seconded.

"I ask you, how many other towns between here and Denver can boast of a doctor of their own?"

"Would that be one-handed, or two?" Harvey Pease called out, soliciting another round of hilarity.

"I hear there's enough cold wind between the doctor and Miss Olivia to freeze an Eskimo," rancher Jeb Grosset remarked once things quieted down. "It'll be a miracle if the two of 'em don't do each other in."

"Well, any kind of wind is better than your wind," quipped his lunch partner, Ingersoll, with a quick glance at proprietor Wanda Neff. "No offense to your cooking, ma'am. 'Specially whilst you got that pot of hot coffee in your hand."

Outside the curtained doors of Neff's Café, Ethan paused, hearing the sound of hearty male laughter from within. Though he'd been only too happy to leave Boston and the venality of his private practice, he was an outsider in this tiny town. Initial mistrust he had expected, but not immediate and ongoing opposition between himself and the resident midwife. Everyone, it seemed, was taking sides—or, at the very least, was greatly interested in every new development.

It wasn't easy to admit after making such a drastic change in his life, but deep down Ethan missed the stimulation of the hospital, the surgeries, his day-to-day association with other medical practitioners. He glanced at his bandaged hand. Even if he were to leave Tristan and return to Boston, how long would it be until he was able to perform surgery again? Weeks? Months?

Another burst of laughter broke out. If he were a betting man, Ethan would have placed money on odds that, in some respect, he was the object of the townsfolk's entertainment.

"They're having themselves a grand time today," Marshal Briggs commented from behind him. "Go on in, Gray. I promised you a lunch you wouldn't forget. I don't know what kind of edibles you had back East, but one bite of Wanda Neff's cookin' will make you wonder if you ain't already passed through the pearly gates."

Ethan hadn't thought himself hungry until he stepped into

the homespun establishment and inhaled. "Beef stew," the slate read. His mouth watered at the warm, tantalizing aromas of meat and vegetables, biscuits, coffee, and something sweet but indefinable that enveloped him like a mother's hug. The ever present pain in his hand faded as he stood in the doorway and simply *breathed*.

"Told you so," Briggs boasted, reading his mind. "I figured you can't have been eatin' anythin' decent, cookin' for yourself. Come on over here, Doc, where Johnson's sittin'. We gotta be able to see out the window, you know."

They joined the deputy at his table, and gradually the silence that had exploded over the room upon their entry began filling in with low conversation. The marshal greeted several of his cronies in his usual booming voice before making a to-do of introducing Ethan to the slight, apron-clad woman who made haste between tables, swinging a large, black coffeepot and filling cup after cup with practiced ease.

The interior of the restaurant was plain, its walls and floors made of the same rough pine. The relative smoothness of the floor existed only because of washing and wear, Ethan guessed, but the splinters promised by any contact with the structure's walls would be most unpleasant. The room's plainness was relieved by the cheerful blue-and-white-checked cloths on the tables and at the front windows. Neff's Café was nothing like the stylish Boston restaurants he'd frequented, but if the food tasted even half as good as it looked and smelled, he'd be back. Regularly.

"Afternoon, Doc." The deputy nodded. "How's it going with Miss Olivia?"

"Miss Olivia? Yes." Ethan forced a smile and attempted, unsuccessfully, to quell the annoyance that rose inside him upon hearing the name of his mandated assistant. He cleared his throat. "I imagine such speculation was the cause of all the merriment before we walked in."

"Ah . . . I . . ." The fastidious-looking deputy was at a loss for words and looked to the marshal for help.

Briggs shrugged and took his seat. "I'm figuring that's what the hootin' and hollerin' was about. Don't be bashful, Johnson. Tell the man the truth—it'll never serve you wrong."

"Talk's going around that the two of you don't get on so well."

"We don't."

"Appears Miss Olivia's been trying," Briggs remarked, barely raising his cup before Wanda swooped over to fill it and Ethan's with steaming, strong-smelling coffee. "Your office looks spanking fine for the Colorado prairie. Don't think there's many even in Denver that could hold a candle to it."

The brown-haired woman had indeed invested an impressive amount of elbow grease in setting his office to rights. She worked hard and didn't complain. But he hadn't been able to forget the look of amusement she'd shot him over Delores Wimbers's head yesterday morning. Since then her manner had been much less prickly, and for some reason that annoyed him more.

In a day and a half, only four other patients had been presented for treatment. Two were human, with minor ailments and enormous curiosity; the other two were dog and goat, respectively. For some perverse reason he bade Olivia to treat the animals—and to his surprise, she did so willingly, displaying genuine warmth and kindness to their owners. For the goat's malaise she had prescribed warm gruel to be fed to the animal until she was restored to her usual vigor and milk-giving capacity. The wide gash on the dog's leg had already clotted over, so Olivia merely applied a coat of dark-colored salve to the wound, sending the owner on his way with enough ointment to last the week.

To his grumbling remarks about having attended Harvard Medical College for the purpose of treating creatures with two legs, not four, she'd shrugged and said mildly, "If folks trust you with their animals, they might take a chance on you with themselves one day. They're merely seeing what you're about."

"How's your hand comin' along, Doc?" The marshal broke

into his thoughts with a question and a noisy slurp of coffee. "You got it wrapped up real pretty."

"It's better." That was true enough, Ethan thought. The pain was no longer as severe. However, his fingers remained useless, and he wondered if the damage done to the nerves would reverse itself or not.

"That's . . . ah, *that's* it!" The marshal's eyes lit up at something over Ethan's head, and it was obvious that the big man's reply was not intended for him. A second later, three plates of fragrant, steaming beef stew were placed on the table. "Father, Son, Holy Ghost," Briggs intoned with a wink. "Whoever eats the fastest gets the most. Amen. Now, pass that salt, will you, Johnson?"

For the time being, all else was forgotten as the men dug heartily into their meals.

❧

Olivia nibbled on her hard-boiled egg and gazed around the schoolroom while Janet spoke to a pupil who had come in from lunch recess complaining of a sore finger. A kiss to the affected area seemed to bring about an immediate cure, and the youngster skipped back outdoors to rejoin her schoolmates.

"If only my problems could be solved so easily," Olivia commented with a sigh once the door had closed. "One kiss . . . all better."

Janet's giggle was mischievous. "I don't know. It might not be so bad to kiss Dr. Gray. After all, he's got such nice brown eyes."

"*Nice* brown eyes? You mean eyes that could bore holes through solid rock. There's nothing nice about them."

Janet shrugged. "If you say so."

"Shame on you, anyway, Janet Winter. What if the school board knew you said such things? Schoolmarms ought not have such a saucy bent."

"I beg your pardon, Miss Olivia Plummer? Who was it who told me Dr. Gray was nothing but a stuffy old sourpuss?"

Olivia frowned. "Well, he is."

"At least he's a stuffy old sourpuss with nice brown eyes. Tell me honestly you haven't noticed." She took a bite of her apple and chewed before a chuckle escaped her. "I'd bet a nickel Delores Wimbers has already paid a call on him for one reason or another."

"First thing Monday morning." Olivia finished her egg and wiped her mouth and fingers with her napkin. Feeling surprisingly discomfited by her friend's words about the doctor, she decided it was time to turn the tables. "But I'm wondering why you have interest in Dr. Gray's eyes so soon after your drive with Marshal Briggs. Perhaps the marshal's brand of manliness no longer appeals to you . . . ?"

"I was merely pointing out . . . oh, never mind. Would you like to share this apple with me?" Ducking her head, Janet rifled through her sack while attempting to hide her blush. "And for your information, I had a very nice drive with the marshal on Sunday."

"Very nice or *very* nice?"

"Olivia!" The petite Janet made no further pretense of hiding her reddened features. She reached for a sheaf of papers on her desk and vigorously fanned her face. "He didn't kiss me, if that's what you're asking."

"Well, I wasn't asking, but seeing as how you were the one talking about kissing . . . the thought did cross my mind."

"Actually, Livvie, you brought it up. Remember? You said you wished a kiss could make your problems all better."

After a pause, the two women burst into laughter, their mirth mingling with the happy sounds of the children playing outdoors. The brightness of the autumn day illuminated the schoolroom, its warmth releasing the evocative scents of chalk, wood, and wax.

Olivia shook her head and rolled her eyes heavenward. "Well and good. I admit I *did* say that, but not with any reference toward Dr. Gray. Besides, I'm not sure there's a woman on earth he would deem worthy of kissing." Another chuckle escaped her. "Maybe he should have kissed Patrick Mulgrew's goat yesterday."

"Patrick Mulgrew's goat! What on earth are you talking about?"

"Apparently she's been languishing for the past several days, so Mr. Mulgrew brought her in for Dr. Gray to take a look at."

"And?" Janet could barely formulate the word through her laughter.

"You should have seen him—fit to be tied! Lucky for the goat, she didn't mess his floor. And that was after Jim Snow brought his dog by for a cut leg."

"Besides Mrs. Wimbers, has Dr. Gray seen any *people?*" Janet wiped a tear from the corner of her eye.

"A few. So far, he treats the people and allows me to tend the animals."

"Is that so?" Janet's expression cooled. "Then I'm sorry for laughing. We're talking about your livelihood, Olivia! I can't believe the man actually wrote the Colorado Medical Society to complain about you. What does he expect, that after the years you and your grandmother have put into caring for the people of Tristan, you'll just quietly step back and allow him to take over?"

Olivia nodded, touched by her friend's loyalty. She toyed with her napkin. "I'd say that's just what he expects to happen."

"But . . ."

"Don't worry, Janet. If he tries running me out of business, I don't intend to sit idly by."

"What if he has the law on his side?"

"I'm no lawbreaker. How can using my healing touch be a criminal act?" Olivia shook her napkin smartly. "Dr. Ethan Gray is so full of himself and his fine education. What could he possibly have learned in his Harvard medical training that I haven't already learned by experience?"

"I don't know, Livvie, probably nothing. I wish we could

keep talking, but . . ." Janet glanced at the clock with an apologetic expression.

"I know, time's up. The good doctor is probably checking his watch right about now, anyway, thinking I've been gone three minutes too long." She stood and stretched her legs. "It's good to talk to you, Janet. I don't know what I'd do if I couldn't unburden myself to someone."

"Don't forget who's always willing to shoulder your burdens, dear friend, any time of the day or night. He's as close as a prayer."

The friends parted with a hug and plans to share their noon meal again tomorrow. Walking down the building's steps, Olivia smiled at the groans of the schoolchildren when Janet rang the bell. They sang out bright greetings as they rushed passed her, still flushed with the excitement of their noontime games. In some respects, Olivia reflected, it seemed not so long ago that she and Romy and Elena had been pupils of Miss Johanna Caswell in St. Louis.

Yet seven years had passed since those lighthearted days, fate scattering the three friends far and wide. And now a terrible accident had befallen Romy, Elena remained missing, and Olivia was herself in danger of being stripped of her vocation. What events would the next half score of years bring?

And what of the promise the three of them had made that late summer night so long ago: that no matter what happened, they would always be best friends? Romy, ever practical—and now the schoolteacher—had at first argued that only one person could be another's best friend. After all, best was . . . well, *best*, she'd argued.

Lying on blankets beneath the stars, bellies still stretched to their limits by Mrs. Schmitt's delicious dinner of chicken and dumplings, corn on the cob, and mixed berry cobbler, the three young women had continued their debate. Olivia smiled, remembering how many times they'd started and stopped talking, oohing and ahing, instead, at the incredible display of shooting stars that velvety August night.

Finally, after Elena had contended that *best* could mean "excellent" or "in the best way" rather than arranging your friends like stock at the county fair and sticking first-, second-, and third-place ribbons on each of them, the three had agreed to remain best friends their whole lives through.

Where *was* Elena? Olivia wondered, missing her spunky, fair-haired friend so deeply that her chest ached. What had happened to her? If Elena was alive, did she even remember that wonderful night . . . or her two best friends? Olivia sighed.

The walk from the schoolhouse to Dr. Gray's office took only a few minutes. Sunshine drenched the little town and the countryside beyond, and the temperature had grown pleasant. It felt more like spring going on summer rather than fall heading into winter.

Rather than giving herself over to enjoying the beautiful weather, Olivia's thoughts turned from her friends to her arrangement with Dr. Gray. It just wasn't fair. Marshal Briggs had said she was to be the physician's assistant until his hand healed, but so far her purpose in serving him had been limited to unpacking boxes and managing animals.

As far as illness and injury, Tristan had been unusually quiet. Did the townspeople truly have no need of healing this week, or were they as wary and unsettled by the changes as she? Talk of the marshal's arrangement ran rampant. But perhaps there was no actual need of her spending her days with the doctor. So far they had not been summoned out of the office for any reason. She would talk to Marshal Briggs about calling off this enforced partnership, for the good doctor seemed to be handling things well enough with one hand.

She yearned for the return of her independence, for the freedom of coming and going as she pleased. She missed seeing town and country folk alike, without the tension the new doctor had brought to the community. Yesterday she had taken the long way home and called on Cora Skeever. The new mother and her infant son were doing well; Cora's sister had arrived from North Platte and had things running smoothly.

It seemed so long ago she'd delivered Cora of her son; how was it possible so much had happened in such a short period of time? Setting her hand on the knob, she sighed. Surely Marshal Briggs would see things from her point of view. She would speak to him on her way home.

❧

The afternoon passed without event. At three, Warren Hawley and Mayor Weeks stopped by to say hello, but not even one soul sought care. Dr. Gray puttered in his examination room, finding places for the seemingly endless quantity of equipment he'd had shipped from Boston and Philadelphia. He commented briefly on what good food Neff's Café served but otherwise spoke only to direct her arrangement of the drugs and pharmaceuticals in the cupboards and cases. This tedious task prevented her from further exploration of the books and journals she had finished putting away yesterday.

By the time four-thirty arrived, Olivia's temples throbbed. There was much work yet to be done with the various bottles, jars, and pots, but with any luck, she wouldn't be the one doing it. She couldn't wait to find the marshal and plead her position.

Dr. Gray was lifting a heavy case with his left arm when she walked into the examination room. Weariness showed in his movements and on his features, and a brownish red stain marred the whiteness of his bandage. What had he done to his wound? she wondered.

Surely he had to be in pain. Despite her dislike of the man, a stirring of sympathy tugged at her heartstrings. As far as she knew, he had not taken any opiates for his discomfort, nor did he imbibe in drink. He seemed a decent enough fellow in some respects. If only he wasn't such an arrogant, insufferable, overbearing . . .

"Time to go?" he asked, setting the case on the complex-looking surgery table. The shadows beneath his eyes made his gaze darker than usual. Yes, there was pain there.

"I made fair headway on the pharmaceuticals," she began, when a ruckus sounded from the front of the building. "Doc! Doc Gray!" a male voice called with urgency. "Come here, quick!"

The physician brushed past her with long strides. "I'm here. What is it?"

Quickly Olivia followed. Jeb Grosset stood in the doorway, wearing an anxious expression. "It's Miss Ella, sir. I found her." The farmer pointed out the door, toward the street. "I was bringin' a load of pumpkins into town an' I found Miss Farwell out on the prairie."

Olivia followed the men outdoors to the large, flat-bottomed wagon heaped with orange fruit. Hitched to the dray was a matched team with a single horse tied on behind. The short farmer hastened to throw aside a musty-smelling tarp, revealing the body of Tristan's milliner and dressmaker. Her taut expression and unnatural positioning gave Olivia no reason to hope the woman's body might hold any spark of life.

"What happened?" she asked, stunned at the sight.

"I don't know for sure, ma'am," Grosset replied before turning his attention toward Dr. Gray. "I was just ridin' along to town, mindin' my own business, an' I saw her horse. Her little buggy was tipped over on its side, an' there she lay on the ground, deader than a doornail. Sometimes women ain't the best drivers . . . or maybe she was tryin' to go too fast . . . or maybe her horse spooked. Hard to say. She prob'ly clonked her head or busted her neck, huh, Doc?" He took a breath, adding sadly, "She never was the friendly sort, but she sure was handy with a needle and thread. It won't be long before we'll be missin' her, and how."

A small crowd had gathered around the wagon, and it was mere moments before Marshal Briggs appeared. "What's going on?" his voice boomed as he approached. Taking in the sight before him, he shook his head. "What a shame. Anyone know what happened?"

"Miss Farwell had an accident, Marshal. She's dead," Grosset supplied, repeating his tale.

When Grosset had concluded, Briggs looked around at the crowd assembling in the waning sunlight. "We got enough for an inquisition here? Six willing?"

Several men acknowledged in subdued voices.

"Raise your right hand. Do you solemnly affirm that you will diligently inquire, and true presentment make, when, how, by what means the person whose body lies here dead came to her death, according to your knowledge and the evidence given you, so help you God?"

Dr. Gray interrupted the chorus of ayes. "Now wait just one minute, Briggs. Don't tell me you're marshal, newspaper editor, *and* coroner?"

The big man shrugged. "I threw my hat in the ring last term."

"And this woman's cause of death will be determined by a half dozen sworn-in onlookers standing around, making their best guesses?"

Olivia noticed Dr. Gray's gaze was darker than ever, his jaw rigid.

"Seems clear she lost control of her animal," Grosset reasoned. "Except for takin' the horse, I left everythin' the way it was. You can go look, if you like."

"We'll be ridin' out shortly." Marshal Briggs's expression had toughened, and he folded his arms across his chest. "Like I keep remindin' you, Doc, this ain't Boston. If you think you've got another way to handle things, I'm all ears."

"Bring her inside, and I will conduct a proper postmortem examination. You will have a full report of my findings."

"Is that really necessary, Dr. Gray?" Hawley stepped forward, palms upward in appeal. "Seems the least we can do is leave the poor woman her dignity. As justice of the peace, I am satisfied that the elements of this case point toward accidental death. Herb Greenfield's our undertaker. Why don't we just take her over there?"

Several in the crowd voiced their agreement.

Briggs studied the physician for a long moment. "How do you aim to conduct this examination, Doc?" he finally spoke. "Did you forget you only got one good hand?"

Dr. Gray turned to Olivia, his gaze shrewd. "You assigned me a pair of hands last week, Marshal. They'll do."

Before she could speak, Briggs ordered the jurymen to bring Ella's body into Dr. Gray's office. "And somebody find Johnson, too!" he hollered. "We need to leave right now if we're goin' to take a look at Miss Ella's buggy in any sort of daylight."

Agitation built inside Olivia as she studied the uncompromising set of the physician's features. None of this was necessary. Anyone with half a mind could see the dressmaker had met with an unfortunate accident, yet the new doctor insisted on another display of superiority by calling for a "proper" postmortem examination.

As Ella's body was carried into Dr. Gray's office, Olivia felt like stamping her foot. Was Briggs blind to the physician's motivation? Ella didn't deserve to be treated in such a manner in order to prove the Boston man's medical prowess, she fumed, especially after the unfortunate way the poor woman had met her end. While Dr. Ethan Gray might have learned a thing or two back East, he needed an education about how things were done in the West.

"You gonna be able to handle this, Livvie?" Briggs asked, after the doctor had followed the men inside. Though the remainder of the townspeople had drifted away from the wagon, he walked over to her and lowered his voice. "I don't rightly know what all his examination is going to entail, but I'm pretty sure I ain't got the stomach for it."

"Why are you going along with this?" Olivia hissed. "No one else thinks this is necessary. Can't you see what the doctor is up to?"

Beneath the brim of his hat, the marshal's gaze was perceptive. "You figure he's blowin' hot air to sound smart and attract attention? That might well be the case, but we don't know that at this point. I figure there's no harm in givin' his scientific Boston ways a try."

"But what about Ella? She should be laid to rest!"

"Ella's past the point of carin' what we do with her. In a few days' time, she'll have a funeral and a proper burial. Don't worry, Livvie, she'll get her due."

With a sound of exasperation, she whirled on her heel and strode into Dr. Gray's office. She would help him with his "examination," but not without telling him just how far out of line he was.

Chapter 5

After the townsmen laid Miss Farwell's body on the surgery table, Ethan bade one of the taller fellows to light the wall lamps. The man hastened to do as he was asked before departing on the heels of his speedily retreating companions. It was amazing a collision hadn't occurred in the hallway, for Olivia burst into the room a second later, gray eyes sparking mutiny.

Angrily she gestured toward the woman's black-cloaked figure. "This is wrong!"

"Miss Farwell's cause of death is unknown."

"Unknown? She had an accident! Why are you the only one having trouble putting two and two together?"

"If you find yourself incapable of assisting me, Miss Plummer, please find someone who can." Ethan was determined to remain unprovoked by the midwife's challenges. His key objective was to discover the reason for Ella Farwell's untimely death. Already he was thinking through the series of steps involved in making his examination, realizing that with his injury, there was no way he could do everything himself.

"I'll help you." Olivia turned up the left cuff of her blouse, her voice as unyielding and steely as the twin tracks of the new Colorado Central. "And we aren't going to find one thing out of the ordinary—except that she was killed as the result of a buggy accident."

Ethan wondered how he had ever thought Miss Olivia Plummer drab. He'd seen glimpses of her temper during the past week, but nothing like the display before him right now. Color-flushed cheeks brought her even features to life. He knew she was at least six inches shorter than he, yet her spine was stiff as a poker, giving her the impression of much greater stature. With brisk movements she continued turning up her sleeves, eyes flashing emotion.

"Just because you went to medical school in Boston, you think you know everything, don't you? You're so educated . . . so lofty . . . so *arrogant!*"

"Are you quite ready, Miss Plummer? We have a great deal of work to do." With his bandaged hand he pointed toward a pad of paper on the counter. Already he had made several mental notes about the deceased's physical appearance. "You'll need to record our findings as we go."

"One word—*dead*—ought to suffice."

"How can you be certain Miss Farwell is dead?" he asked, recalling Professor Bowditch's physiology laboratories. Nothing was taken for granted; everything was questioned.

She shook her head as if he were the most feebleminded fool on earth. "Well, look!"

"Yes, Miss Plummer, I have looked. Now tell me what *you* see." With concentration, he stepped alongside the corpse, noticing more precisely the positioning and skin tones, trying to reticulate this information with what the farmer had reported.

Olivia drew in a deep breath and released it in a controlled manner while she walked to the opposite side of the table. "Her arms and legs are stiff. The left side of her face is lavender from where she lay on the ground; the other side is abnormally pale. The eyes are dull." Touching Ella's exposed flesh, she added, "She's cold."

Ethan was surprised at the number of things the midwife had thought to mention. "How long has she been dead?"

"Since yesterday sometime."

"By what reasoning?"

"Because this darker-colored skin doesn't blanch when I press on it."

She had just given a perfect description of fixed lividity. Ethan watched the movements of her hands, which were sure and respectful. She didn't appear at all squeamish to touch the deceased, and seemed to have some knowledge of the normal physiologic processes occurring after death. *She might prove to be a capable assistant, after all,* he thought. "Remove her bonnet, please."

Olivia's graceful fingers untied the knot beneath Ella's chin and eased the cap from the woman's head. Gently, she moved her fingertips across every part of Ella's scalp. "I don't find anything here. She must have broken her neck when she struck the ground."

"We'll get there, eventually."

"Eventually? What else is there to do?" Her gaze was filled with challenge. "I won't allow you to disfigure this woman's body merely to puff up your own pride."

"My pride?" Despite his intentions of keeping his temper reined and focusing on the tasks at hand, the midwife's opposition sparked Ethan's ire. "This is not," he bit out, "about my pride. Conducting a thorough and proper postmortem examination is simply what any self-respecting, well-trained doctor of medicine *does* in situations such as this." He took a deep breath and let it out, determined to press on. "You discovered no lacerations, bumps, or depressions on the deceased's scalp?"

"Didn't I just say so? For a well-trained medical doctor, your memory is rather lacking."

Ignoring her spiny comment, he continued. "Now we'll move to the eyes." Lifting the delicate flesh of the eyelid, he was startled by what he saw. Quickly he examined the undersurface of the lower lid. "Check the other eye," he ordered, disturbed by the implications of his finding.

She did as he asked, a furrow marring her forehead. "I've never seen such a thing. The insides of the lids are all red."

"Yes," he said in a grim tone. "Ecchymoses of the conjunctivae."

He watched some of the fight go out of Olivia and wariness settle in its place. "What does that mean?"

"You might want to check the *Manuel Complet de Médecine Légale*. Some very important discoveries made by Auguste Tardieu are discussed in detail in volume one. You do read French, don't you?" Ethan couldn't resist the gibe.

Olivia's chin went up a notch, and she answered with bravado, "No, I do not read French, nor do I see the importance of red eyelids. Now, if you would be so kind as to call it a day—"

"I would wager that Ella Farwell did not die accidentally."

"What?" At his shocking statement, Olivia froze, her eyes widening. "What . . . how . . . how can you be certain?"

"I have examined the bodies of persons who have died of suffocation . . . and I've seen this before. Do you notice these scattered pinpoint spots on her face?"

"Yes?"

"If she was asphyxiated, her lungs will reveal the same sort of spots, only to a greater degree. Next we will examine her nose and mouth."

The midwife's gaze left his face and studied the former dressmaker's features. "For what? Feathers?"

"You catch on quickly, Miss Plummer. Now, would you be so good as to record our findings?"

The next several minutes passed while he and Olivia made careful, tedious inspection of Ella's nose, mouth, neck, and hands. They discovered nothing distinctly amiss, and Ethan could sense his assistant's growing skepticism while they removed the dressmaker's clothing. He did not doubt that further examination would bear out his suspicions, yet he was frustrated by the lack of any other physical evidence pointing to foul play.

"I just don't believe Ella was killed." Olivia's voice was terse as she draped a sheet over the inert form. "Don't you think we would see some sign of struggle? So far, we haven't—" She pulled the sheet back down, her gaze sharp. "Oh my." Pointing to the faint line of pigmentation beginning at the woman's navel, she traced it downward before placing her hands on the abdomen and palpating its contours.

"She's with child," she said softly, wonderingly.

"How far along?"

"In her sixth month, I'd guess."

"You did say it was *Miss* Farwell, didn't you?"

"Yes, she isn't—I mean, wasn't—married."

"Who was her . . . gentleman caller?"

"No one, as far as I know. Donal Connally courted her for a time last year, but she sent him packing."

"Who's Donal Connally?"

"My neighbor, widowed two years ago. The word was, Ella didn't fancy taking up where Deborah Connally left off. Since then, Donal just drinks and lets his children do the farming."

"He's in town often?"

Olivia nodded. "At Kelly's Saloon."

Ethan turned this information over in his mind. "There are many more examinations we need to make, Miss Plummer. Are you up to the task?" He nodded toward the polished wood autopsy case on the counter. Beneath its gleaming lid was a tray containing a hammer, an enterotome, scissors, and scalpels of various sizes. The lower compartment held heavier equipment. This postmortem kit had cost a pretty penny, and he almost hadn't made its acquisition.

Certainly he hadn't expected to use it so soon.

"Not only Ella, but a defenseless little babe lost, as well. I can't believe Donal would do such a thing. I pray it isn't so." Olivia's voice was sober as she walked to the case and opened its lid. She gazed at the contents a long moment before turning her head toward him. Her complexion had paled, and he noticed that she swallowed hard. "I'll do what I can to help you," she said, her gaze steady nonetheless. "But I must tell you I've never—"

"You'll do well." He hadn't meant to say such a thing, but the encouraging words escaped him quite honestly. She was a plucky woman, ever proving herself to be a more-than-capable assistant. Since the day she'd sutured his wound, he'd found he couldn't stop watching her hands. So small yet so steady and gifted.

Frustration rose within him when he glanced down at his own hands. Beneath the bandage the cut healed without sign of infection, but his right thumb and forefinger remained paralyzed. "Let's continue," he said curtly, breaking off his thoughts before they hurtled to their inevitable, worst-possible conclusion: He'd never use his right hand again.

Marshal Briggs returned just as they finished the examination, well after dark. He and Deputy Johnson walked into the room, their faces shadowed beneath their hats. With sorrow, Olivia washed and wrapped the tiny infant while the physician shared his medical conclusions with the lawmen.

Never had she been through such a grueling experience as this postmortem, nor had she ever, in her wildest imaginings, conceived of making such a tour of the human body's inner workings. She was completely worn out from the experience, both physically and mentally. Dr. Gray's knowledge of anatomy was exhaustive, his investigative techniques meticulous.

The only thing over which they'd found themselves at odds was the womb. Olivia had wanted to leave it closed, allowing the fetus to remain undisturbed, but Ethan had been insistent. There was only one chance to gather evidence, and he didn't intend to miss the tiniest detail.

The baby she held in her arms was perfectly formed, a boy. Ten little fingers, ten tiny toes, a faint covering of dark fuzz on his miniature head. Not even two pounds, yet human in every regard. How had Ella carried this child secretly within her, going about her business as usual? Who was his father? Tears welled up in Olivia's eyes at the scope of this double tragedy. She hoped the killer would be brought to swift justice.

"So her neck was broken. What do you make of all this?" Deputy Johnson sidled up to Olivia and removed his hat. He glanced at the sheet-draped form, then focused his attention on the wee, still infant.

"The hyoid bone in the front of Ella's neck was crushed inward."

"Terrible tragedy, her crashing like that." Johnson made a clucking sound and shook his head.

"Dr. Gray thinks an accident was unlikely. He believes she was strangled." A shiver ran through Olivia as she recalled each horrifying discovery they'd made. "Her liver was also lacerated by her broken ribs."

"Well, surely that happened in the smashup," Johnson supplied.

Olivia chose her words carefully. "Yes, I'm sure it did, but the absence of hemorrhage from the liver speaks to the fact that she was already dead when she crashed."

The deputy was silent a long moment. "You know anything about the baby?"

"No, I never even suspected."

"It's small," the assistant lawman observed. "Looks about the size of a newborn pup."

"He," Olivia amended, her throat thick. "The child is male."

Johnson nodded. "How early you figure it is?"

"I believe he would have been due sometime after the new year. Without knowing when . . . " Her words trailed off in a sigh. "Well, it's hard to be certain."

Head canted to the side, the deputy appeared to digest her words while he studied the infant. Olivia had witnessed many stillborn infants in the course of her work, but seeing such things had to be difficult for a bachelor.

"What do you think, Johnson?" Briggs's voice was troubled, deeper than usual in pitch. Strain lined his features. "Do we play this close to our vests till we visit Connally?"

"There's something else." Dr. Gray cleared his throat. "In the course of our examination, we also discovered evidence of Miss Farwell's having recently lain with a man. There appeared to be no force."

"How recent?" Losing interest in the baby, the deputy turned on his heel and rejoined the men. "How can you tell?"

"It's impossible to give you a time, but I'd guess shortly before she died. The proof is beneath my microscope."

Olivia glanced at the wondrous invention that, beneath its lenses, had enabled her to view a whole new world. Until today, she'd only heard of such devices.

". . . and then we find out where Donal was yesterday," the deputy was saying. "If he can't account for his whereabouts, then we—"

"Hold on a minute, Johnson," Briggs interrupted. "They haven't had anything to do with each other for well over a year."

"That you know of."

Briggs folded his arms across his chest. "I keep close enough tabs on this town that I think I'd know. Trouble is, I have no idea who else she might have been seein', either."

"Did you know about the baby?" Johnson challenged.

The big man was quiet, mulling over his deputy's words. "Go on and get him then. This time of night, he's probably on his stool at Kelly's."

Briggs released an enormous sigh when Johnson strode from the room, his smooth features fixed with determination. "And I thought things in this town couldn't get any worse. I owe you an apology, Doc. It appears that this postmortem was indeed called for. You knew what you were doin', after all."

"No, I didn't *know* any of this before I started, Marshal. I've just learned over the years that things are not always as they appear to be. When there's an unexplained death, it's always better to be safe than . . . well, having a murderer go free."

Olivia's heart beat harder while the men continued talking, a flush of shame stealing up her cheeks. She was as guilty—if not more so—as the townsmen for opposing Dr. Gray's convictions regarding this matter. At every turn she had refuted and contradicted him, until she could no longer ignore the evidence: Ella's death was not accidental.

Could Donal Connally truly be a murderer? Or was there another man with whom Ella had been involved? With a long, final look at the baby, Olivia pulled the blanket over his porcelain features and laid him in a basin. If Donal had done this terrible thing, what would become of Susan? of Seamus? of their farm? The poor children had already lost their mother; would another, worse tragedy visit their young lives?

"No, I don't believe Ella had family," the marshal replied to the physician. "Did you know of any relations, Livvie?"

"No. She told me once she had no family remaining."

"What will happen to her?" Dr. Gray asked, inclining his head toward her body.

"She'll be buried tomorrow. If you're done with everythin', we'll get her over to the undertaker's and call for Deacon Carlisle in the morning. I'll have to swear Herb Greenfield to secrecy about the baby, at least for the time being—"

"Hello? Anyone here?" a distressed female voice called from the front of the office. "Please, is anyone here?"

In the dim lantern glow of the front office stood Mabel Lepper, a middle-aged woman who lived with her husband and children on a small ranch north of town. Her lean, careworn face was streaked with tears. "It's Luther! I think he's dying."

"I'm Dr. Gray, madam." Ethan spoke to the rancher's wife as if she were his only concern on earth. "Please take a seat and tell me what ails your—"

"I can't do that. . . . Luther—my husband—needs help right away. Please, can you come? Or Miss Olivia?"

"What are his symptoms?"

She wrung her hands and took a step toward the door, appearing torn between staying long enough to describe his illness and wanting to be back at his side. "Oh, he's in terrible pain. His face is pinched and white, and his eyes are sunk in. He's been vomiting all day and can't move his bowels."

"It sounds as though he may have an intestinal obstruction." Ethan turned and looked at Olivia, who hung toward the rear of the front room with the marshal. "Do you know where they live?"

She nodded, remembering something. "I think my grandmother saw Mr. Lepper once for his hernia." She spoke in a low voice.

"Yes!" Mabel seized on Olivia's words. "But when Granny Esmond saw him, it wasn't nearly as bad as this."

"Guess I'll park myself here till you're back," Marshal Briggs spoke wearily, leaning against the door frame of the hallway. "Mark my words, you'll never again hear me say things can't get worse."

Chapter 6

A three-quarter moon provided sufficient light by which to travel. Dr. Gray's new carriage was larger and more finely sprung than Olivia's, making for a smoother ride over the rutted prairie track than she was accustomed to. Mrs. Lepper was probably back at her husband's side by now, for the ranch wife had departed for home immediately after seeking their assistance.

Olivia shivered and snuggled more deeply within the folds of her cloak. The night was cold, but even more chilling was the thought of poor Ella lying out on the prairie overnight after having met her end. Who could have committed such a heinous crime? Had the person who killed her also fathered her child? That was what Briggs, Johnson, and Dr. Gray had discussed.

Weariness hummed behind her eyes, and she closed her lids. Fatigue and unremitting activity were things to which she had grown accustomed over the years, but never accompanied by a feeling of such uneasiness. To think that someone in their community could have . . .

Opening her eyes, she glanced sidelong at the doctor's profile. What was he thinking? Was he sorry he'd come to Tristan? Beneath the black felt-rimmed hat, his expression appeared resolute. She knew he had to be tired as well, but he'd insisted on driving, managing the reins in his left hand and with the third and fourth fingers of his right.

The star-spattered sky stretched over the grassland as far as the eye could see. Some nights Olivia thought the astral bodies appeared close enough to touch, but tonight it seemed as though a wide chasm separated the heavens from the earth.

The Leppers' ranch lay yet two miles north. If Mabel had presented an accurate picture of her husband's symptoms, he was in grave danger. *Please, Father,* she prayed, *rest your hands on Luther until we arrive, then lend ours your help as we tend him.*

"Tell me what your grandmother did for Mr. Lepper's hernia." Olivia started at the physician's voice. His words to her were stiff as ever, but had she detected a hint of softening in his tone?

"I wasn't with her, so I can't be certain," she replied. "I'll check her books in the morning, though I know that doesn't help right now."

"She kept records?"

"Oh, yes, her books are very detailed. They've been of help to me more times than I can count." Beyond that, though, Olivia treasured the thin-lined volumes as timeless links to her mother's mother, the woman who had raised her as her own. Adeline Esmond's sepia-colored script left a legacy of love, as well as valuable information about the people she'd treated.

"Am I to assume, then, that you keep records as well?"

"Of course." She was surprised he asked, for she'd peeked into the formidable log he'd brought from Boston. He'd begun a new one upon his arrival in Tristan, his penmanship crisp and bold . . . until his injury. She hadn't been able to decide if the few untidy entries since then had been made with his left hand or somehow with his right.

A long sigh issued from him, audible over the *clippety-clop* of the horses' hooves. "You're a disconcerting woman, Miss Plummer."

"How so?"

"Because the more I know about you, the less I know about you."

"But you don't really know me." After a pause, she ventured, "You assumed you knew all about me when you came here, didn't you?"

Turning his head, he regarded her with eyes too shadowed to read. "That's a fair enough question."

After an uncomfortable silence ensued, she asked, "If it's a fair question, why don't you answer? I answered plenty of yours while I stitched your hand."

Something between a snort and a chuckle escaped him. "You told me the townspeople thought I was putting out to pasture."

"Well, you asked . . . and you never gave your reply about why you came to Tristan, either. I don't understand. With all your wealth and education, why would you choose to settle in a town such as ours?"

She sensed him stiffen beside her. "You think me a wealthy man?"

"Your clothes are finer than anyone's around here." Gesturing at the carriage, she added, "You seem to have no shortage of nice things. And with all your equipment, you could open a brace of hospitals."

Another long sigh floated upward, lost in the vastness of the night. "I came to Tristan to simplify my life. It had gotten to be quite . . . complicated."

"Are you running away from something?"

"You have no trouble asking questions, do you, Miss Plummer?"

"I beg your pardon," she apologized, abashed at her lack of manners. "I'm not usually so presumptuous. Please forgive me."

"Maybe I am running from something," he replied in a musing tone. "Or maybe I'm trying to run toward something else. Perhaps one day I'll tell you why I came—not that you probably won't ask again. You seem to have no qualms whatsoever about speaking your mind."

But I'm really not that way, she wanted to protest. If only she could explain, without compounding her troubles, that there was just something about him that aroused such passion within her. When she thought of the way she'd spoken to him during the postmortem, she wanted to sink low in her padded leather seat. Especially since the examination had borne out the true cause of Ella's death.

Had she hurt his feelings? she wondered. It was hard to believe a man such as he could be affected by mere words, but maybe her incivility had affected him. Marshal Briggs had apologized; was she no less wrong than the burly lawman?

"How did you learn so much?" he asked, allowing her to set aside for now the idea of asking his forgiveness. The memory of his calling for her arrest upon their initial meeting remained a bitter taste in her mouth.

"Granny Esmond taught me what she knew."

"And she learned . . .?"

"By doing. In St. Louis, she mostly attended births. When we moved here, out of necessity she was called for other things. There was no one else."

"So she treated hernias."

"Among other things."

"And she required you to pray before every procedure?"

"She did so herself. To her, failing to pray was doing only half a job."

"And you agree? Do you believe the same?"

Did he ridicule her? At his dry tone, she cocked her head, shifting herself in the seat so she could more fully see him. "Aren't you a God-fearing man, Dr. Gray?"

"I am."

"Then why do you disparage the idea of seeking the Lord's help for your patients?" Perhaps graduates of Harvard's medical school considered themselves too lofty to require divine assistance, she thought, smarting at the implied challenge of his words.

"I'm not disparaging the idea of prayer itself. I merely consider it a private matter between a man and his Creator."

To Granny Esmond, prayer had been a private matter, a public matter, and everything in between. "Think of it, Livvie," she'd said many times in varying ways, "when our time on earth is up, how many folk we will have prayed for. Some of them might not have had a single word to the Lord spoken on their behalf otherwise. When it feels burdensome, you think on that and keep praying."

"Why were you raised by your grandmother?" he asked.

Apparently the subject of faith was now closed. "Cholera. Both parents," she replied. At the time of their deaths she had been so young that the few remaining memories of them lingered in her mind, hazy and dim.

"Please accept my sympathies."

She nodded, oddly touched by his formal-sounding condolence. "What about you? Are your parents living?"

"My father ran off to the gold fields and was never heard of again. My mother died when I was twelve."

"Who cared for you? Your grandparents?"

"No."

"Aunts or uncles? A neighbor? Surely you didn't raise yourself."

"You might be surprised." The grimness in his voice should have discouraged further questioning, but Olivia's curiosity burned beyond her control.

"You grew up on your own . . . yet you attended *Harvard University?* How can that be?"

"Let it suffice to say I worked very hard."

Olivia clearly understood the message behind these terse words: ask no more. She returned to her front-facing position and rearranged the folds of her cloak while her mind turned over the physician's spare revelations. An orphaned, impoverished youth had somehow, on his own, transformed himself into a highly educated medical doctor. Suddenly Ethan Gray's uncompromising, perfectionistic manner began making a great deal of sense to her. As for discovering the reason—or reasons—he'd left Boston, she would have to wait. His life story promised to be more fascinating than that of a Dickens character.

"I see a light. Is that their place?" he asked from beside her, interrupting her introspection.

"Yes. We're nearly there."

Time to turn her thoughts back to the task at hand. She prayed for wisdom as they approached the Leppers' modest home, hoping Luther's condition could be somehow reversed. Ever the self-sufficient rancher, he had undoubtedly disguised his condition until he had fallen deathly ill. Perhaps Dr. Gray would know of some treatment she didn't, she thought, quickly reminding herself that she was merely the doctor's assigned pair of hands until such time as he was fit to use his own again.

And don't forget he's contacted the Colorado Medical Society, Livvie. When this is over, he plans to run you out of business any way he can.

❧

"We have two choices."

The sweat-drenched rancher moaned with pain in the next room of the simple abode while the blond physician spoke gravely to his wife. To their credit, the Lepper children did not fuss during this time of fear and uncertainty, but quiet as mice they drew close as they dared to overhear the doctor's words.

"I have examined your husband and confirmed that he does, indeed, have a strangulated hernia of moderate size," Dr. Gray went on. "Taxis—manual replacement of the hernia—may be successful, but if not, it's imperative we operate without delay."

Operate? Olivia intercepted the doctor's glance, an icy finger of fear running down her spine at the thought. Assisting with Ella Farwell's postmortem examination was one thing . . . but operating on a live person was quite another. Granny Esmond had, obviously, manually returned the outpouching of Luther

Lepper's bowels through the ring of muscle back to its proper place. But as Dr. Gray was explaining, this method might not be effective. *Oh, God in heaven,* she prayed, *I do not know if I am equal to the tasks that may be asked of me this night. In your mercy, I ask you to spare Luther his life and any unnecessary trouble or suffering.*

The next few hours passed in a blur. Before beginning anesthesia, the affected area was prepared for surgery so no time would be lost if taxis was not successful. Given the rancher's condition, Dr. Gray was reluctant to use chloroform. However, he said he preferred its relaxative effects over those of ether, so he proceeded to administer the drops of liquid sleep with caution, allowing Luther to inhale their anesthetic qualities through a clean, folded cloth.

When their patient lay in a deep, restful state, Ethan gave Olivia precise instructions on how she should manipulate the hernia. To their great relief, the tumor grew smaller and smaller with the maneuvers, finally returning to the abdominal cavity with a gurgling sound.

Dr. Gray called Mrs. Lepper into the room then and spoke with her while Olivia returned the physician's instruments and supplies to his bag. "Things look promising, madam. Your husband should stay in bed for the next twenty-four hours. Allow him no food." Silent tears, testimony of her unbearable strain, slipped down the ranch wife's cheeks even while she nodded her understanding. The children hovered at the doorway, peeking through the gap between the door and the jamb to see whether their father had lived or died.

Olivia gave them an encouraging smile before pointing toward the bed and making a gesture indicating he was asleep. This elicited smiles of relief from the older ones. Glancing up, she saw Dr. Gray had noticed her movements. Frowning slightly, he continued. "He'll be fully awake soon. We'll return tomorrow and fit your husband with a truss. My fee is fifteen dollars. You may pay me now or on the morrow."

"Fifteen . . . dollars? But I don't . . . we don't—" Fresh tears formed, and the ranch wife's face crumpled with distress. She bowed her head and buried her face in her hands.

Olivia's heart went out to her, and she walked quickly to Mabel's side. "Don't give the money a thought," she soothed, laying her hand across the woman's trembling shoulders. "Having Luther up and about is more valuable than all the ore in the Leadville mines. We'll work something out. Now, do you have any questions about what Dr. Gray told you? Luther will probably be wanting his bacon and eggs in the morning, but you're going to have to hold him off and let his system rest."

Meeting Ethan's gaze over Mrs. Lepper's head, Olivia was shocked at the thundercloud of expression on his face. Surely he wasn't upset about the money. Didn't he know cash was in precious short supply?

He said nothing to her as they departed the Leppers', but his silence reeked of his disapproval. He sat so stiffly at the reins he appeared to be starched. She looked at the sky, noticing that the crisp wedge of moon had traveled far across the sky while they had seen to the rancher. Its dim illumination spread across the prairie.

Finally, when the carriage was clear of the house, he spoke. "Don't ever do that again."

"Do what?" Olivia replied with equal censure in her tone. "Would you really see these good people sell off their necessities in order to pay you cash?"

"What do you propose, Miss Plummer? That I just accept whatever token of gratitude they see fit to bestow? Medicine is a profession, and if it is to be treated as such, certain rules of order must be followed. I have adjusted downward my schedule of fees, realizing Boston's economy is no doubt more prosperous than Tristan's." He cleared his throat and inclined his head toward her. "What system of remuneration do you employ? Chickens? Dry goods? Guns and blankets?"

"You're more right than you know. These people are generous with what they have. I doubt Claude Harker was home five minutes with his broken ankle before he sent Mickey over with more potatoes than I can probably eat all winter."

"Potatoes. You're telling me I missed out on a winter's worth of potatoes by not setting that man's ankle? Miss Plummer, you must set your price and hold fast, or people will simply walk all over you."

"You really don't understand, do you?" she sputtered. "People can't give you what they don't have. Times are hard and there just *isn't* money. You take what you get."

"You're telling me you're never paid in cash?" His tone was incredulous.

"Some folks can pay a little. I've managed to put aside some savings."

"Well, I'm prepared to pay full price and wish to settle my account with you at once." He gestured with his bandaged hand. "You've never mentioned your fee for your work."

"Fifteen dollars," she replied, thinking swiftly. "And you may immediately apply the money to Luther Lepper's bill."

"You can't do that." He turned his whole body and leaned forward in order to stare at her, challenge in his hardened eyes.

"I can't? You may pay me then, and I'll just hand Mabel your fifteen dollars tomorrow. The math's the same." Why was he such an impossible man? Exasperation made her tongue reckless. "For growing up in want, you seem to have forgotten where you came from." She saw her words land like a blow, and she immediately regretted them.

Eyes narrowed, Ethan returned to his former position, presenting a profile so rocky it appeared to have been hewn from solid stone. When he spoke, his voice was low. "I have never met a more *difficult* person in my entire life than you, Olivia Plummer."

She was difficult? He was *beyond* difficult. She very nearly told him so, lifting her hands from her lap to make her point. A second later, she dropped them, frustrated at her lack of humility and self-control. Why was she so hateful where Ethan Gray was concerned? she asked herself. She had no right to pass judgment on him or anyone else. "I'm sorry," she said, knowing her voice sounded tense. "My words were uncalled for."

He made no reply. A mile passed before he spoke again. "You will be paid the moment we return. You may keep your money, and I will cancel the Lepper account entirely. Will that please you?"

"No," she replied without thinking. "I don't want your money."

"What *do* you want, then?"

I want you to understand our people and our ways, she thought, not knowing how to articulate her passion. *For you to not be so stuffy and formal about everything, proving your superiority at every turn.*

"Why the hesitation? You had no problem speaking your mind a short while ago . . . or for that matter, ever since I made your acquaintance."

"Once again, I must beg your pardon," she said inelegantly. "I was raised better than that."

To her admission he made no reply, and they passed the remainder of the drive to town in silence. Exhaustion settled heavily upon her while she reviewed the events of this arduous day. With longing, she thought of her bed and the comfort she would find in her little cabin. Sunrise would be here too quickly, but she was sure even a few hours in her home would restore her equilibrium, her perspective.

It was a good thing Granny Esmond had already departed this life, for she would have been shocked at Olivia's behavior of late. She longed for the older woman's wisdom and guidance. Adeline Esmond would have known exactly how to deal with Dr. Ethan Gray in a firm, no-nonsense, and godly manner.

Marshal Briggs met them at the livery, apparently having been watching for their return. "We need to talk," he said, guiding them down the street to his office. Neither of the two jail cells was occupied, Olivia noticed. She saw that Dr. Gray had made the same observation, giving the marshal a questioning gaze.

"For the time being, I have deemed Ella Farwell's death accidental." Briggs's bleary-eyed face was stubbled with beard. He sighed and readjusted his hat. "Before you get your feathers all ruffled, Doc, let me finish."

"Please do." Ethan folded his arms across his chest, resting his wounded hand on the biceps of his opposite arm.

"Besides the killings of a couple of no-goods passing through the area, we've never had a crime of this sort in Tristan," the marshal went on. "Now, I don't want the townsfolk up in arms about there being a murderer on the loose."

"I hate to disagree with you, Marshal," the physician said dryly, "but there *is* a murderer on the loose. The evidence I discovered is irrefutable."

"I know that, Doc. I'm getting there. We're going to be digging up some evidence ourselves when we comb through Ella's things. I'm confident we'll find something that will lead us to the guilty party. Until then, I don't want him skipping town— or his due."

"But what about Donal?" Olivia asked, worried about the children's safety.

"We took Connally for a walk and questioned him about his relationship with Ella. He says it never progressed beyond a single kiss, and that he hasn't seen her since before Christmas. A half dozen of Kelly's regulars said he was on his stool at the saloon earlier than usual Monday and didn't leave till closing."

"You're wrong to take the word of a bunch of drunks," Johnson said, materializing from the darkness on the far side of the room. "One lies, and they all swear to it."

The big lawman frowned. "Johnson and I aren't in perfect harmony on this matter. John Kelly told me the same as his regulars—and Kelly's as dry as a tobacco box. If he says Donal Connally was on his stool all day until closing, I can take his word on it."

"Do you remember Ella's visit Monday morning?" Olivia glanced at the physician and the deputy before turning her attention toward Briggs. "She was talking with Dr. Gray when Mr.

Johnson and I walked in. She said she was just welcoming the new doctor, but she seemed as nervous as a cat in a roomful of rockers. I wonder if she was there about her pregnancy?"

"She made a point of saying there wasn't anything the matter with her." Ethan's tone was thoughtful. "I wonder what she might have told me if we hadn't been interrupted?"

Olivia went on. "And then when she left, she said she had to make a delivery. I don't know where she was going, but I think we must have been the last people to see her alive."

"Obviously Donal Connally was the last to see her alive." Cynicism was evident in Dermot Johnson's tone. *Did the man's shirt ever wrinkle?* Olivia wondered, looking the man over. Even at this hour, the deputy's appearance was as neat as the marshal's was rumpled.

Briggs held up his hands and shook his head. "Hold your horses, Johnson. He told me Miss Farwell had hinted to him of another man, a gunman. We'll find something in her things that will lead to his identity . . . and his arrest." An expression of regret crossed his weary face, and he faced Olivia. "But until that time, Livvie, I can't allow you to be out at your place alone."

"You . . . what?"

"Even though I don't think Donal Connally is behind Miss Farwell's demise, I'm not taking any chances. I don't want you out there by yourself." Briggs's boots made a scuffing sound against the wood floor. "And after Mabel Lepper rode to town as if the hounds of hell were on her heels, I got to wondering what the doc is supposed to do if he gets another such call after you've gone home for the day. Precious time could be lost if someone has to ride out for you. But the longer I live, the more I've been realizing that the solutions to problems are often staring a man right in the eye. Livvie, you'll move into Ella's shop until we have the killer behind bars."

Disbelief suspended Olivia's anger at his pronouncement. She'd been stripped of everything else and now—just like that!— she was to leave her home and move into the house of a dead woman? She could find no reply. Tears welled in her eyes, and her shoulders slumped with defeat.

"Aw, Livvie, don't do that," Briggs said awkwardly, fumbling for his handkerchief. "Please? The situation's just temporary. . . . Look at it this way; you can spend more time with Janet," he added with anemic optimism. "Maybe have your dinners together."

She swallowed, fighting to control her emotions. "Am I allowed to get my things?"

"Of course," the lawman hastened to reply. "I'll take you out there myself, first thing in the morning. That is, of course, if you can spare her for a while, Doc."

Ethan nodded, his expression impassive.

"Come on then, Livvie," Briggs said with a heavy sigh. "Let's get you settled in your new home."

Chapter 7

Olivia awakened with a start in Ella Farwell's tiny bedchamber. After passing a few hours of fitful rest, she was convinced she might feel better if she hadn't bothered sleeping at all. Wearily she pushed herself to a sitting position on the side of the bed and stretched. The base of her neck felt knotted, her head cloudy.

Watery light entered the room around well-tailored drapes, providing enough light for her to study the former dressmaker's furnishings. Made of wine-colored brocade, the bed's coverlet matched the drapes. The sheets were muslin, but of a tight weave. Olivia had noticed their freshness at once, which told of a recent washing. A wardrobe stood opposite the iron bed; the only other piece of furniture was a small table on which rested a basin, brush, comb, and hand mirror.

The walls were papered in a beige *fleur-de-lis*, giving the modest room a tasteful look not commonly found in these parts. A few pictures dotted the walls, and three braided rugs covered most of the clean-swept wooden floor. Upon entering the shop last night, Olivia had noticed that the dressmaker had allotted most of her space to her business, leaving only a few rooms for personal use. Ella Farwell had kept a neat house, and her fabrics and millinery goods were equally orderly. Rising, Olivia longed for a long, hot bath, knowing there was no chance of having such a luxury this morning. A splash of water on her face would have to suffice.

She descended the L-shaped staircase and saw that the clock in the kitchen read seven-twenty. She held little hope that Irvin Briggs would change his mind about his latest decree, for as he'd walked her to her temporary home earlier this morning, he'd impressed upon her the need for secrecy about both Ella's pregnancy and her murder.

Glancing at the cloth-wrapped loaf of bread and knife on the cutting table, she shook her head. Just two days earlier, Ella Farwell had had no idea she'd made her last breakfast. The dressmaker had to have known about the baby, though. What had been her thoughts about the life growing within her? And who was the wee one's father?

So much turmoil. So much to think of. Only a scant two weeks ago, Dr. Ethan Gray had burst into Tristan like a crate of sparking Chinese fireworks, threatening to shoot the pieces of her well-ordered life as high as the moon. And now together, in the midst of Ella Farwell's death, they had discovered this complex tangle of ugly, secret sin. If not for Dr. Gray's dogged insistence on performing a postmortem examination, the evil might never have been exposed. Grudging admiration for him arose inside her.

A picture of the physician's face came to mind. If he ever smiled, he could be a handsome man, she allowed. But more than good-looking features in a man, she valued kindness and a heart for God. Did Ethan Gray possess either? she wondered. Since his arrival, he'd seemed anything but kind to her. He had also made references to suggest her faith was silly, trivial, even superstitious.

But what about his offer to waive Luther Lepper's charges? she asked herself. *If things like that weren't done in Boston, he's made quite a concession. He also told you he was a God-fearing man . . . and you know plenty of people who hold a deep but private faith in the Lord. Given his upbringing, isn't it possible he's put together like that?*

One opinion about the man she'd revised was that of his eyes: she no longer thought his gaze merely cold and remote. On the contrary, she now knew a deep intelligence burned in their umber depths. She'd first been aware of it upon their inspection of Ella Farwell's body. Ethan Gray was systematic and single-minded, nothing escaping his scrutiny. Later, watching him examine Mr. Lepper, she again detected the same keenness in his manner and gaze. Janet might simply think he had nice brown eyes, but Olivia knew there was much, much more behind them.

Her stomach growled, and she looked at the clock. Seven-thirty. No time to eat. She needed to get to her cabin, collect her things, and report to Dr. Gray's office. With a little luck, she might be back to town by ten. Susan would be wondering what had happened to her; thank goodness for the girl's willingness to look after her home while she was away. Olivia had no worries about her little cabin or her cow, but she was concerned for the Connally children. She hoped they had drunk every last drop of what Susan had milked.

Though Olivia didn't really believe Donal Connally could have committed either crime against Ella Farwell, her worries for his children had now multiplied. It was ironic: perhaps her biggest objection to leaving her cabin was that she would no longer be near the Connallys . . . and that was precisely the reason Briggs wanted her away.

"I wish you knew how bad I felt about this, Livvie," the marshal said on their ride back to town. Olivia's clothes, foodstuffs, and healing goods were stacked in the back of his wagon. "I realize I'm uprootin' you from your home, but for the time bein' I don't see a better way to do things."

She nodded, wrapped in sorrow at her parting from Susan. Only ten minutes earlier, the skinny girl had thrown her arms around Olivia and convulsed with tears at the news her neighbor would be moving to town. She had nearly offered to take Susan

with her but realized she couldn't take Seamus away from bringing in the crops. The Connally children were as loving and
protective of one another as any two siblings could hope to be,
and she didn't have the heart to separate them.

The skies were drab, corresponding with her mood. Ahead,
the faint outline of the town appeared amidst the vista of sere
prairie grass. What choices did she have about anything anymore?
she asked herself. She'd been told where to live, with whom to
practice . . . and Dr. Ethan Gray certainly told her what to do in
that regard, governing her every movement. Perhaps she ought to
think of moving on. It shouldn't be difficult to establish herself in
another community.

"You just ain't been yourself since this all started, Livvie,"
Briggs spoke. "Not that I can blame you, of course. But for what
it's worth, the doc thinks you're doin' a real fine job."

She bit back a tart response.

"What he said is that you've got good hands."

An unladylike snort escaped her.

Briggs glanced over, his gaze serious. "You managed a
number of things for the doc yesterday, Livvie, and that couldn't
have been easy for him. What you maybe don't understand in all
this is a man's pride."

"Ethan Gray has no shortage of pride."

"I don't mean it in that way. I'm talkin' about pride as in
competence and ability. It's everythin' to a man to be good at
what he does. That's just something the Lord put into our
nature."

"So you're saying women don't take satisfaction in
performing their tasks—whatever they may be—to the best of
their ability? That I don't give folks my best effort . . . or Janet
doesn't care deeply about the welfare of each one of her pupils?"

"Aw, come on, Livvie, you're makin' me out to be as
chuckleheaded as a prairie dog. Do you think I want both you
and Janet packin' a grudge against me? Of course I know women
take their work seriously. But with men, it's different. Just hear

me out. I've put some thought into this and boiled it down to three *P*s."

"Three *P*s. I suppose you're going to tell me what they are."

"Sure am." Briggs smiled with relief, Olivia assumed, at being out of the dangerous territory he'd skirted.

Despite her mood, she felt the corners of her mouth turn upward. Irvin Briggs was sometimes blustery and overbearing, but he was a caring, good-hearted man. She had never felt romantic inclination toward him, thinking of him, instead, in a brotherly fashion, but she knew Janet would do well to have the lawman at her side the rest of her days.

"All right now," he went on. "These are my three *P*s: pursue, provide, and protect. That's what the Almighty put into man: the need to pursue, provide, and protect." He looked at her, satisfied with himself.

"And he put into women the need to procure, prepare, and prevail," she shot back.

"Blast it, Livvie. Your mind works faster than chain lightnin'." A scowl replaced the big man's pleased expression. "It took me a long time to think that up." He *harrumphed,* then added, "All I was tryin' to say was that after your troubled beginnin' with the doc, he said a few complimentary things about you. I just thought you might want to know."

"Thank you for passing along his sentiments." She patted the marshal's thick forearm, hoping his feelings weren't truly injured. Not that she necessarily believed what he'd said about Dr. Gray. From their first meeting, the physician had made no disguise of his opinion about her.

But what if it's true? an inner voice questioned. *What if Dr. Gray really spoke in your favor?*

"Thank you, Marshal," she repeated, asking herself if it really mattered what thoughts lay behind the physician's intelligent brown eyes. *No!* she wanted to shout, but at the same time she could not deny a small, oddly buoyant feeling at the notion that Ethan Gray had been pleased with something about her.

❧

My Dearest Romy,

By now, hopefully, you will have received the last letter I sent, congratulating you on your marriage. It will again seem strange to address this envelope to Mrs. Jeremiah Landis rather than Miss Romy Schmitt!

I have written to you about my friend Janet's infatuation with the marshal. They took a drive after church a few weeks ago, and I continue to have high hopes for their gradual courtship progressing toward the matrimonial state. I am certain wedded life would agree with them as it no doubt has with you and your new husband.

How is your leg coming? Are you of a mind to elaborate on the details of your accident? I didn't ask in my last letter, but must confess to my curiosity getting the better of me. If you don't feel up to telling that tale . . . perhaps you will sketch in the details of your wedding?

Circumstances in Tristan continue to be challenging. Remember how I wrote about the new physician injuring his hand, and Marshal Briggs appointing me as the doctor's deputy, so to speak? My hands have had to serve as his since that time, and oh, the tales my fingers could tell!

Olivia set the pen in its rest and took a sip of tea. The spicy-sweet aroma of baked beans filled the air, making her mouth water. During the two weeks she'd lived in Ella Farwell's house, her life had slowly taken on a new routine. Rise, work, read, sleep. This little kitchen was cozy enough, she supposed, but it would never be home. How she longed to be back at her cabin for good, instead of riding out to make visits whenever she was able.

Across the table, the kerosene lamp sputtered, sending up a curl of smoke. She wished, too, that she could tell Romy the truth about the dressmaker's death. But she had given her word to Briggs; she would not reveal the details of the postmortem examination to anyone until he gave the go-ahead. He and Deputy Johnson had spent days going through Ella's possessions, failing to discover any definitive evidence leading to her murderer.

After another sip of tea, she continued writing.

The townspeople turned out last week for the funeral of Ella Farwell, our dressmaker, who met a tragic end. The marshal has asked me to live in her quarters, for the time being, so as to better be available to assist the doctor. Now he is right down the street.

Dr. Gray is a most vexing man. Sure of himself to the point of arrogance, yet possessing a truly brilliant mind. He has taken to questioning me on all manner of subjects—to amuse himself, perhaps? Some things I can answer, but mostly I feel foolish because I don't know even a fraction of the things he does. I've taken to smuggling his textbooks and journals home in the evenings in the hopes of surprising him with one correct reply. I fear for the use of his hand—it is not healing quickly.

I also worry about the Connally children, but Susan looked fit when I saw her yesterday. Miraculously, their father seems to be of a mind to lay aside his bottle. I pray his temperance will continue.

After expressing her love and best wishes, Olivia laid the letter aside to dry while she addressed the envelope. It was strange to think of her friend's familiar surname being replaced by another. Just like that, Romy Schmitt had become Romy Landis. Was Elena married? she wondered, remembering the beauty of her long-lost friend's golden voice. Olivia hoped she'd found happiness in the theater, for she knew Elena's home life hadn't been pleasant. It troubled her greatly that her friend hadn't written in so long. Once again, she hoped nothing terrible had befallen her.

The beans were smelling done, and Olivia looked forward to her meal. The day had been a busy one, beginning before dawn with a case of croup. Though some of the townspeople remained mistrustful of the new physician, many more were seeking his services. During odd moments, she found herself wondering what things would be like if circumstances between her and the physician were different, for she had seen his winning manner with their patients.

In the back of her mind, however, lurked the specter of the Colorado Medical Society and the memories of Dr. Gray's first days in town. To her knowledge, the medical association had not yet replied to his formal complaint, but she worried what their determination of her livelihood might be.

The scope of Granny Esmond's—and her—practice was limited to the body's exterior. Dr. Gray, however, possessed both the knowledge and training to open the flesh and correct illness and disease surgically in ways she'd never dreamed of. His vast assets of medical references fascinated her; she had lost more than a little sleep poring over their pages.

By far the most intriguing volume lining the doctor's book-shelves was the *Illustrated Manual of Operative Surgery and Surgical Anatomy*, a title she had discovered upon unpacking his boxes. Bones, musculature, organs, and the circulatory system were depicted in breathtaking detail by artists' renderings, as were the many operative procedures to restore a body's health. It was this book she planned to read tonight after supper. She had learned so much in such a short period of time.

A wry smile on her lips, she rose from the table. She might be woefully unprepared to answer the doctor's questions, but what would he say if he knew his peremptory quizzes were actually guiding the course of her study?

❧

It seemed as though Ethan had barely fallen asleep when he was awakened by a loud pounding.

"Doctor! Doctor Gray! Open up!"

In the dark, he pulled on his trousers and stumbled toward the front door. Using his left hand, it seemed to take an eternity of awkward groping before he managed the lock and swung the door open wide. "What is it?" he spoke to the tall, skinny man garbed in farm dress, holding a lantern aloft. "What time is it?"

"Three or four, sir, I'm not sure. Maude . . . my wife . . . she's had an easy time of it in the past, but there's something wrong with this one. It won't come. Emily Marlow's been with her since suppertime. They said to come for Miss Olivia and you." Glancing up, Ethan saw the midwife standing in the outer ring of the lantern's glow. Though she was swathed securely against the cold of the late-autumn night, she looked small and cold and tired. "Come inside," he urged, aware of the chill seeping up his legs from his bare feet.

"We need to hurry. Mr. Hogan offered to take us both ways." Olivia inclined her head toward the street. "They live over by the creek. My things are already in his wagon."

"I'll bring mine too, if you don't mind," he retorted needlessly, trying to flex his bandaged hand into a fist, his effort in vain. How much longer until his fingers obeyed the commands he sent them? The wound itself had granulated with shiny, healthy pink tissue, but his damaged nerves kept to a timetable of their own.

He knew it could be months before his thumb and forefinger were functioning again, but still he worried that the detriment to his hand might be permanent. Then what? He couldn't very well keep Olivia Plummer at his side for the rest of his life.

By now she had to be wondering why his hand was still bandaged. She knew enough about healing to expect that the laceration would be closed, but she had not asked him about his wound since the day after the incident. However, he'd seen her gaze on his hand from time to time—silent, assessing. Managing his clothing was still a challenge, but he lit a lantern, finished dressing, and added the necessary obstetrical items to his bag as quickly as he could.

Conversation was sparse on the trip to the Hogan farm, with Olivia asking questions about what had occurred thus far in Maude's labor, and her husband answering that he didn't know, that it was his custom to stay as far out of the way as possible for the birth of each of his children.

A glow in the eastern sky heralded dawn as they reached

the Hogan farm. Yellow lamplight shone out the lower-story windows of the house, a cut above the many soddies to which Ethan and Olivia had paid visit since his arrival. Here, closer to the South Platte River, trees broke what often seemed to him an unending eyeful of northeastern Colorado grassland. His wish to leave behind the things of Boston had come true in one respect: the sights and smells of this landlocked prairie were as different from those of the bustling port city as were cow and fish.

Even before the wagon came to a stop in the yard outside the house, they heard the screams of their patient. "Oh, Lord, what am I going to do without her?" Shoulders slumping, the farmer hung his head and covered his face with his hands. A sound of despair escaped his throat, commingled with the anguished cries coming from the house, and disappeared into the dawn.

"No one's said you'll have to do without her, Mr. Hogan." Olivia quietly spoke to the grieving man. "You can be assured our heavenly Father knows her plight and is ever merciful to the cries of his children. Have you some chores to occupy your time? The milking, perhaps? We'll send for you just as soon as the babe arrives."

"Yes . . . no . . . I don't know. Maybe I'll milk the cows and take a drive. The young'uns are over at the Marlows'."

"Why, you'd be there just in time for breakfast. They'll be so glad to see you."

Russell Hogan nodded. "Maude sent along three pies and a mess of rolls when I took them over last night. With as big an' uncomfortable as she was, I couldn't believe all the cookin' and cleanin' she got done yesterday."

"It is amazing, isn't it?" Olivia smiled in agreement. "But then, Maude's quite a woman."

Having already dismounted the wagon, Ethan watched this interchange with interest, seeing the farmer's posture straighten somewhat. Olivia's manner with people was so genuine, so compassionate and reassuring. It was clear she was well loved in this community.

He set his bag on the ground and extended his left hand. Since they had been working together, he had performed small acts of courtesy for her, but she usually tried to avoid them. This time, she glanced at him in the ghostly light and accepted his offer of assistance.

The scene that greeted them in the farmhouse was chaotic. The laboring woman's screams had just faded to a rhythmic, piteous moaning as they entered through the kitchen door. A hot fire burned in the stove, causing the enormous copper wash-kettle upon its top to billow forth steam. Items sat in disarray about the room. Pantry doors hung open, revealing their contents.

"Oh, Livvie, I'm so glad you're here." A worry-eyed woman, whom Dr. Gray assumed to be Emily Marlow, ran into the room. Tendrils of blond hair hung around her pinched, exhausted face. "Doctor," she acknowledged, "we thought she'd be done so fast that we wouldn't have to call for you. But now—" she shrugged as a tear trickled down the dry skin of her cheek, and her voice dropped to a whisper—"the baby won't come. She's been bearing down since midnight."

"What is the presenting part?" Ethan asked, removing his coat with haste as the agonized screams began again.

"Presenting part of what?" The panicked gaze swung toward him. "I don't know. Please, you have to help her." The woman's eyes pleaded with him to fix things as he mentally ticked off possible causes of obstructed labor.

Olivia, too, swiftly removed her cloak and rolled her sleeves above her elbows. When he glanced up again, she was at the sink, giving her hands and arms a thorough scrubbing. Though many of his colleagues remained skeptical of Listerism, Ethan's own experience had made him a believer of the English physician's methods of disinfecting wounds, bandages, and instruments. Surely Olivia Plummer had never heard of Joseph Lister. Why, then, did she cleanse her hands so thoroughly before touching her patients, when many of his own contemporaries preferred washing only after performing their operations?

She remained an enigma, this woman, one he doubted he'd ever understand.

After she was finished, he followed suit and found their patient in the bedroom next to the kitchen. Maude Hogan writhed upon a tangle of sheets, her face swollen and blotchy, her hair matted to her head with perspiration. Her expression was a rictus of agony, her screams wild and hoarse. Olivia sat next to the woman upon the bed, one hand on the swollen belly, the other clasped with the laboring woman's.

The midwife's words were gentle and soothing, and gradually the agonized woman quieted, focusing on Olivia's encouragement.

"Something's . . . wrong, Livvie," she managed, when the contraction had at last receded. "The pains . . . are . . . so hard. My . . . back."

"Will you let me examine you?"

The woman nodded, closing her eyes in surrender. "Oh no," she moaned just a second later, her spine arching as if she'd been stabbed. "Not another one . . . not so soon!"

Ethan watched as Olivia spoke to the farmwife all through the next contraction, her efforts yielding marked relaxation in the laboring woman. There were no screams. When the contraction had withdrawn, Olivia's hands moved deftly over the enormous expanse of belly. Then after an interior examination, she glanced at Ethan before regarding their patient who, eyes closed, gasped for breath.

"Henry was close to ten pounds, wasn't he, Maude?"

She nodded, not opening her eyes.

"I'd say you've got another one his size, but this little one's head needs to come around some yet." She spoke to the other woman, a thread of quiet command running through her voice. "Emily, we'll need the washtub filled with water so she can soak. Will you prepare that while I get her up? I'll also need a cup of water for tea."

The other woman nodded, her relief at being asked to leave the room obvious.

"Get her up to *soak?* You're going to give her a bath and tea at this stage of labor?" Ethan had never heard such a ridiculous thing in all his days. "Is the dilation complete? The head engaged?" To Olivia's nod, he went on. "Then she needs to be delivered as soon as possible."

Another contraction commenced, drawing Olivia's attention from his line of questioning. Emily scurried into the room and thrust a cup of steaming water into his hands, leaving just as quickly as she came. His displeasure grew as the midwife uttered several even more preposterous suggestions. "Can you roll to the other side, Maude?" she urged, assisting her patient to a lateral position and praising her efforts. "That's right, all the way over. Well done. And next time, we'll get you on all fours."

All fours? This case begged for ether and forceps, the sooner the better. Inwardly he cursed his wounded hand, knowing he wouldn't be able to manage the metal device necessary for delivering the woman of her child. Up to this point, Olivia had proven apt at following his directions, seeming to have a natural touch. Would he be able to explain the motions necessary to secure a good fit of the instruments about the fetal head? Poor application of the forceps could result in damage to both mother and infant.

"Madam," Ethan began, stepping to the bed, setting the cup of water on the nightstand. A pair of bleary blue eyes focused upon him. "You have made a valiant effort here this night, but I see you have lost your strength."

"Nonsense. Maude is a strong, healthy woman." Olivia stiffened, her eyes slapping him with censure. A graceful hand stroked the patient's shoulder reassuringly. "She's given birth to five hale children, and it will soon be an even half dozen."

From the next room came the sounds of a bath being prepared. Ethan's vexation increased, and he felt his eyes narrow. "Step into the kitchen with me."

Another contraction gripped the depleted woman, and he watched with disbelief as Olivia urged her completely over onto her hands and knees, all the while commending her for her exertions. Once Maude was in this ludicrous position, Olivia's lithe hands applied surprising pressure to the small of Maude's back, to the patient's obvious relief.

"Now drop your head on the pillow and rest," Olivia said when the pain had passed. "I'm going to make you some tea, and then we'll get you into the bath." With a reassuring squeeze of Maude's shoulder, she turned to the nearby basin of water and began washing as if he hadn't spoken to her.

"Miss Plummer," he ground out, "I wish to have a word with you."

She glanced at him as she dried her hands, then rifled through her bag for a small pouch. Extracting a bit of substance from the bag, she dropped it into the steaming cup of water. Only then did she give him her attention, motioning him over to the side of the room.

"I'll thank you not to discourage this good woman." Though she whispered, her eyes were as dark as a gathering storm. "She'll need every bit of strength she can muster."

His voice left him in a low growl. "What she needs is an operative delivery. The forceps are in my bag; if you listen carefully to my instructions, I think you can manage them."

Her eyes widened, and livid color highlighted her features. "I will do no such thing. Granny Esmond told me about doctors like you, avid to apply your shiny instruments . . . and in the process, ripping women to pieces."

Doctors like him . . . ripping women to pieces? The cadence of Maude's breathing changed, signaling the start of another contraction. Frustration boiled up inside him as he felt Olivia's attention slipping away.

"If you don't do as I say," he warned in an urgent whisper, "the lives of this woman and child rest upon your shoulders."

Her spine stiffened at his words, assuming the ramrod straightness with which he was becoming so familiar. She took a quick step toward him, coming near enough that her breath fanned his chin.

"That's precisely what I fear if I *do* as you say. Surely you can humor these humble endeavors. They've served me well in the past." Olivia's voice remained low, but she faced him squarely, thunder in her gaze. "And my grandmother before me."

Maude was midway through the contraction, huffing into her pillow. Ethan sensed the midwife was torn between defending her actions and wanting to be at her patient's side.

"The bath's ready, Livvie," Emily called from the kitchen, adding even more tension to the moment.

The bath. He released a sigh at being trapped in the midst of such an unorthodox, unscientific affair—the very sort of thing against which he had rallied so vigorously in Boston. Though his vexation and cynicism abounded, for some reason he found himself opening his vest and taking out his watch. Morbid curiosity, perhaps.

"Very well then. You have an hour," he said, raising his brows in a way that had never failed to intimidate medical students and interns alike. "One hour to deliver this woman of her child, and not a second more."

"The Lord willing, we'll be done well before that," she countered, appearing undaunted. Staring at him for a heartbeat longer, she turned on her heel and went back to her patient.

Chapter 8

Five minutes later, Ethan found himself entangled in an affair against which every fiber of his body protested, which made a mockery of modern medical practice, which flew in the face of—

"That's it, Maude, just a few more steps and we'll be in the kitchen. Have you got another pain coming? You do? Well, that's fine. Each one helps. Let's stop here at the wall. . . . Don't worry, Dr. Gray will hold you up." Olivia rewarded her patient with a bright smile. "You're doing so well, my dear, and that bath is going to feel heavenly. Try not to bear down, if you can help it." Avoiding his gaze, Olivia continued her stream of one-sided conversation.

Inwardly, Ethan growled while Maude Hogan leaned against him on one side and Olivia on the other. Her body radiated heat like a well-stoked furnace, and she moaned loudly through the height of her contraction, her hand clamping his forearm with the force of a vise.

"Well done, Maude. I'm so proud of you. Lean forward a bit more . . . that's it. Does that help your back?"

Who was this woman—this Olivia Plummer? He had dismissed her initially as no one of consequence. As time passed, he'd begun seeing that she could hold her own against both adversity and the unknown. But tonight? She'd gone far beyond either, metamorphosing into a military magpie. He'd had no intention of participating in this travesty of obstetrics upon which she insisted, but she hadn't given him a choice while she conscripted him into service.

The contraction abated, he guessed, for the moaning ceased and the pressure on his arm lessened.

"Along we go, into the kitchen," Olivia chirped. "Look at the nice bath Emily's prepared for you." Doing a six-legged dance at a snail's pace, the trio made their way to the metal washtub while the neighbor woman hovered before them, hands fluttering.

"Could we have some towels, Emily?" Olivia asked, giving purpose to the blond's nervous movements. "Maude, Dr. Gray will look away while we get you situated in the tub. This shift is soiled anyhow. Once you're done, we'll get you a nice fresh one—"

"Oh . . . oh! . . . I feel it! . . . It's . . . turning! Liv-*vie!*" The second syllable of the midwife's name was a deep, guttural grunt, and Maude's hand gripped Ethan's forearm with pulverizing force.

"Let's go!" Ethan's assistant gave the order with fire in her eyes, forcibly turning the straining woman back in the direction from which they'd come. "Come on, Maude," she urged with a unique blend of sweetness and insistence, "we've no longer any need of this bath. I promise, the instant you're in bed, you can push this lollygagger right out."

"Oh! . . . I feel it! . . . It's coming!"

Constance Leola Hogan arrived just two minutes later, lusty and pink. Olivia attended the birth with natural dexterity, exclaiming with joy as she raised up the plump, wailing infant.

"What a glorious daughter you have, Maude. Look at her! Thank you, Father, for keeping them safe," Olivia openly praised. "Oh, Jesus, what a good and loving Shepherd you are."

The farmwife fairly glowed with beauty and bliss, every last trace of agony wiped from her countenance. "My baby . . . oh, my sweet baby," she wept with rapture, reaching for her infant.

Ethan waited for Olivia to comment on the rapidity of the delivery, occurring well under the hour he'd allotted, but he waited in vain. Instead, she attended to the many details requiring her attention, all the while marveling over the new baby with the other women. How different this birth had been from those he attended in the moneyed sector of Boston. There, obstetrical anesthesia was desired—nay, demanded—by upper-class women who wanted the same pain relief Queen Victoria had lauded a quarter century earlier.

But many of those women who insisted on such remained limp and languorous after birth, not even interested in their babies, preferring the insensate experience of their anesthetic sleep. Against that he contrasted his years of training, of delivering poor women in the crowded maternity hospital ward, most of them suffering their lot without benefit of pain relief. Their screams and cries had convinced him that the administration of ether, more popular than chloroform in the northeastern states, was the only humane course of action for a woman in travail.

Maude Hogan was a farmwife. Although not dirt poor, her means were far from upper-class. She had suffered greatly—his aching forearm bore witness to the depth of her agony. Yet how different she was from either type of woman he had attended. What was the difference? Her expression, so suffused with love and tenderness as she gazed at her newborn child, attracted his attention. Again he asked himself, what was the difference?

Pacing about, feeling like a fifth wheel, he watched Olivia's efficient movements. After tying the umbilical cord with a length of cotton twill, she snipped through the thick, gelatinous rope with a sturdy pair of scissors. The afterbirth delivered without fanfare into a basin.

Emily had thrown open the shade, allowing the morning light to illuminate the bedchamber. When Olivia finally turned to him, her face carried a glow not unlike that upon her patient's, and the thought struck him: she is beautiful.

Her natural, easy smile revealed a row of milky teeth, the left eyetooth overlapping a bit onto its neighboring incisor. Her eyes sparkled like gray pearls, framed by brunette wisps that had escaped the confines of the thick knot atop her head. She stood then, entering a pool of sunshine as she walked to the basin.

He found himself utterly entranced by her appearance, unable to look away. Rivulets of water glistened upon her forearms and lissome hands while she washed, the sunlight playing up the red highlights in her hair, glossy and smooth. Her shoulders were strong and square beneath her homespun blouse, the line of her skirt sliding gracefully from waist to floor in a cascade of even gathers. How had he missed the brilliance of this plain Colorado midwife?

"She's lovely, isn't she?"

Olivia turned, gracing him with a grin. Never before had she smiled at him, nor had he imagined she was capable of such a delightful expression.

Immediately averting his gaze, he shrugged, embarrassed at having been caught staring . . . caught so completely off guard. It had to be the lack of sleep. "Yes, she's . . . ah—"

"Oh, Doctor, I want to thank you for your help," Maude praised. "I don't know what I would have done without your strength."

"Madam, I beg to differ with you," he said quite honestly, relieved to direct his attention elsewhere. "It was your fortitude that made this remarkable delivery possible." Walking nearer to the bed, he examined the swaddled, red-faced infant nestled in her mother's arms. "Your daughter is indeed a lovely creature. I heard she's joining what . . . five others?"

While they talked, Olivia and Emily made short work of freshening the room. "Why don't you and Dr. Gray go over to your place and give Mr. Hogan the good news?" the midwife suggested. "That way he can take the doctor back to town. I'll stay for a spell . . . if that's agreeable with you, of course," she added deferentially, with a nod toward Ethan.

If he found her plans agreeable? Did she think he hadn't noticed how she'd maneuvered him time and time again during the course of this short morning? And then had the gall to turn a face of shining, artless beauty toward him?

Yes, he would ride with Emily Marlow to release Mr. Hogan from his night-long sentence of worry. And as Olivia had suggested, he would return to Tristan and open the office for the day. He would do these things not out of mere acquiescence, nor because he hadn't thought of them himself, but to escape her presence and the disturbing feelings she raised within him.

Russell Hogan didn't seem to mind making his third trip to town in one day. On the contrary, the exhilarated new father chattered with Olivia all the way to Tristan. They had left Maude in sound condition, sleeping off the effects of her exertion, baby Constance snuggled in the crook of her arm. Emily Marlow had returned with a basketful of fixings later in the morning, turning the kitchen into a one-woman beehive of activity. The Hogans would be eating well for days, Olivia surmised, allowing her mind to wander.

The noon sun emitted only frail warmth. What would Ethan say to her when she returned? she wondered, shivering inside the folds of her cloak. Now that she'd had time to reflect on the bustle and ado of the dawn delivery, she realized she had not only defied the doctor, she had bossed him about shamelessly.

Her only defense was that she had just *known*, deep in her heart, there was no need for forceps. Over the years, Granny Esmond had taught her many tricks for coaxing along a recalcitrant labor. Olivia had been certain Maude would benefit from a change of position, for that often helped rotate the baby's head into the proper position for birth. Her opposition to Dr. Gray's desire to use forceps had been borne not because she'd wanted her own way but because she believed walking and a relaxing, warm-water soak would produce a delivery all the same.

And she'd been right, she thought smugly, recalling that

Maude hadn't even needed the decoction of pine bark to increase the strength of her labor contractions, an Indian remedy Granny Esmond had culled from a healer back in Missouri.

Olivia's self-satisfaction dwindled as they passed Briggs's office. She recalled the burly marshal's words about how important it was for a man to be good at what he did. Dr. Gray was surely displeased with her overbearing manner . . . no doubt that was why his dark eyes had smoldered upon her while she washed her hands after attending the birth.

Hogan fell silent as they entered town and pulled up in front of the doctor's office. "I can't thank you enough, Miss Olivia." His slow words stood in sharp contrast to his garrulous speech during the journey. Reaching deep into his pocket, he retrieved his handkerchief. "Things are a little better for us now than they were when you delivered Henry. I've never felt right about you forgivin' our debt—"

"Mr. Hogan, please. I didn't forgive your debt . . . we called it even. You gave me a great deal of wool, don't you remember?"

He cleared his throat several times and nodded. "I remember. But this time I intend to pay you properly." With work-roughened hands he unfolded the fabric, revealing a ten-dollar gold piece. "Will an eagle be enough?" he asked, extending the coin to her.

"More than enough," she whispered, realizing what an enormous amount of money he surrendered.

"I don't want to hear no arguin'. Just take it," he said, pressing the money into her hands. "God bless you."

"May God continue to bless you, too, Mr. Hogan," she said to the farmer, who, after assisting her from the wagon, averted his gaze, responding to her words with only a nod.

A sharp wind blew down the street as he departed. She glanced up the walk, in the direction of the former dressmaker's building, tempted to seek a little quiet time before facing the physician. She sighed, knowing it would only delay the inevitable. He'd probably already seen her and was eager to give her a piece of his mind for her behavior this morning.

But how could she apologize for insisting upon something that had clearly been in their patient's best interest? She opened the door to the office, the gold eagle as heavy in her hand as the cumbrous thoughts weighing upon her heart. As coin seemed to hold premier value to the doctor, perhaps offering him the entire ten dollars would appease his offended nature.

She had grown accustomed to seeing him sit at his big desk, but the front room of the office was empty when she let herself in. The sound of his voice, farther off, greeted her ears, followed by the tearful voice of . . . Susan? Alarmed, she set down her things and walked across the room toward the hallway. The door to the examination room stood slightly ajar.

"I just didn't know what to do . . . so I came to see Miss Olivia," came the girl's voice, followed by a snuffle.

"I realize I'm a poor substitute for Miss Plummer, but I hope I have removed your fears."

"Oh no . . . I mean, yes. You've been so nice. I thought something inside me was hurt bad. I was so scared . . . I just didn't know."

Olivia stopped short of entering the hall, listening, for some reason unwilling to reveal her presence. The young voice belonged to Susan Connally; she was certain of it. But what had brought her to town?

"On the contrary," Ethan went on with a tender note she had never before heard from him. "One day you may be called to motherhood. Right now, your body is preparing to bear the fruit of married love, and what has happened is as normal and healthy as can be. In fact, it is a cause for reverence and celebration in many cultures all over the world."

"It is?" she asked with wonder.

"Indeed it is. May I tell you a little more?"

"Yes, please," came Susan's reply. "I never knew about any of this."

Olivia's eyes filled with tears at the thought of her young, motherless friend passing into maturity without any preparation whatsoever. She had failed Susan in overlooking this eventuality, thinking the girl too young to be troubled by such matters. At the same time, she was transfixed by the warmth and gentleness radiating from Ethan Gray's earnest tone.

"You are in perfect health, Miss Connally, and other than tending to the discharge, your menstruation need not trouble you in the least. Now, there are some women who view this most natural event as something evil or dire, or as a means to gain sympathy or attention or some sort of indulgence."

Olivia immediately thought of Delores Wimbers.

"They do? Why would they want to do that?"

"Oh . . . for a variety of reasons, I suppose. But very often these are the sorts of women who don a cargo-load of bands and binders and heavy clothing, in the process restricting every vital organ. Their diets are poor, their digestion imperfect, and their lungs so pinched they can scarcely draw breath. Do you ever run or skip or climb a fence, Miss Connally? Jump over puddles? Take the stairs two at a time?"

"Ah . . . yes, sir . . . I . . . am I not supposed to?"

The sound of Ethan Gray's reassuring laughter did something peculiar to Olivia's chest.

"On the contrary—I want you never to stop! Exercise and fresh air are the best medicine in the world. You should have seen some of the women I treated in Boston." A shuffling sound ensued, followed by Susan's silvery giggles.

"What a funny face! Did they really look like that? walk like that?"

"If they walked at all. Some of them used their menses as an excuse to stay in bed for days."

"They would stay in bed? I've never seen Miss Olivia act like that."

"No, I can't imagine she would. She's an active woman, and very healthy herself."

"Do you like her?" Susan asked suddenly, candidly, causing Olivia's heart to pound and her hands to grow clammy.

"Such a question, Miss Connally," he answered after a pause. "What makes you ask?"

"I heard that on the day you got here, you tried getting Marshal Briggs to put her in jail because she fixed Claude Harker's broken leg."

"Well, it's not as simple as all that—"

"And that the marshal had to *order* you to work together until your hand gets better."

"He did say something to that effect, yes."

"I thought you must be a mean old man because Miss Olivia was so unhappy about working with you. She even cried when she told me she had to move to town," the girl revealed. "But you don't seem mean at all."

"I certainly hope not."

"So, do you?"

"Do I what?"

"Do you like her?" Without giving him time to respond, she went on. "You should. Miss Olivia's the finest person I ever met. She's nice and kind and likes to laugh a lot. Since my mama died, she's been my best friend in the whole world. Do you know that I see to her place every single day," she announced proudly, "and take care of her cow and do whatever needs doing?" Even from where Olivia stood, she heard Susan's sigh. "I wish she could come home. I miss her so much."

"Well, then—," he began, only to be interrupted by another question.

"Do you really believe all healers need a high education? That's what she told me, that you think she needs a high education. But she says Granny Esmond taught her what she needs to know."

Ethan was quiet a long moment. "I can't argue that Miss Olivia doesn't know many things." His next words were indulgent, carrying a hint of humor. "And I can tell you have spent time in her company, young miss, for your speech is as straightforward as hers."

"Mama always taught me and Seamus to say the truth."

"Your mother was right. Being from the East, I'm not acquainted with such plain talk, but I believe it saves a good deal of time in getting to the heart of a matter. You see, in Boston society it is considered polite to disguise what you really wanted to say with a lot of unessential words."

"Well, that's just silly."

Again came that rolling, warm male laughter, doing riotous things to Olivia's insides. "I agree. So I'll endeavor to answer your questions as best I can." More seriously, he went on. "Back in Boston—and everywhere, really—there are many persons called doctors and healers and midwives who do a great deal of harm. They haven't had any education or training, and often-times people are hurt because of that. Infections are passed. Unnecessary pain and death result. My colleagues in Boston are trying to change that, to make sure doctors go to good medical schools, not bad ones, so they're well prepared to care for their patients."

Olivia let out her breath, willing her hammering heart to slow, afraid of what he would say next.

"But Miss Olivia takes good care of people," Susan argued. "She doesn't hurt them."

"She has a natural touch, I would agree. And she is good and kind and all those things you said—"

"But do you like her?"

"We tend to nettle one another, but yes, I . . . ah, have come to respect her."

"She's pretty, isn't she? I like how she smiles."

Olivia nearly stopped breathing while waiting for Ethan Gray's response. What he thought of her appearance didn't matter in the least. Not one whit. Not in the slightest. Why, oh, why then, did his next words fill her with such a strange, light-headed feeling?

"Her smile . . . yes. I saw it this morning." His deep voice was thoughtful, contemplative. "Have you any more questions for me, Miss Connally? I expect Miss Plummer will be back before too long. If you'd like, you can wait out in the front with me."

With as much stealth as she could manage, Olivia hurried

back to the entrance of the office before her presence was detected. She felt hypocritical as she opened the door and closed it with more force than was necessary, as if she had just arrived and not heard one word of their most disconcerting conversation.

❧

Olivia was on edge the remainder of the afternoon, even though she and Susan had passed an enjoyable hour over tea in Ella's little kitchen. Her father was still sober, the girl reported, and had taken an interest in the farm. He had not returned to his stool at Kelly's since Ella's death.

If Olivia had thought Dr. Gray's consideration of her this morning was disturbing, the glance he had directed her way when he escorted Susan from the examination room was even more unsettling. On top of that, with his bandaged hand he had waved her off, suggesting that she and Miss Connally might enjoy spending some time together . . . further delaying their inevitable conflict.

When she returned, he was occupied with something in the rear of the building, calling out that she should make herself useful in the front. After giving the waiting room a thorough dusting, she knelt before the bookshelf, eager to find a new topic to take home and study. She had smuggled the surgery book back into place, hoping it had not been missed.

Her fingers skipped over the spines of Dr. Gray's books until they reached *Man and Medicine*. Selecting this weighty manual, she skimmed over several chapters, seeing pages laden with dense descriptions of disease and indisposition. More than an evening or two would be required to do justice to these teachings. Readjusting the neighboring volumes to disguise the hole left by its removal, she turned to rise, nearly bumping into the fine wool of Ethan Gray's trousers.

"Oh!" she uttered, nearly dropping the manual. How had his entrance escaped her notice? Her heart raced from startlement . . . and an indefinable something else. The charged air between them had still not been cleared. Perhaps the storm was about to break.

"'Oh,' indeed, Miss Plummer. May I ask what you're doing?" In his voice was none of the warmth she had heard him use earlier. "Stealing another of my books, perhaps?"

"Stealing? I may be many things, but I am not a thief," she retorted, scrambling to her feet while maintaining her hold on the cumbersome book. "I have just *borrowed* a few of your medical volumes."

He just looked at her—deeply.

"I've brought them all back," she added defensively, feeling heat flick up her cheeks. She knew full well that taking something without permission was as good as stealing. What made her think she was justified in removing his books to her home?

"I'll thank you to put that back where you got it," he said with such haughtiness that Olivia's temper immediately flared. It was as if they were standing on Main Street in front of Claude Harker's wagon all over again, the tall, arrogant doctor having just called for her arrest.

"Put it back yourself," she challenged, watching his expression darken. This man was responsible for each and every one of the wretched changes wrought in her life, not to mention the imperilment of her future practice. Her anger bloomed; her tongue grew reckless.

"Go on," she taunted, wanting to hurt him. She held the heavy volume out between them. "Go on and take it, if you want it back."

With a scowl marring his features, he reached with his left hand, but she sidestepped, pulling the book from his range.

"No. With your *right* hand." Holding his gaze, she was stunned to see the fight leave his eyes. Even more shocking was the subtle sagging of his shoulders.

After a long silence, he said, "I can't. My fingers are numb."

"Ohh," she breathed, overcome by a painful blend of remorse and compassion. For days she had suspected what he had just admitted. Why couldn't she simply have *asked* him about his still-wrapped injury? How could she have been so deliberately cruel? Oh, Lord, how could this man infuriate her one second and rend her heart the next?

He held up his bandaged hand, his expression beaten. "There is no feeling in my thumb or index finger."

"Let me see." She gave him no choice as she led him to his chair at the desk, setting the offending book on its surface with a loud *thump*. Wordless, he sat while she knelt before him, allowing her to unwrap the dressing and study his hand.

His fingers were lean and well formed, radiating a disturbing amount of heat to her smaller hands. In the fading light, she saw that the injury had healed well. The skin edges had knitted together without furrow or pucker, and the crooked pink scar would fade to white in time. But what of his damaged nerves? Would they reawaken? She turned his hand palm side up, then back over again, studying its contours from every angle.

What would Ethan Gray do if his fingers never regained their feeling? All his education . . . all his training . . . to what end? A fresh wave of sorrow flooded her soul to think that such a hand might never again perform useful service. Without conscious thought, she bent her head and brushed her lips against his knuckles.

With that, the air in the twilight-shadowed room became electrified. God in heaven, what had she just done? Her head jerked up, only to be immobilized by the look on the physician's face. In his eyes was something she'd never before seen. Tenderness? Longing? Her breath caught, the moment going on and on while answering, undefinable emotions inside her sprang to life.

Things softened, then ran hot between them as he cupped her face in his hands.

Chapter 9

"Olivia . . . Livvie," he murmured, gazing into her eyes. "May I call you that? So bright and genuine, so caring. This morning when you smiled . . . " His words broke off with a sigh.

The touch of his hands was foreign to Olivia but every bit as breath-stealing and intoxicating as his words. Slowly, disappointingly, he drew them back and folded them across his lap.

"B-but I thought you were angry with me." She seized on something—anything—to say.

"I was. I am. But I also recognize that you have some truly amazing talents." With a wry chuckle, he continued beholding her with eyes as warm as molasses. "Maybe it's just taken me this long to come to my senses." More seriously he added, "Little by little you've grown in my heart, Livvie, even when I acted like anything *but* that was happening. I'm not good at admitting my faults . . . but I've treated you wretchedly from the moment we met. Do you think you can forgive me?"

"Forgive you?" Her heart melted like butter on a griddle, her words pouring forth. "If Granny Esmond were alive, she'd have had my hide for the way I've spoken to you, especially a man the Lord placed in my hands for healing. I've done nothing but seethe and spout off and talk back—I've been just awful. I'm the one who needs forgiveness, from both you and him."

"Shall we call a truce then?" He smiled, giving his face an amiable expression she found infinitely appealing. "Start over? I'll even share my books with you."

She looked away, feeling a shy, answering smile steal across her face. Heavens, she'd had no idea Ethan Gray possessed so much charm.

Was this the appeal of which Janet had spoken that day in the schoolroom? Of one thing she was certain: if he had turned this sort of attention on her the day he'd arrived, she'd be head over heels in love with him by now.

In love?

A shiver ran through her. From where had an outlandish idea like that come? "Does this mean you'll continue quizzing me about anatomy and disease and anything else you can think of?" she asked lightly, steering her unsteady thoughts toward a more stable subject. She slipped into the chair beside his desk.

"Probably twice as much as before."

An awkward silence passed. "What about your hand?" she ventured.

"Do you mean the one you kissed, or the other one?"

Her cheeks burned brighter than a bed of live coals. "With God as my witness, I've never done anything like that before in my life."

"I believe you, Livvie. I'm only teasing." His voice washed over her, tender and gentle, its sensation every bit as warm as the caress of his hands. "Would you be surprised if I told you I admire the way you have with people? That doesn't come second nature for me the way it does for you."

Yesterday she wouldn't have argued with him . . . but today? Right now? She couldn't imagine what would be happening to her insides if he were any more engaging.

"Your hands first caught my attention," he mused. "Next was your indomitable spirit. You don't let anything stand in your way, do you? If you're willing, I would like to ask for your continued help until the feeling in my hand has returned. Nerves can take some months to heal, and you seem to have a natural touch—"

"A healing touch," she corrected, marveling at the fact that he had sought her agreement about their continuing on together. Before he'd arrived, she had hoped and prayed they might make some sort of amicable working arrangements. Today the answer to that prayer was unfolding before her, if only a bit delayed.

"That's what Granny Esmond called it, anyway," she explained. "It passed over my mother, but my grandmother and I were both given the healing touch. She said we were born with it, to do God's work."

"To do God's work." In the fading daylight, Ethan rubbed his good hand across his jaw, as if thinking. "His will, too?"

"Of course. To the Lord goes the glory; his will is merely worked through our hands."

"Everything we do, then, is his will?"

"No, not everything. We *were* given a will of our own. It's in surrendering it to his own that his will is done and he is exalted."

"How can you be sure you're always doing his will?" He moved his chair closer and leaned toward her, over the corner of his desk.

"Well," she began, choosing her words with care, for he seemed most intent on her reply. "For me it's this way: Granny taught me to pray for all my patients and submit each situation to God for guidance. For example, when I came to stitch your hand, I called upon the Lord to lead me the whole way through."

"For a safe journey to town? To wipe away the blood? To place each and every suture?" His head cocked to the side. "Are you ever *not* engaged in prayer?"

"You should know the answer to that," she replied with a rueful smile. "As you are no doubt well aware, my temper and my tongue tend to run away with the best of my intentions. Perhaps some of the saints were able to pray every moment of every day, but I don't have that kind of piety."

"That's admirable, Livvie, but hardly practical. There is the business of living to attend to."

She nodded. "I know. But Granny Esmond set such an example; she walked with one hand in the Lord's the whole day through. And it's what the Scriptures exhort, to pray without ceasing. A missionary came through here once. Every hour he stopped to worship and acknowledge the Lord . . . and I'm certain he did not limit himself to that. Deacon Carlisle says we need to cultivate an awareness of always being in the Father's presence—even if we don't feel like it, or if it doesn't seem that way. We need to offer him every duty and interruption. . . ." Wondering if she'd lost him, she said, "You once said you were a praying man."

He nodded, looking uncomfortable. "I did, but—"

"But you've never thought of troubling him with small matters?"

Another nod followed a more contemplative jaw rub.

"Praying for life's little things isn't a waste of God's time. He's always delighted to hear from us. It's yet another way we can yield our will to be conformed to his."

"That's all well and good, but what if we're still not doing his will?"

"He'll let us know, one way or the other. Depending on the stiffness of a person's neck, some lessons are learned more painfully than others."

Ethan had just opened his mouth to respond when the door swung open, admitting Marshal Briggs. Of the three, it was hard to say who was the most startled. The lawman's eyebrows lifted in amazement as Olivia and Ethan simultaneously scooted their chairs in opposing directions.

"Well, well, well. I've come to expect you not to be speakin' to one another . . . or to be at each other's throats. But what do I see here?"

"We were just talking about . . . things," Olivia offered, feeling the all-too-familiar warmth suffuse her face.

"Seems like a right cozy atmosphere to talk about such 'things,' whatever they may be. I suppose neither of you has noticed it's all but dark."

With his left hand, Ethan awkwardly struck a match and lit the lantern on the opposite corner of his desk. "Actually, I just asked Miss Plummer if she would be willing to stay on as my assistant. As she rightly deduced, my hand suffers the effects of nerve damage."

"For good, Doc?" Ever blunt, Briggs took off his hat and walked toward them, peering down at the physician's hand. "Your scar doesn't look so bad."

"No, but nerves can take much longer to regenerate than flesh." Making a fist of his left hand and squeezing it a few times, Ethan added, "In the meanwhile, I'm getting a little better at navigating with this hand. My penmanship has gone from so many chicken scratchings to being nearly legible."

"*Nearly* legible is all," Olivia seconded, forgetting her discomfiture. "I was *almost* able to read your record of Mrs. Hogan's delivery."

Briggs canted his head as he looked first at her, then at Ethan, then back to her. "I hate to point this out, Livvie, but you just smiled at the same time you said something to the doc. That's got to be a first."

The heat in her face intensified. Wearing an enigmatic expression, the sandy-haired physician came to her rescue, bringing up a darker subject . . . one that never strayed far from the back of her mind. "I've been meaning to ask you, Marshal, have you turned up anything pointing to Miss Farwell's killer?"

"Johnson thinks Connally's the man, no question about it. We just have no proof. The fact he suddenly quit drinking and is acting the part of a model citizen makes him appear more guilty, to the deputy's way of thinking."

"What do you think?" questioned Olivia, knowing how Donal's arrest would destroy the tenuous relationships he was beginning to rebuild with his children.

"Obviously, if I agreed, he'd already be behind bars. Connally had it in him to be a mean drunk now and again, but he seemed more intent on destroying himself than anyone else. He insists Ella told him more than once about another man, a gunfighter."

"An outlaw?" Olivia asked. "But we haven't had any trouble around these parts for some time."

"I know. But I reckon an unsavory character could have hung around without my knowledge. Especially if she was meeting him outside of town somewhere. That's more the idea I'm inclined to go with. As you know, we turned her shop inside out and upside down, but we didn't find a blessed thing."

"If that's the case, the man could be a thousand miles away by now." Ethan shook his head, his expression sober.

"And probably is, if he has any smarts. Well, I just stopped to say hello. Livvie, can I walk you home?" Briggs toyed with the brim of his hat.

"That would be nice," she replied, rising from her chair, secretly disappointed that this unexpected and most remarkable interlude with Ethan Gray had come to a close. But there was tomorrow, she thought with a tingle of excitement, and many tomorrows after that. "I'll just get my coat—oh! I almost forgot."

Reaching into her pocket, she retrieved the gold piece and set it on the desk.

"What's this?" Ethan asked, puzzled.

"It's for the Hogan delivery."

"You charged them an eagle?" Ethan's eyebrows shot upward. "After the way you took me to task for billing the Leppers—"

"Of course not," she interrupted. "It's what Mr. Hogan insisted on paying . . . he said part of it was to make up for last time, when they couldn't pay."

"Then you keep it." Pushing the coin back toward her, he looked at her. "All I did was go along for the ride." The corners of his mouth twitched. "And suffer a bit of bossing."

Briggs chuckled. "Don't feel bad, Doc. In the heat of the moment, I've seen many a grown man scurrying to boil water and do Livvie's bidding."

"Until tomorrow then, Miss Plummer. Don't forget your book." Ethan inclined his head toward the medical volume. "I'll have a few questions prepared for you."

Olivia couldn't stop the thrill that shot through her at his words. As she donned her cloak, however, the niggling thought arose that Ethan had not addressed the future beyond when his hand healed. What would happen to their working relationship then? Recalling his words to Susan about the importance of proper medical training, she promptly cast them aside. The threat of the Colorado Medical Society notwithstanding, she focused instead on his admission of her natural abilities . . . his acknowledgment of her healing touch. His warm brown eyes. His smile.

Good heavens, what was happening to her? she thought, preparing to leave. Only yesterday she had dreaded being in this man's company, and now she could hardly wait for the next day to dawn.

After a quiet, solitary supper, Ethan went to bed both elated and troubled. The thought of Olivia Plummer's shining gray eyes and lovely smile gave his heart a turn, but he continued thinking about their conversation well into the night, especially the things she'd said about prayer.

Some nights he forgot to pray or was otherwise occupied, but for the most part he was faithful to this childhood teaching from his mother, who had instilled in him a fear of the Lord. His faith, however, was quiet and individual, his alone, and not to be witnessed by strangers. He could no more imagine crying out his thanks to the Almighty for a baby safely delivered than publicly shouting out any other intimate detail of his private life.

His confidence in God's goodness and individual care, however, had taken a beating along with every blow and thrashing he'd endured during the two years he'd spent on the streets. Left alone after his mother's death, his adolescent years had begun a constant scrabbling for shelter, food, work, and money.

Finally, when he was fourteen, he found a position as a clerk for a druggist named Nathan Broder. For some reason

Ethan still didn't understand, Broder took a liking to him at once, perhaps seeing the potential of his young, inquisitive mind. Ethan's initial duties of washing bottles and scouring the brass pans of the counter scales gradually gave way to such responsibilities as opening the store for the day and mixing up elixirs, tinctures, pills, and plasters. A small room at the back of the stairs was provided for him, and the two often took their meals together.

An intellectual and a brilliant chemist, Broder had challenged Ethan to resume his studies, tutoring him in a wide variety of subjects. The older man subscribed to the theory of deism, believing in God but denying the Almighty's interference with natural law. Whenever Ethan tried making sense of his childhood—his father's abandonment, his mother's death, the years spent on the streets—Broder's philosophy seemed to hold water. To God he gave the honor and respect due the almighty Creator, subconsciously not believing the Lord's involvement in a person's daily life.

By the time Ethan was seventeen, the druggist had him translating a page of Greek and Latin every day and was propelling him toward quadratic forms and solid geometry. Those were good years, Ethan reflected, thinking of the older man's many kindnesses to him.

To Ethan's amazement, Broder secured him a Harvard admittance examination. In the months leading up to the interview, his benefactor stretched his mind without relent. Passing the examinations, Ethan was admitted to the college and began his first year of studies, planning to pursue the same process of chemistry as had his mentor.

But Broder's sudden illness shifted Ethan's focus to medicine. And when his patron and protector died before Ethan's first year of college was out—leaving him sole heir to the drugstore and modest estate—he decided then and there to become a physician. To be truthful, human science and the workings of the body had always fascinated him more than the study of chemistry. He realized his career change would not bring Nathan

Broder back from the dead, but he vowed to honor the older man's memory by devoting himself single-mindedly to the pursuit of becoming the most excellent physician he could be.

So he had sold the store and applied the monies toward his tuition. In that day, Harvard's medical school was in the midst of sweeping reforms, and he was among the first wave of students to benefit from the more rigorous standards, the modern laboratories, the practical application of their studies. Not once did he regret his decision to become a doctor. He loved medicine and dedicated himself to the betterment of the practice, rooting out sickness and disease, and even preventing infirmity by promoting good health.

And where had that led him? To partnership in a powerful, moneyed practice . . . to treating the wealthy . . . to disillusionment . . . to Tristan, Colorado.

How did God's will fit into all this? he asked himself, wondering if it fit in at all. Ethan had always ascribed his ascent from poverty to being at the right place at the right time and, of course, to his own hard work. But the Nathan Broders of the world were few and far between. So much sadness and suffering abounded.

On the other hand, Ethan had seen many inexplicable things in his years of practice, things that flew in the face of natural law. Were those called marvels? mysteries? or miracles? How did such things jibe with Broder's perception of a God who had created the world and its physical principles, then dusted off his hands and sat back to watch things play out?

Tonight, after talking with Olivia, he questioned whether God could have actually led him to the druggist's doorstep, having had in mind the ultimate plan of his becoming a physician. If so, what was God's will for the rest of Ethan's life?

In the dark, Olivia's fluid voice came back to him. *We were given a will of our own . . . it's in surrendering it to his own that his will is done and he is exalted.*

Based on his initial knowledge of Olivia Plummer, Ethan hadn't wanted the least bit to do with the prairie healer. And he certainly hadn't wanted to respect her. More troubling than all that was the fact that recently everything about the woman had begun to fascinate him. What had happened in the velvet twilight of his office this evening? he asked himself, tossing from one side to the other. The covers tangled at his waist, and he tugged at them impatiently. His body demanded rest, yet the disquieting thoughts of his mind would not cease.

The humble, impulsive kiss Olivia . . . Livvie . . . had pressed against his injured hand had evoked a flood of feeling in his heart, a deep and painful yearning for something more. He couldn't explain what had come over him then, or that he had very nearly kissed her himself, pulling back at the last second to allow himself the pleasure of holding her beautiful face within his hands for a few fleeting seconds.

Her thoughts on prayer came back to him, of her desire to offer every situation up to God, of the importance of praying for life's "little things," as she had called them. He recalled a professor once joking that God never heard from so many students as he did on examination days. However, Olivia Plummer's faith was so integrated with her life that praying came as naturally as breathing. Did that have anything to do with her empathetic, easy manner with people?

He allowed that there were people who led lives wholly devoted to prayer. The abundance of monasteries and convents on the Continent gave evidence to that. Some nights during his routine prayers, he remembered to ask a miracle on behalf of his sickest patients. But to pray for them as he cared for them? To openly proclaim the Lord's goodness as he worked to whomever might be listening?

That wasn't for him.

There was another question he had wanted to ask Olivia, right before Marshal Briggs had come in. She maintained that she had some sort of right to exercise her "healing touch" as her grandmother had before her. He had to concede that her knowledge and skill were impressive. But what if the Colorado Medical

Society replied that her practice was not within the bounds of legality? What then?

Nor could he deny his attraction to the woman. What might happen now that their reciprocal dislike had sparked into . . . into what? What exactly *were* her feelings for him? Would she have objected if he *had* kissed her?

Leaning up on his elbow, he pummeled his pillow into a more comfortable shape and flopped back down upon it. With the demands of his education and career, he had not had free time to devote to courtship. Consequently, he was not certain of what had transpired between him and Olivia this afternoon. Why was he so drawn to this woman . . . the very antithesis of what he stood for? What had changed between them? After seeing her smile this morning, what had made him want to elicit another . . . and another . . . and another?

While his head was busy trying to rationalize these troubling, unknowable things, far beneath his conscious reasoning his heart sent up a plea to the God he knew was there—but to what degree of involvement in human affairs?—to somehow assist in sorting out this entire, tangled, increasingly complicated situation.

Chapter 10

"Explain a diluent."

"A substance that thins a liquid . . . that which dilutes."

"Where is the eustachian valve?"

Eustachian *valve?* The warm, soapy cloth in Olivia's hands stilled while she pondered the physician's question. She remembered that the eustachian *tube* was in the ear. Where on earth was the eustachian valve?

"Ah, so I have you on that one?" Glancing up from the pharmaceuticals he mixed, Ethan raised his eyebrows. "The eustachian valve is located at the entrance of the inferior vena cava."

The heart. She had only begun learning the anatomy of the circulatory system. "How can two places so far apart have the same name?" she protested. "That's just plain confusing." After a series of busy days, today had been slow; consequently, Ethan peppered her with questions on a wide variety of topics. She resumed washing the jars into which he would place the medicated ointment he prepared for Hubert Zellickson's foot.

Amusement lent his face a boyish expression, and he chuckled. "You're a few centuries too late to register your complaints. Bartolommeo Eustachio has been dead for three hundred years."

While he laughed, Olivia once again marveled at the changes that had taken place during the past month. While winter's snowflakes blew into town on the biting northwesterly wind, Ethan Gray's brusque exterior thawed a little more every day, leaving behind a charitable man who seemed to enjoy engaging in good-natured banter. Had she not heard his tenderness with Susan that day, she might have wondered more at his change of disposition. But because of that secret knowledge, she discerned that his initial bluster and ill humor had been but a disguise for a heart that, deep down, beat with goodness and compassion.

After their extraordinary encounter that dusky afternoon, she and Ethan had resumed their regular routines, pulling back into what could most accurately be described as overformality. However, the sparks of attraction between them burned warm and undeniable. She often felt his lingering look on her and, in return, found herself watching him far more than was mannerly. Each contact they shared—from the briefest brush of their arms as they worked, to his warm hand over hers as he assisted her from the carriage—evoked breathless, giddy feelings inside her.

And how did he know so many things? she wondered with both frustration and admiration. Even if she did nothing else in life but study his textbooks from cover to cover, she would never possess his effortless recall of information. She realized she was fortunate to have gotten the schooling she had, but her learning was no match for his keen intelligence or premium education.

Initially, he had used his intellect to manifest his medical superiority, but now he seemed to enjoy sharing what he knew. Some days the gap between his knowledge and hers seemed too wide, too discouraging, but a secret kernel of competitiveness within her wouldn't allow her to remain disheartened for long. Back she would go to the books and read until the wee hours of the morning.

"Can you give me the common name for *Gelsemium sempervirens?*" he asked, measuring a scoop of white powder and tapping it carefully into his mixture.

"Oh—now it's botany?" she asked, trying to gain a little time as she endeavored to recall the names of the plants and flowers she'd read the other day. "What's next . . . chemistry? calculus? conjugation of Latin verbs?"

An indolent smile lit his lips. "All of the above, if you wish. But for now, with no further delay, it's *Gelsemium*, Miss Plummer."

She sighed and ventured, "Goldenseal?" knowing she was most likely mistaken.

"That's *Hydrastis*," he corrected, blending the unguent with his left hand. "*Gelsemium sempervirens* is yellow jessamine." After a pause, he went on. "By the way, I've been wanting to ask you about your herbals."

"What do you want to know?"

"The lotion you gave Mrs. Fossum the other day. What was in it?"

"Oh, that was a decoction of elderberry flowers to calm the itching she suffers during the cold months. Granny Esmond used to make it up for her every winter. It also has usefulness for soothing sprains and sores, and a tea taken internally can quiet an upset stomach. A tisane of the inner bark, however, produces strong vomiting."

"Similar in action to ipecac. Interesting. How did your grandmother come to know these treatments?"

"Several were passed on to her or she discovered them on her own, but some are Indian remedies she learned from a healer when we lived in St. Louis."

"I don't believe I've ever asked. How long did you live in Missouri?"

"I was raised there. We came west seven years ago, when I was seventeen. I'm still not sure why Granny decided to settle in Tristan, but she was sure this was the place the Lord wanted her."

"Was it hard to leave?" Over the past weeks, his questions had gradually become more familiar.

"It was hardest leaving Romy." In response to his questioning look, she went on. "She and Elena were my best friends when I was growing up."

"Have you ever gone back to visit them?".

"There's no one to visit anymore. Romy teaches school in Washington Territory, and Elena ran away from home the year before Granny and I left. No one knows where she is . . . or what's become of her."

"I take it you and Romy correspond?"

She nodded, idly twisting the rag in her hands. "Not long ago I learned she suffered the amputation of a leg due to some sort of accident."

"She lived?"

"Yes—and got married, besides. I can't imagine what she's been through, but I'm sure she'll make her new husband a wonderful wife. A person couldn't ask for a nicer or more loyal friend than Romy Schmitt—I mean, Landis. I wish you could meet her. She's dark-haired and petite and sweet as a stick of candy. Of the three of us, she made the highest marks in school and was the best behaved." She smiled, remembering old times. "Elena called Romy a goody-goody and was always daring her to break the rules. And every once in a while, she succeeded."

"This Elena doesn't sound like the most upright sort."

"Elena Breen was . . . wonderful." Olivia sprang to her friend's defense. "She wasn't afraid of anything. I'll admit she could be a little fractious at times, but she had a father who, in my opinion, made Simon Legree look like a saint." Her spine prickled at the memory of Andrew Breen's loud voice and cold, mean eyes. His sons, Elena's younger brothers, were cut from the same cloth. It had been Granny Esmond's opinion that Katherine Breen had died simply to escape the menfolk of her household, and in the years following Mrs. Breen's death, the older woman had gone out of her way to shower Elena with as much love and kindness as possible.

"Elena was as fair as Romy was dark," Olivia went on, "and had the most wondrous singing voice. She joined the theater when she ran away. She wrote for a while, but then her letters stopped coming. I know it's probably silly, but every time I see a big-city newspaper I check for her name," she confessed. "I feel like I can't stop looking until I know what's happened to her."

"I don't think that's silly at all. Your friend is quite fortunate to have someone like you to love her." After his quiet reply, Ethan busied himself with his blending.

"Who loved you, Ethan?" Olivia risked in the ensuing silence. "After your mother died, I mean. Were you really left on your own?" Since the night of their ride to the Lepper farm, her curiosity about his upbringing had grown into monstrous proportions.

His movements stilled, then slowly resumed. "I was."

"How did you live?"

"If a boy doesn't learn to live by his wits, he dies. But I was luckier than most. After a couple of years on the streets, I found both job and home with a druggist."

"Oh, thank God for that. Are there many children on the streets of Boston?"

His expression answered her question, leaving no room for doubt.

"Oh, Ethan. How did you manage?" Sympathy for this fine, tall man rushed up from the depths of her heart. "This druggist who took you in, was he kind?"

"He was a good man," he said, nodding, with a faraway expression. "I owe my education entirely to him."

She wanted to add, "And to the Lord," but since their discussion of God's will, they had not talked again about matters of faith. Instead, she asked, "You said he 'was' a good man? Has he passed on?"

"During my first year of college."

There was much more Olivia wanted to ask, but the office door opened.

"Hello, Livvie! Dr. Gray," rang Janet Winter's pert greeting. She came in, her nose and cheeks reddened by the cold, and wiped her feet on the rug. "You've been so busy, Livvie, I've hardly seen you. Can you believe Christmas will be here before too much longer? I forgot to ask you the other day, but would you like to take Christmas dinner with me again this year? Mrs. Thatcher says you're welcome."

"Instead of burdening the Thatchers with another mouth at the table, how about you celebrate with me?" Olivia impulsively offered. "We'll open up my cabin—"

Her words were interrupted by the entrance of Irvin Briggs. "I thought I saw you come in here," he said, tipping his hat to Janet. "Good afternoon, Doc. Livvie." Glancing back and forth at the two women, he looked abashed. "You two look like you're up to something. Am I interrupting?"

"Not at all," Janet replied coyly. "I came to invite Livvie to have Christmas with me at the Thatchers', but she had an even better idea."

"And what might that be?"

"She just invited me to celebrate Christmas at her cabin."

Olivia didn't miss the way her friend's face lit up at the lawman's entrance. As busy as she'd been of late, she hadn't been sharing her lunches with Janet, nor had she any opportunity to prod along Briggs's slow-moving courtship. This might be an excellent opportunity to do just that. "You don't have any family in the area either, Marshal. Why don't you join us?" she asked spontaneously. "And if you're worried about our safety, you can protect us from danger."

"What danger?" Janet asked, eyes widening in question.

"Aw, she was only joshing you," Irvin Briggs replied, admonishing Olivia with a glance. "There should be no danger."

"You'll come then?"

"Only if the doc comes along. What do you think, Gray? Do you think these ladies can cook us up a meal as good as Mama used to make? Or Wanda Neff, anyway."

"Well . . ." As Ethan hedged, bending over his mixture, Olivia was chagrined by her thoughtlessness in failing to include him in their impromptu plans. As a newcomer to town, he must feel doubly out of place.

Setting down her cloth, she shyly approached the now-silent physician. "The marshal's manners are much better than mine. We would love to have you along," she seconded, realizing she very much wanted Ethan Gray to join their party.

His eyes lifted and briefly met her own, causing her heart to pound within her chest. "I'll come," he said simply, causing Olivia to let out a breath she didn't know she was holding.

Briggs clapped his hands together heartily. "It's settled then. You ladies tell us the time, and we'll be there."

⁂

A rash of minor ailments was seen and treated by Tristan's healers in the days preceding the holiday, but nothing of a serious nature. It was as if an unwritten ordinance had been proclaimed by Mayor Weeks, prohibiting any grave illness during the advent of Christmas. Even though the economy remained in decline, spirits quickened in anticipation of the holiday.

A lacy blanket of white had settled across the prairie, winter snowfall being as scarce as summer rains. Unchecked, the wind blustered across the flatland from the northwest, biting cheeks and stinging ears. This time of year, lunches at Neff's proceeded at a more leisurely pace, while the checkerboard at Young's Mercantile scarcely rested between games.

During the first part of December, Delores Wimbers organized her third annual "winter fancy," a pretentious name hung upon an ordinary covered-dish dinner held in the town hall. Still, the event was widely attended and received a favorable write-up in the following Tuesday's *Tribune*.

Olivia and Ethan missed the affair due to Warren Hawley's ingrown toenail, an affliction that had been long-neglected by the attorney. Just before the party, Hawley limped into Ethan's office in apologetic agony. Shaking his head as he examined the painfully inflamed great toe, Ethan determined the wisest course of action was to remove the entire outer half of the nail and obliterate the nail matrix. That half of Hawley's nail would never grow again, but neither would it grow in.

Janet listened in horrified fascination as Olivia described the operation she'd performed under the physician's direction. "I've seen him limping around," the schoolteacher declared when Olivia concluded her tale, "but I had no idea you did all that to the poor man."

"It wasn't anything I'd care to do again, either," Olivia confided as she stuffed onion-and-sage dressing into the first of three chickens lined up on the table, "but Ethan says that in a month he'll be as good as new." The two women chattered with light hearts as they prepared for their Christmas Eve dinner.

Olivia overflowed with joy at returning to her own home. Even though the quiet excitement of being near Ethan made staying in town worth bearing, she had missed her familiar cabin and all her things, her customary routines. Susan had taken good care of her home during the weeks she'd been away, even going so far as keeping up with the housework. Olivia had been astonished to find not a speck of dirt or dust when she and Janet had crossed the threshold this morning.

Today her little cabin was filled with fun and laughter and many good smells. After the experiences of the past several weeks, it was like stepping into another time and place. In addition, the anticipation of the company with whom they would share their hospitality was like a sweet, delicious secret shared between them.

"Do you suppose the marshal will like my cake?" Janet wondered aloud, creaming butter and sugar and eggs in a ceramic bowl. "I brought some wild strawberry–rhubarb jam to spread between the layers and on top. It's not fancy, but—"

"I'm sure the marshal will love *anything* Janet Winter's hands have touched," Olivia said in such an exaggerated manner that her friend made a face.

"Oh, yes? While we're speaking of love, Miss Olivia Plummer, you might be interested in knowing what folks are saying about you and the doctor."

Olivia felt a shock course through her. Were her growing feelings for Ethan Gray so apparent? "I don't know what you're talking about," she denied, industriously filling the cavity of the third chicken with savory stuffing.

"Then why are your cheeks pink?"

"It must be the onions."

"I don't think so." Casting a dubious look her way, Janet first added flour, then buttermilk to her mixture. "Irvin told me there's been plenty of talk about the doctor at Neff's lately. You know . . . about how he came to town as conceited as a flea full of blood, and then how the two of you started making war on each other."

Olivia was silent, listening as a stranger would to this bit of small-town gossip. So far Janet had not said anything objectionable or untrue.

"Now the bets are changing," Janet said with a saucy twinkle in her eyes. "Instead of figuring how long it's going to take for the two of you to do each other in, people are starting to wonder how long it's going to take for Dr. Gray to get down on one knee."

Olivia blushed to the roots of her hair. People had actually *said* such things? It had to be an excess of idle time on their hands. Seeing amusement, sympathy, and inquiry written on Janet's features, Olivia was caught between wanting to deny everything outright and pouring out her heart to her friend. Yet how could she admit she'd done something so impetuous and forward as kiss Ethan Gray's scar . . . or that he'd gathered her face between his hands and looked at her in a way that had stolen both her breath and her heart?

"Is there something between you and the doctor, Livvie?" Janet asked gently. "I'm sorry if I hurt your feelings. It's just that you've teased me about the marshal for so long that I couldn't resist."

"Oh, Janet . . . I don't know," she replied miserably, wiping the seasoned mixture from her hands. "So much has happened, and I don't understand any of it. Before he came to Tristan, I wanted to like him. But once he got here and called for my arrest, I couldn't stand the sight of him. Then he got hurt and the marshal made us work together, and I despised him even more for the changes he wrought in my life. Some admission from a God-fearing woman, wouldn't you say?"

"It's honest, Livvie." Janet's stirring motions slowed while she listened.

Olivia's words came faster now, tripping over one another with the force of her emotion. "He would be perfectly civil to other people, but never to me. There was always some kind of . . . *attitude* in his eyes when he looked at me. To top that off, there didn't seem to be one thing he didn't know. He knew everything and was always right about everything too. It made me feel mad and stupid and ashamed all at once, so I started taking his books home to read. Then one day last month, he caught me . . . and accused me of thievery."

She paused, reflecting on the events of that extraordinary afternoon. Janet waited, giving her batter a few halfhearted stirs. The stove popped and crackled, indicating its readiness to accept whatever they wished to bake. Sighing, Olivia spoke again, this time in a different vein.

"Until I heard him talk with Susan that day, I never thought he could be gentle and kind. But he was, and now Susan worships the ground he walks on. Later that day, he talked the same way to me."

Janet tipped her head to the side, eyebrows cocked, while she studied Olivia. The set of her lips lingered somewhere between a musing expression and a smile. "I think there are several things you must have left out in between those two events, but I'll let them go for now."

Olivia smiled her gratefulness, remembering the touch of Ethan's hands on her face, the tender words he'd spoken.

"So he's declared his feelings for you. How does that affect your work? And what about the letter he sent to the Colorado Medical Society?"

"Well, he hasn't declared himself in so many words. He asked if he could call me Livvie, but since then he continues addressing me as 'Miss Plummer.' He's been so courteous and respectful . . . and he even asked my forgiveness for the way he treated me at first. He's never mentioned the letter again. It's been long enough now . . . I would think the Colorado Medical Society would have written back by now if they were going to. I'm just not going to worry about it anymore."

Janet shrugged, an uneasy expression crossing her face.

Olivia smiled, feeling both hopefulness and exuberance return. "We've actually been getting on quite well this past month. Between my reading and his questions, I've learned so much. You know I've always loved being a healer, Janet, but the study of *medicine* is something I don't think I could ever get enough of."

"Well, why don't you become a doctor then?"

Olivia smiled at the thought, dismissing it immediately. "How could I do that? There aren't any medical schools around the corner."

"I suppose not. How is Dr. Gray's hand?"

"He told me the other day he *thinks* a little of the feeling has returned. That's a very good sign, you know."

"And what happens to the two of you when his hand is back to normal?"

Olivia dropped her gaze under Janet's steady stare. "I suppose things will work out. He'll treat some people, and I'll treat others."

Janet nodded, changing the subject. The spoon moved swiftly in her hand. "It will be good to hear Reverend Todd tonight. I believe it's been over a year since he's come to Tristan."

"Reverend Todd is indeed a man filled with the Holy Ghost," Olivia agreed, her mind slowly shifting from thoughts of Ethan Gray. "That must be how he gets the stamina to keep the pace he does."

During most of the year, Tristan's religious services were conducted by Norman Carlisle, a middle-aged Congregational deacon elected by the townsfolk to serve as spiritual leader. Every so often a circuit rider, an ordained pastor, would come through—Methodist, Baptist, Presbyterian, Roman Catholic,

Episcopalian—and conduct Sunday services. Though some townsfolk were particular to one church or another, Olivia appreciated each clergyman's spiritual guidance, garnering precious nuggets of wisdom upon which to dwell during the ensuing days and weeks.

This year Tristanites would enjoy a midnight Christmas Eve service given by Reverend Jack Todd, an ambitious circuit rider whose sermons were enthusiastically received by citizens of Wyoming, Nebraska, and Colorado alike. This was a break from tradition, for Deacon Carlisle usually conducted a Christmas morning worship.

"So, Livvie, what kind of potatoes do you think will give these men the stamina to sit through a midnight service?" Janet asked, dividing the cake batter between two greased and floured pans. "Mashed?"

"Do men like anything else?" she quipped, feeling the lighthearted atmosphere resettle between them. "Granny Esmond always said if you give a man mashed potatoes and plenty of gravy, he'll be as happy as a dog with two tails."

"Well then, we'd better start peeling soon. I don't know about the doctor, but I have an idea the marshal can eat quite a few spuds."

"Livvie, Janet, I don't know when I've had a better meal." Irvin Briggs pushed back his chair and patted his belly. "I'd say I couldn't eat another bite, but I see that cake over there, just begging to be cut."

"Is that so?" Olivia rose to clear the dishes from the table, catching a warm glance from Ethan. Yet another shiver of pleasure ran through her at his look. A convivial aspect of his normally intellectual personality had emerged this evening, a delightful surprise to her, Janet, and Briggs. The four had shared many laughs over dinner.

within a person for days on end. His messages required action, change, and conversion—both new and ongoing. Silently, Olivia prayed for God's will to be done with Ethan Gray, for the old hurts within him to be healed, and for an outpouring of grace that would transform the faith he had into something both liberating and monumental.

Chapter 11

"Do you believe God has a plan for your life?"

Pastor Jack Todd's words resounded throughout the candlelit church, effectively silencing every sniffle, cough, and shuffle. Delores Wimbers's quartet of warblers had already led the congregation in several rousing carols, and Deacon Carlisle had just taken his seat after reading Luke's account of the Christ child's birth.

Ethan studied the man standing at the pulpit. Everything about him—from his height and weight to his medium brown hair—at first glance appeared average. Garbed in a white shirt, tie, and tired-looking but clean brown suit, Pastor Todd patiently and gently studied the flock gathered before him. He took his time, making certain not one face escaped his notice.

Ethan had been to enough Christmas services over the years to be relatively certain of what content the man's sermon might hold. Olivia, Janet, and Briggs, however, had spoken highly of this particular preacher during the hayride, each trying to describe what it was about him that was so compelling. As they had not managed to come to a consensus on the matter, Ethan had decided privately to judge the man for himself. Olivia was seated at his right side, her attention glued to the man in the front; Janet and the marshal were to Ethan's left.

"My brothers and sisters," Pastor Todd assured the gathering, speaking as intimately as he might to a group of his closest friends, "the almighty God does indeed have a plan for your life. But before we dwell on that, let's step back in time to a manger in the city of Bethlehem, where the Son of God enters the world as a newborn baby. . . ."

The man had undeniable charisma, Ethan decided, listening to and watching him speak of the Savior's lowly birth. Whether his skill was natural or had been developed was hard to say, but his voice and facial mannerisms were remarkable—powerful— tools that held the members of his audience rapt.

"But God's plan of salvation was in action long before that day." The unpretentious circuit rider spoke softly, building an air of suspense with his skillfully woven words. "Salvation *history* began with a couple: Adam and Eve. From there it was carried to the family of Noah . . . the tribe of Abraham . . . the nation of Moses . . . the kingdom of David . . . and then to the birth, death, and resurrection of Jesus the Christ—and the establishment of his church here on earth."

Ethan shifted in his seat, thinking he'd not heard things presented quite like this in the past. From beneath a fringe of feminine lashes, Olivia gave him a quick glance and reassuring smile. They'd had a marvelous time on the hayride, but he sensed a growing apprehension within her since their arrival at church. Was that because of him? he wondered, massaging the benumbed fingers of his right hand with his left. A few encouraging, tingling feelings had returned in the past week.

"You might ask, what does this mean to you? In other words, how does the magnificent plan of God have anything to do with any one of you sitting here in Tristan, Colorado, tonight?"

Despite himself, Ethan found himself falling under the preacher's spell. The man's words of faith—and his way of reasoning—struck a chord inside Ethan.

"The Lord is eager to communicate with you." As he pointed at various people seated on the wooden benches, Pastor

Todd's voice grew in strength. "And you and you and you! Each and every one of you. In fact, I believe you would be shocked to know how often he speaks to you." He sighed and shook his head. "But are you listening? Do you *know* he speaks to you? Are you *assured* that he loves you beyond all reckoning? Tell me if you're *convinced* he knows your every thought and deed. And I ask you again: Do you *believe* he has a specific plan for your life? Just as he planned for the birth of his Son, he plans for you, as well. You have to believe that before you can go any further in your faith."

Pastor Todd's words were in direct conflict with Nathan Broder's belief in a rational God who worked only through the laws of nature. Before Ethan's mind could systematically sort through and weigh the minister's bold statements, the man spoke again.

"So you say, 'Pastor Todd, I believe! I believe the Lord has a plan for my life.' Then what?"

Then what, indeed? Ethan thought, giving up his analyzing to hearken to the extraordinary convictions of this most ordinary-appearing man. The atmosphere within the church remained one of expectancy and rapt attention. Not one child fussed.

"Do you delight to do his will?" The minister's words were slow and mesmerizing. He leaned forward, as if revealing a great secret. "Do you *want* his will and his wisdom for your life . . . or do you want your own?"

Ethan glanced at Olivia, recalling their conversation about God's will. Though he had appreciated the sincerity of what she'd tried to explain that afternoon, he was not convinced why its application should make a difference in one's life.

Sadly, the pastor shook his head and repeated, "Do you want wisdom? Or do you think you already have all you'll ever need? Personally, I don't believe there's a man, woman, or child on earth who would not benefit from more wisdom." While he straightened, seeming to grow taller by several inches, his voice rose with passion. "Brothers and sisters, that's why I *ask* the almighty Lord for wisdom! The first chapter of James says, 'If any of you lack wisdom, let him ask of God, that giveth to all men liberally, and upbraideth not; and it shall be given him.' *Ask!* It's as simple as opening your mouth! And once you have asked—"

Ethan heard the soft catch of Olivia's breath as the pastor threw his arms open wide and cried out, "Abandon yourself to the will of God!" Casting his gaze heavenward, the pastor sank to his knees. "Thy will be done, Father, not mine."

Far from appearing the fool, Jack Todd seemed to glow with an otherworldly holiness. Ethan had always glanced askance at the corner evangelists hawking their messages of God's love and salvation. But tonight, as he stared at this man who had humbled himself so completely before this assembly of persons—as well as before the Lord above—he sensed no disingenuousness whatsoever. Instinctively, Ethan knew there was something special about this man of the cloth.

Or was it the message he bore?

Ethan's heart beat faster as he reflexively leaned forward, wondering if Todd was prepared to offer any solid, practical information about how he practiced what he preached. Tonight, for the first time, none of this sounded silly or vaporous. He wanted to hear more . . . he was *eager* to hear more. Much of what Olivia had said was beginning to make sense.

"You need one another." From his knees, Pastor Todd expounded. "I repeat: You need one another. You are members of one body, and any doctor worth his beans can tell you about the trouble created when one part of the body falls out of unity with all the others. The Lord will use your brothers and sisters to help you discern his will. You were not meant to go it alone. And once you have reached this point—"

Ethan blinked. When had the pastor returned to his feet? A peculiar, stirring feeling surged through his chest and outward to his limbs, making him feel nearly the same as he had, some years back, on the occasion of being in proximity to a lightning strike. Quickly, he glanced at Briggs, to see whether the marshal was similarly affected. The big man's gaze was focused on Todd, his head nodding his agreement with the preacher's words. But before Ethan could observe him more closely, Todd went on, his voice slowing in measure.

"Once you have reached this point, be prepared to wait. Perhaps even a very long time. But as you wait, continue moving forward with your life. And as you go about your daily business, one fine day, out of the blue, you will receive that knowledge of God's will that you so desire to have. Act on it. Test it out. Sometimes you may not get it exactly right, but as you live with this sort of faith, you develop your 'hearing' for the things God is telling you."

But how can God tell you anything? Ethan wanted to ask in frustration. About doing the Lord's will, Olivia had simply said, "He'll let us know, one way or the other." To Ethan, that concept was as clear as mud. In what way would he let a person know?

Mercifully, Pastor Todd addressed this next. "How does God speak to you? you might ask. One way is through the written word, his Word—the Bible. I cannot be more insistent: Read the Scriptures. Feel free to think of them as his love letter to mankind. God will also speak to you when you pray or have quiet moments. Sometimes he sends a stranger to deliver his messages, sometimes your friends. Then there are random events, flukes, or coincidences—though we call them thusly, God often arranges happenings and events in such ways we cannot ignore. In time, your heart will begin to recognize who is behind them. Knowing and living and operating in the will of God will fill you with a peace you never imagined. Do you long for that kind of peace? It can be yours."

Ethan's mind whirled with the implications of Todd's assertions. If the circuit rider was right, then there was much more to this business of life than a man's using his learning and common sense to his best advantage. Ethan felt strange, as if he wanted both to flee and to remain seated at the same time. His hands trembled. Could Broder have been so very wrong after all?

There was only one way to find out, and Todd had said as much himself: Test it. Act on it. At least Ethan's mentor would have approved of that scientific methodology, though he would have scoffed at the idea of God being involved with human affairs. Was God involved or wasn't he? Jack Todd's initial words came back to ring in his ears: *Do you believe God has a plan for your life?*

I don't know, Ethan cried out from within his mind. Was it enough to *hope* there might be a plan and to submit oneself to it in the manner Pastor Todd had described? *Is it enough, Father?* he asked, uttering a prayer—albeit silent—in public. He felt disoriented as the others around him rose and began singing "O Come, All Ye Faithful." Standing, he wondered how he'd been so lost in his thoughts that he'd missed the end of the sermon. Things like that didn't happen to him.

Olivia touched his arm and smiled up at him, her eyes sparkling. It was plain to see she'd been invigorated by the traveling minister. Something twisted in his heart at the sight of her lovely face wreathed with such joy. Was it too much to hope that any affection for him shone in those dove-colored depths? For the first time in his life, he longed for a woman's affections . . . and not those of just any woman.

He wanted the love of Olivia Plummer.

Her gaze lingered on him a moment longer before returning frontward as she joined the congregation in song. From his other side came Briggs's booming voice, lacking finesse but full of heart. How could a year make such a difference in a man's life? he asked himself. Last Christmas Eve he'd worked, dined alone, and gone to bed.

But tonight he stood in the company of these fine friends in a tiny church more than halfway across the country from the place he'd always lived. Hardship and difficulty had befallen him, yes, but it was with warmth and gratitude that he thought of his new home, his fellow townspeople.

And if that wasn't enough, he also stood on the threshold of offering his will to the Lord above . . . and his heart to the woman beside him.

❧

The hour being late, people did not tarry as they normally did after services. Even so, an uncommon joy and enthusiasm suffused the congregants. Christmas blessings and well-wishes rang out in the crisp, starlit night. More than a few had hung bells on their horses, and the cheerful jingling added to the festive air.

"That was some sermon, huh, Doc?" Briggs proclaimed, walking down the church steps. "You ever hear anything like that back in Boston?"

"Nothing quite like that," the blond man affirmed with a rueful smile. "And I thought I'd heard it all."

"Sure makes a fellow think, doesn't it?"

"Sure does," Janet replied in a mock basso, eliciting a round of laughter.

Olivia couldn't remember when she'd been more inspired or moved by a preaching. But was that really the case? Smile fading, she wondered if her emotions had to do less with the sermon and more with her increasing feelings for Ethan Gray.

"Would you like to ride up front with me again, Miss Janet?" the marshal inquired, stopping before the wagon. "You two don't mind riding in the back, do you?" He glanced between Ethan and Olivia, and by the light of the lantern, Olivia could have sworn he winked at Ethan as he turned to help Janet into the wagon.

As he had on the way to the church, Briggs began a circuitous route once they left town. His loud humming soon gave way to verse, and he led them in a series of carols and hymns beneath the wintry moon. In addition to their merriment, however, another note was present in the hay-filled wagon box.

Amidst the pungent-smelling grasses, Olivia and Ethan sat facing one another, each nestled beneath a warm traveling robe. From time to time their gazes met, and no matter how hard she tried, Olivia could not help the shy smile that stole across her lips. Ethan Gray was such a fine figure of a man . . . how could she have ever thought she despised him?

"You two warm enough back there?" Briggs called when "God Rest Ye Merry, Gentlemen" had come to a close.

"Just fine," Olivia replied, snuggling deeper within the folds of her blanket.

Ethan, however, gave her a roguish look and leaned forward. "Actually, I am a little cold," he whispered, motioning for her to join him.

No conscious thought went into her decision. A few short seconds later, she sat snugly next to him in the circle of his strong arm, her heart leaping with both wonder and joy. Through the thicknesses of coats between them, she felt him take a deep breath, hold it, and release it slowly. Did his pulse race as wildly as hers? Did her presence do to him what his did to her?

Her answer came a moment later when his other arm encircled her. Instinctively, she turned her face toward his. To his smile of tenderness and question, her lips curved in wordless assent. With his left hand—which was not cold but warm as a summer's day—he gently cupped her cheek. A long sigh escaped him, and she read vulnerability in his eyes.

"Livvie," he murmured, "I don't know what's been happening between us, but I don't want to pretend anymore that it's not happening."

"I don't either," she said softly.

A low chuckle escaped him. "Well, then . . . what comes next? I've never been in such a position before."

"Nor I."

"I've always kept busy with my work, seeing patients—"

"Yes," she replied, nodding, knowing exactly what he meant.

"Does that mean no one's come courting, Livvie?"

"Yes . . . I mean, no. I've never had a beau. There's been no time."

"Do you think you might have a little time right now?"

"Just whom did you have in mind?" she asked with false innocence. "Briggs? Johnson? Hawley with his poor toe, maybe?"

The brown gaze was potent upon her. "I have another suggestion."

Just then Briggs shouted, "Whoa!" and the wagon lurched to an abrupt halt, sending her and Ethan sprawling sideways into the straw, toward the front of the box. Olivia was momentarily disoriented until the lawman's booming laughter, accompanied by Janet's hearty giggles, rang out across the prairie.

"I noticed it was gettin' mighty quiet back there, didn't you, Miss Janet?" Briggs said with a wide grin. "You did a fine job of bracin' yourself." He and Janet turned in the front bench to watch Olivia and Ethan extricate themselves from the hay. "Say, you weren't fallin' asleep back there, Doc, were you?"

"Nooo," Ethan replied, an answering grin tugging at the corners of his mouth. He brushed a clump of hay from his shoulder and gave Olivia a special, private glance as he helped her regain her seat.

"And ain't it peculiar, Miss Janet," the marshal went on, pointing, "that from where Livvie was sittin' clear across the wagon, she somehow fell right beside the doc? I don't believe I've ever seen anythin' like it."

"The science of matter and motion can be a fantastic thing, Marshal," Ethan allowed, settling his arm around Olivia's shoulders and pulling her close. "I also notice that you and Miss Janet seem to be conserving so much space on that bench up there that you could take on another half-dozen riders."

"I'm usin' my warmth to protect the schoolmarm from frostbite," quipped Briggs, waggling his brows. "It's what any decent, self-respectin' John Law would do."

Olivia's heart soared when she saw the expressions on both Janet's and Briggs's faces. She'd been so enthralled with Ethan that she'd failed to notice the flowering of her friends' romance.

"And speakin' of decency," the marshal went on, "we probably ought to get you ladies safely home. It's got to be gettin' close to three o'clock. Did you mention you're both stayin' at

Livvie's tonight?" Olivia noticed the lawman's eyebrows drew together, expressing his misgivings.

"For what's left of the night, anyway," Olivia said lightly. "We'll be back to town after breakfast."

"Breakfast? Did you just hear someone say *breakfast*, Doc?"

Ethan chuckled from beside Olivia, the sound wrapping around her like a mantle of warmth. "I did indeed."

Briggs sighed and affected a forlorn expression. "And after a long, hard hayride, wouldn't you say, Doc, that a late Christmas mornin' breakfast would be just the thing to refresh a man? That's if we have the strength to make it back out to Olivia's again, of course."

"If you bring along some eggs, you can come at eleven," Olivia invited, seeing pleasure spread across Janet's face.

"I thought you'd never ask. Back to Livvie's it is then." Briggs turned around and shook the reins.

The wagon lurched forward, causing Ethan to list in Olivia's direction. His arm tightened, holding her securely, the feel of his strong body against hers both foreign and sheltering. She felt as though she could sit here forever. Her heart swelled with joy, with exultation, with emotion utterly indescribable. So this was love. Many times she had read the Song of Solomon, wondering at the meaning of the lushly written verses.

Now, for the first time, she thought she perhaps grasped just a little of the beloved's feelings for her lover.

In the darkness of Olivia's cabin, Janet whispered, "Oh, Livvie, what do you think is going to happen? Will we have a double wedding one day, I wonder? And if I marry the marshal, do I get my own star and gun?" Tristan's schoolteacher dissolved into a fit of giggles. "That ought to go a long way toward keeping those Sullivan boys in order."

The pair had been in bed for an hour, with Janet showing no signs of winding down. So far they had discussed every aspect of the evening—twice. Olivia was long past ready to call it a night, but Janet continued her chatter.

"I told you it wouldn't be so bad to kiss the doctor, Livvie. He's such a nice-looking man."

"Maybe one day . . . soon." Olivia sighed, reliving the glorious feeling of being held in Ethan's arms. "I love him, Janet," she confessed.

"You love him!" The cornhusk mattress rustled with Janet's wriggling display of delight. "Oh, Livvie, does he love you, too? Oooh, this is so exciting!"

"I declare, Janet Winter, you are two different people living in the same body. The school board would *never* believe their ears if they could hear you tonight."

"I don't believe there are any members of the school board within earshot of us right now—and you never answered me: Does he love you?"

"He hasn't said exactly that," Olivia said, "but he said he knew something was happening between us."

Janet was quiet, then responded, "What does your friend Romy write of being wed? She was married . . . when, last summer?"

"Now that I think about it, she really hasn't said much about it at all," Olivia mused. "She lost her leg, you know, and is having her troubles with that. But you'd think she would write something about her husband. For the past few years she managed to work Jeremiah Landis's name into every letter she wrote, but now that she's married to him, she hasn't mentioned him at all."

"That's peculiar."

"Yes. It makes me wonder if there isn't some sort of trouble."

"Shall we end this night with a prayer, Livvie? We'll pray for Romy and her husband, and then we'll thank the Father for these two wonderful men the Lord has placed in our lives. You've kept me up so long that I think the sky is beginning to get light."

"I've kept *you* up so long?"

Janet giggled. "All right. I kept you up. But I'm so happy. And you have to be too. Things are going so well; it's like we're living a dream come true. Dr. Gray is courting you, and I think maybe the marshal is courting me."

"After all this time, I think maybe he finally is!" Olivia laughed. "It took him long enough to get around to it."

"For all his bluster, Irvin Briggs can be downright bashful. It's rather delicious to know a mere schoolmarm can cause a burly marshal to blush."

Olivia's heart expanded as Janet lifted her voice in a prayer of thanksgiving and praise, her friend's warm hand seeking hers. Despite all the problems she and Ethan had started out having, perhaps God's larger plan was to see them together. Could she surrender herself to that plan?

Yes, her heart sang. *Yes, yes, yes.*

Chapter 12

Breakfast for four grew into a meal for seven. Not long after Olivia rose and stoked the fire in the stove, Susan Connally knocked at the door, having noticed the smoke. After the girl gobbled down the last slice of the cake Briggs had loved so dearly, Olivia impulsively sent her home with an invitation for the Connallys to join them for their Christmas repast. From the brief conversation she and Susan shared, it sounded that while many things were looking up as a result of Donal Connally's sobriety, his cooking was not one of them.

"Come on, Janet Lazybones Winter," Olivia called after Susan departed. "We've got even more to do now. I just invited three more quests! And I know you're awake."

A groan sounded from the bed. "How can you be so chipper after such a short night? You're already washed and dressed, aren't you?"

Olivia smiled and set out two large bowls. "I've had years of practice of living on little bits of sleep."

Slowly Janet pushed herself to a sitting position. The hair that had escaped her braid stuck out in all directions. "What are we making? I think we talked about everything else but that last night."

"Your hair is really . . . something," Olivia observed with amusement. "If only Irvin Briggs could see you now."

One hand smoothing her hair, Janet shot her a grimace and shuffled to the table. Sitting down, she asked, "What do you want me to do?"

"We don't have time to properly steam a pudding, so we'll have to make do with quicker fare. I thought maybe flapjacks, or biscuits and gravy. I have salt pork and sausage—and plenty of potatoes. We could fry the potatoes or make hash with the cold chicken from last night. And what do you think about a nice plum cobbler in lieu of plum pudding?"

"I think it sounds like too many choices. You pick. I'll sit and peel potatoes."

After making three trips to the root cellar for the things they needed, Olivia found her friend finishing her ablutions, looking slightly more alert. She set an apron and a bowl of potatoes on the table, and the women began preparing the meal in companionable silence.

"What did Dr. Gray say about the sermon last night?" Janet finally spoke, stripping the potatoes of their peels. "Or was he too busy making eyes at you?"

"Oh . . . we talked about other things." Olivia felt her cheeks pinken while she rolled cobbler dough.

"Mmm-hmm. You know, Livvie, I realized what a shame it is that we didn't think of making a pot of kiss pudding for the doctor. I'm sure he would have enjoyed a dish immensely."

"I'm sure you're right." Despite her discomfiture, Olivia enjoyed the humorous moment with her friend, wondering if people in Boston were even acquainted with the meringue-topped, sweet vanilla pudding.

As their laughter wound down, a serious expression replaced her friend's saucy countenance. "I've been wondering, Olivia . . . exactly where is Dr. Gray's faith?"

Giving the matter some thought, Olivia eventually replied, "Well, I believe he fears the Lord. But given his upbringing and those who influenced him, he stands at a distance from God. Or perhaps it's more accurate to say he believes God stands at a distance from him."

"How was he raised?"

"He's an only child. His father ran off to California with gold fever when Ethan was a baby. His mother died when he was twelve. After that, he was on his own. Some time later, a kindly druggist took him in and gave him a job."

"Mercy!" Janet exclaimed. "That would explain much."

"I can't imagine living such a life. But look how successfully he turned out. I've been praying . . . and I hope last night's sermon did something to help close the gap between him and the Lord. When Pastor Todd was finished, I was struck by the expression on Ethan's face. . . . For a moment, he looked just like a little boy."

"Yes, well, before you give your heart to that little boy, make sure you know to whom his belongs."

Olivia nodded, solemn, while Janet continued.

"But you know as well as I, Livvie, that if the Lord wants you and the doctor together, there is no difficulty too great to be surmounted. Not the problems of the past, the present, or even the future."

At those words, fresh optimism tingled in Olivia's breast. She and Ethan . . . together? Could something so unimaginable actually be happening to her? She set down the rolling pin and dusted off her hands. *Oh, Father,* she prayed, remembering the substance of Pastor Todd's sermon, *not my will be done but thine.*

"And most of all, we thank you for sending us your Son, whose birth we celebrate this day." Briggs's head was bowed as he asked the blessing, his expression devout. "We also thank you for the new birth you have given us through faith in Jesus Christ—the precious gift of salvation you offer to every sinner here on earth. Amen."

Quiet *amens* ensued as Olivia started passing the first dish.

A barrel and an outdoor bench made do as additional seating around the drop-leaf table, but even with both leaves up, there was little room to spare between the diners. Ethan sat across from Olivia, his melting eyes sending shivers down her spine.

"You were kind to invite us over, Miss Olivia." Donal Connally's dark hair was still wet from a careful combing. His cheeks remained gaunt and sallow from many months of excess, but his face was smooth shaven, his eyes clear. In Olivia's opinion, he'd undergone a remarkable transformation.

"We're delighted you could join us," she declared, finding it difficult to believe this regenerate man could have had anything to do with Ella Farwell's demise. Uncomfortable with the direction of her thoughts, she turned to the serious-looking adolescent who helped himself from the heaping bowl of hash. "And, Seamus, I declare you've grown into a man since I've last seen you. I don't remember having to look up to say hello."

Though the youth made no verbal response, a faint, pleased smile tugged at the corners of his lips.

"He's done the work of a man since his mother's passing," his father admitted, shamefaced, "while I've been down at Kelly's—" Voice choked, he broke off. The festive atmosphere evaporated as an uncomfortable silence settled over the group.

"Lord . . . oh, Lord." With a deep, shuddering sob, the farmer broke down. "I hope someday I'll be forgiven for the things I've done."

Briggs's troubled gaze searched Connally's features. Olivia noticed Ethan's dark eyes inspecting the man as well. A glance passed between the marshal and the physician.

"I've no doubt my Deborah has been tossin' in her grave to know how I took to the bottle . . . neglected the children . . . let the farm go. I tried to get the young'uns a mother, but Miss Ella wouldn't have me. And now she's gone too. I just ain't much good for nothin'. I don't even deserve to be sittin' here among you fine people . . . ruinin' your meal." A tear dripped from his cheek and fell onto his plate.

Janet was the first to recover her voice. "There is no sin

greater than the power of Christ's forgiveness, Mr. Connally. If you confess your sins, he is faithful and just to forgive you of them and cleanse you from all unrighteousness."

"I don't deserve to be forgiven," he whispered.

"None of us does," the schoolmarm went on as though she were teaching a Sunday school lesson. "But God's Word does not lie: Confess your sins, and you shall be forgiven."

Head bowed, he nodded.

"There is another matter about which I've been meaning to speak to you, Mr. Connally, and I suppose now is as good a time as any." For a diminutive woman, Janet Winter could easily command the respect of full-grown men. "Now that you have begun to amend your ways," she declared, "I believe it is time for the children to return to school. I'm certain Mrs. Connally would have wanted them to continue their studies."

"Yes, ma'am, she would have," Connally acceded, his words failing to cover his son's muffled groan.

"Oh, Seamus. I *want* to go to school," Susan interjected wistfully, pouring maple syrup over her flapjacks. "I miss it."

"Good for you." Ethan beamed his approval toward the girl. "And perhaps one day you'll attend college. I missed several years of schooling, but I studied hard and managed to further my education. You're never too old to learn."

A shy, adoring smile blossomed across the girl's face while her father blew his nose and wiped his eyes. After clearing his throat, he nodded toward Janet. "They'll both be back in their seats, Miss Winter." Turning to Olivia, he asked, "Are you back home to stay, ma'am? I've been thinkin' I should do somethin' to properly thank you for all you've done for my children . . . Susan, especially."

"You don't have to—"

"She's staying in town for the present," the marshal interrupted Olivia, his gaze fixed on the farmer's face. "At Ella's place. She'll be going back this afternoon."

At the mention of the dressmaker, Connally's thin features became doleful, and he shook his head. "A cryin' shame about

Miss Ella. You single gals can't be too careful, especially out there on the prairie by yourselves. When you're back home for good, Miss Olivia, I'd be honored if you'd call on me for any assistance you might need." That said, he dug into his hash.

Janet, Susan, and Seamus hungrily consumed their food, apparently unaware of the unrest Connally's words had caused those who knew the truth behind Ella Farwell's death. Olivia's appetite fled. Had only simple gratitude and goodwill shone from Donal Connally's eyes, she wondered, or was cunning concealed in their depths? She regretted including the farmer in her impulsive invitation, noticing that neither Ethan nor Briggs ate much either. The joyous Christmas meal she had envisioned as a perfect conclusion to last night's camaraderie passed awkwardly, the remaining conversation strained.

The Connallys took their leave after the plum cobbler was consumed. Once the dishes were done and the cabin secured, the marshal escorted Janet back to the Thatcher home, where she boarded. Olivia rode to town with Dr. Gray in his carriage, both of them wrapped in silence. Main Street was deserted this Christmas afternoon, a lonely, windy place. Stopping the carriage before Ella's building, Ethan turned to Olivia and abruptly said, "You're Donal Connally's next mark."

"What!" she exclaimed, her jaw falling open with shock at the physician's words. From their meal today, had he somehow deduced that Connally was Ella Farwell's killer? What had the farmer said to give it away? How could he be sure?

A muscle flexed in Ethan's jaw. "You once told me Connally courted Ella Farwell after his wife died, intending to make her the second Mrs. Connally."

"Yes . . ."

"Well, it's my observation that he looked at you today with more interest than that of a friendly neighbor. Not only did he play upon your sympathies, he offered you his protection and service. Now that his brain is no longer pickled—at least for the time being—he's come to realize the perfect replacement for his wife has been under his nose this whole time. He can hardly wait for you to move back out to your cabin."

Olivia let out the breath she'd been holding, realizing what Ethan was driving at. "You think Donal Connally wants to *court* me?"

"If the actual thought has not yet crossed his mind, it soon will."

"But do you think he had anything to do with Ella's death?"

He shrugged, eyes narrowing. "All I know is that I don't want you staying out there by yourself."

"But, Ethan, it's my home. Granny Esmond and I have lived there since—" Her voice faltered when he set his left hand over her right.

"I want to take you to church tomorrow, Olivia."

Her heart thumped at the significance of his words. To have him publicly escort her to church would mean . . .

He nodded. "I want to do so for the reasons you're probably thinking. But I also want to because . . ."

Olivia waited while the physician searched for words. In the time she'd known him, he'd not been a man to hesitate or waver. A vulnerable expression swept across his features, and she knew the thoughts with which he wrestled were weighty indeed.

"Whatever you have to say, Ethan, is safe with me."

He nodded, dropping his gaze to their hands. "I've been doing a lot of thinking about the sermon last night. Briggs and I talked on the way home . . . and then I hardly slept. I read some in the Good Book."

"Yes?" Anticipation bubbled up within her.

"I'm going to test out what Pastor Todd said last night . . . believing God has a plan for my life. I never thought of things that way before, but if it's true . . ."

"I promise you, it's true," she whispered, tears of joy stinging her eyes while her heart sent up a silent prayer of thanksgiving.

"I hope you'll be part of that plan, Livvie," he said with

more sureness, looking into her eyes with a tender look as soft and smooth as melted chocolate. His crooked smile made her think once again of the abandoned boy he had been. How she ached to remedy the hurts of his past, to love him so completely that the suffering of his early years would be washed away and never cause him pain again.

But she knew the largest part of that job belonged to the Lord, not to her.

"I hope so, too, Dr. Gray," she replied softly, "and I'd be honored to attend church with you tomorrow morning."

The crooked smile gave way to a breath-stealing grin. "It's settled, then. Unless we're called out, I'll be by for you shortly before nine-thirty."

"I'll be ready," she replied, yielding the deeper meaning of her words to the Lord while Ethan assisted her from the carriage.

I'm ready, Lord, her heart echoed, *for whatever plans you have for Ethan and me. I surrender . . . I abandon myself to your will.*

Though he wasn't a Tristan native, Ethan was aware he'd caused quite a stir by appearing in church with Olivia Plummer on his arm. The little place of worship fairly hummed throughout the service, and just how much of Deacon Carlisle's preaching on the Holy Family was absorbed by the congregation was questionable.

Could I take this woman as my wife? Ethan asked himself, glancing down at Livvie. A warm, floral fragrance rose from her hair—or was it her neck?—and he breathed in deeply, admiring the shape of her dainty hands, folded one over the other in her lap.

That was what courtship was all about, wasn't it? A period of time that most usually led to marriage?

Dressed in a dark gray skirt and matching dark shawl, Olivia Plummer looked particularly fetching this morning. The charcoal color, combined with the visible bits of the soft white blouse she wore, set off her eyes and coloring to perfection. A faint blush tinted her cheeks, due either to the chill wind outdoors or to the draughts of ado they'd stirred indoors, he couldn't say. As he watched her, he answered himself: *Yes, I could marry this woman.*

He thought of her kind and gracious way with patients, and how they responded to her genuineness. With her bright mind and natural skill—her healing touch, as she called it—she would have made a wonderful physician. Though the idea of admitting women to the Massachusetts Medical Society had never caused him any distress, the topic provoked hot feelings and much consternation among its members.

Unlike the New York County Medical Society, which had begun admitting women to membership in 1871, the Massachusetts Medical Society continued denying female affiliation. The majority of voting members believed women belonged in the home and that women doctors were out of their sphere of motherhood. Nor did Harvard Medical School accept women. The attributes that made Olivia a wonderful healer, he realized, would also make her a wonderful mother to their children.

Their children?

He flexed his right hand, relieved beyond belief at the increasing mobility and sensation he felt returning to his thumb and finger. Had this injury been used to bring him and Olivia together? he wondered. Was this all part of God's plan? Were these things even knowable?

Determined to bear out the truth of Pastor Todd's exhortation on God's will, Ethan had been making a point of relinquishing his will to God every time he prayed. As far as he could tell, the Almighty hadn't spoken to him yet in any discernible way, but he felt a rightness in his heart whenever he thought about deepening his relationship with Olivia Plummer.

Finally, the service was over, and the church slowly cleared of people. As he'd suspected, Delores Wimbers was the first person to bustle up and comment on the fact that he'd walked the midwife to church and had sat with her during the assembly.

"Aren't you looking lovely this morning, Miss Olivia?" the matron exclaimed. "And Dr. Gray. How good to see you've begun joining us in worship. I've always said it's a sure sign of a man ready to settle down. Wouldn't you know, just the other day I was predicting the two of you would soon be strolling arm in arm. Louella didn't believe me—*oh, Louella!*" Standing on her tiptoes, she raised a plump arm over her head and called to her friend, nodding. "I told you so! I was right!"

"Really, Mrs. Wimbers—," Ethan began, concerned that Olivia might be upset by the older woman's remarks.

"I take it your courtship is official now?" Delores plowed ahead, unmindful of the fact she'd interrupted. Settling back down on her heels, she peered first at Ethan, then at Olivia.

To Ethan's surprise, Olivia appeared faintly amused. "I'm not sure what you mean by 'official,' Mrs. Wimbers," she demurred. "Dr. Gray merely asked to escort me to church."

"Yes, and I couldn't help but notice that he escorted you to the Christmas Vigil . . . along with the marshal and Miss Winter. I've also heard tell that the two of you have gotten quite cordial as of late. My, oh my, have things changed since your showdown on Main Street last fall!" She clapped her gloved hands together, a broad smile causing her fleshy cheeks to pouch outward. "I have just had the most marvelous idea. You'll come home and take Sunday dinner with me!"

"Oh no, Mrs. Wimbers. You weren't expecting us; we couldn't impose," Ethan protested, envisioning hours of auditory captivity.

"But I insist!" she trilled. "It's no imposition whatsoever. Since Mr. Wimbers has been gone, rest his soul, a single Sunday afternoon can take ever so long to pass. I've got a pot of bean soup bubbling, a baked rabbit, and just last night I mixed up a lovely chocolate cake. You do like chocolate cake with chocolate icing, don't you, Doctor Gray?"

Before he could answer, she went on. "And as neither of you has any kin in the vicinity, I shall take it upon myself to provide chaperonage for you as my Christian duty." Tapping her forefinger to her chin, she glanced between the two of them and shook her head. "Your working together does pose a problem, however."

"Mrs. Wimbers, I can assure you—," Olivia began, faint pink tinting her cheeks.

"Oh my, yes. Propriety would indeed dictate against such an arrangement," the matron interrupted. With a plump arm, she beckoned. Her head was high as she assumed the lead. "Come along now. We'll speak of it over dinner."

Meeting Olivia's gaze, Ethan shrugged in helpless resignation and held out his arm, knowing whatever he said this afternoon would be told and retold over the cracker barrel at Young's Mercantile for months to come. Bending low to Olivia, he whispered, "I suppose it would be a sin to pray for someone to fall sick and need a doctor this afternoon, wouldn't it?"

Merriment bubbled in her. "I was just thinking that if someone was going to be sick *anyway*, this afternoon would be just the time for it." Their gazes met in delicious conspiracy, and Ethan's heart seemed to skip a beat at Olivia's mischievous grin.

Oh yes, he could imagine this woman at his side for the rest of his days.

New Year's passed, then January and most of February. Ethan and Olivia saw to sundry minor ailments, delivered two babies, managed an apparent heart attack, tended several pneumonias, excised a tumor on the wrist of Rex Sulander, treated an accidental gunshot, and removed a dried bean from the left nostril of six-year-old Angie Maghee.

Each Sunday morning at nine-twenty, Ethan called for Olivia and walked her the two blocks to church. In addition to dining at Delores Wimbers's that first Sunday after Christmas, they received a Sunday dinner invitation to the Thatcher home the following week—along with Marshal Briggs—and another from the Leppers two weeks later.

As the days went by, Olivia found it more and more difficult to keep her feelings for Dr. Gray camouflaged. What would
happen when he no longer needed her medical assistance? she
wondered. As swiftly as his hand was now recovering, he would
soon be able to manage on his own.

This noon he had gone to lunch at Neff's with Briggs and
Johnson, while she sorted through and put away a shipment of
pharmaceuticals that had arrived earlier that day. She'd been so
hungry midmorning that she'd already eaten her lunch. The
office was quiet, with only the ticking of the clock to break the
silence.

Glancing at the glass-fronted bookshelves, she smiled,
remembering the battle she and Ethan had waged over the thick
volume of *Man and Medicine*. How much had happened since
that dusky afternoon. What would happen in the future, she
wondered, especially now that his hand was improving so
rapidly? Though they talked about a wide variety of topics, that
wasn't one of them. Olivia wished their present arrangement
could go on indefinitely, but she knew that wasn't possible.

The door opened, admitting a gust of icy air. "Hello, Livvie.
Anyone been by?" Ethan greeted her as he walked inside and
quickly closed the door to the elements. "I'm starting to wonder
who's the better cook—you or Wanda Neff?"

"That kind of flattery will get you nowhere, Doctor. And
no, we still haven't seen a patient yet today. I'm about half done
with the pharmaceuticals."

Last fall, if anyone had told her that a smile would come
easily to Ethan Gray's face, she would have pronounced that
person mad. In the past two months, however, an easygoing,
genial side of the doctor's nature had emerged. Olivia reveled in
his good humor, soaking up his vitality like a flower in the sun.

"Maybe you need to cook for me so I can more closely
compare your cooking to Wanda's." One eyebrow cocked, he
issued the challenge. Walking over to stand beside her, he added,
"For scientific purposes only, of course."

"Of course," she answered, hiding her grin by pretending to give attention to the pharmaceuticals.

With his finger he lifted her chin. "Maybe you should go home early so you can get started."

At his nearness, Olivia was aware of her hastening heartbeat. "Merely for scientific purposes, you say?"

"Completely." His finger stroked her jaw, then tucked a wisp of hair behind her ear.

"Would you like me to leave at once?"

His smile was replaced by an earnest, serious expression. "Actually, Livvie . . . I've been wanting to speak to you about something. Could we talk now?"

"Of course." She nodded, curious. Turning completely toward him, she gave him her full attention, clasping her hands before her. "Have I done something wrong?"

"No . . . no, you've done nothing wrong." Taking a step back, he looked down at his hands. "Do you remember when we talked about God's will . . . and how a person can know for sure he's doing what God wants him to be doing?"

Olivia remembered the conversation well. She nodded, encouraging him to speak.

"I've given that discussion a great deal of thought," he went on, beginning to pace on the colorful oilskin rug. "I've thought on it and prayed on it . . . and when Pastor Todd gave his sermon, I think I began to understand what you were trying to tell me. Something happened to me that night, Livvie, and since then I've been telling God I'm willing to defer to his way of doing things."

"Oh, Ethan," she exhaled, unaware she'd been holding her breath.

"I've known a kind of peace since then," he went on, "and whether that comes from trusting in the Lord's plans for my life or not, I don't know. One thing I do know, though, is that every time I think about you and pray about you, calmness falls over my heart. Calmness and joy."

A smile darted across his features. "I'm a graduate of

Harvard Medical College, yet I've learned so many things from you. I didn't like the type of man I was becoming in Boston . . . or the kind of man I was when I first came to Tristan." His expression unguarded, he continued, "I don't know how to say this, so I'll just say it. Olivia Plummer . . . I am in love with you, and it would honor me if you would consider becoming my wife."

"Oh, Ethan," she cried, flying into his arms. The strength of his chest was solid, comforting, exciting. "I love you too."

"Does that mean—"

"Oh yes," she affirmed, gazing into twin pools of molten brown. "I love you and would be honored to become your wife."

"Oh, Livvie," he said hoarsely, raining kisses on her forehead, her eyes, the bridge of her nose. "When I moved to Colorado, I had no idea anything like this was going to happen to me. What more could a man ask than to have a woman like you at his side? I was thinking, too, that we could ask Pastor Todd to come back and perform the ceremony. Would you like that?"

Elation coursed through her at the thought of becoming Ethan Gray's bride. Could a person die from this much happiness? *Thank you, Father,* she silently prayed. *I never thought I would be married, yet you have provided a more wonderful man than I could ever have imagined.*

"Come spring," he went on, cupping her face in his hands, "we can start building a house right here in town—wherever you choose. My hand has made vast improvements, but if you like, you may continue working as my assistant until the babies start coming."

At those words, Olivia froze. *She could continue working as his* assistant *until the babies started coming?*

He chuckled tenderly. "And believe me, I'll be sorry to lose such a fine assistant."

"But I'm a healer, Ethan. Not an assistant."

"You've been *my* assistant."

She pulled away from his embrace and stiffly repeated, "I'm a *healer.*"

"And you've done well. But Tristan has its own doctor now; it's time to set your healing practice aside."

"Set it . . . aside . . . ," she sputtered, feeling her fingers clench into fists. "I beg your pardon! All the while I've served you, I've waited to get back to my own practice. *My practice.* And because of you, I can't even live in my own home!" In a split second, all the old feelings of dislike and animosity sprang up within her, while her anger ascended to heights too lofty to check. "And if you think I'll continue working as your 'assistant' while you do your best to turn me into a broodmare, Ethan Gray, you've got another think coming!"

"Well, whether you like it or not, you aren't going to have a practice anymore," he challenged, his eyes snapping.

Fear clogged her voice. "What are you talking about?"

Walking to his desk, he opened the top drawer and pulled out a letter. "I'm talking about this." Holding the envelope aloft, he took a deep breath, as if trying to subdue his emotion. "I didn't want to have to do this," he said in quiet appeal.

"Well, you've done it now, so you may as well tell me what this is about."

He nodded, his next words causing the air to leave her lungs. "It's a letter from the Colorado Medical Society."

Chapter 13

"A State Board of Medical Examiners is being established, Livvie. In the next few weeks, the governor is expected to sign legislation that restricts the practice of medicine to those with proper qualifications."

"Which you don't think I have." Olivia became even more distressed at hearing the quaver in her voice. Angrily she brushed a tear from the corner of her eye.

"Which you *don't* have . . . unless you can produce a diploma from a well-accredited medical college in the next few weeks." Ethan sighed, holding up one hand in appeal. The ticking of the clock was loud in the room. Outside, a team and wagon rattled past. "Livvie, honey, it's not that I think you aren't—"

"You can stop right there," she cut him off, hurt and anger writhing inside her. "I am not your 'Livvie, honey,' I'm your assistant—remember?—and apparently a poorly qualified one at that." She stopped, breathing hard, remembering the events of autumn. "You called for my arrest before you even knew me or what I was about. And if that wasn't enough, you fired off a letter of complaint to the state medical society as well." Planting her hands on her hips, she announced, "Guess what, Ethan Gray? I quit! As you seem to think no one can do anything properly without a college certificate, this arrangement is now terminated. There's just one thing I want to know before I leave: How long have you had that letter?"

"A few weeks," he answered straightforwardly.

"A *few weeks!* When did you plan to tell me about it? Or did you at all?" In addition to anger, the bitter acid of betrayal burned in Olivia's breast. "Or maybe you thought that if you married me and quickly begot a child, you wouldn't even have to mention it."

"Olivia . . . I didn't intend for this to . . ."

She saw him swallow, saw the hurt in his eyes, but she didn't care. He had played her false. His next words were soft, sad. "Don't you want children?"

"Of course I want children." Her voice broke as the dam of tears gave way. "I've longed to be a mother, to hold my own babies instead of everyone else's. I never thought I'd be married, much less have children." At that admission, her head drooped forward and her arms sank to her sides.

"Then let's sit down and talk about this reasonably," he urged. "I love you, Livvie, and it hurts me to see you this way."

"Does it really?" she disputed, needing to get away . . . to be alone. Lifting her chin, she said, "I don't believe I can trust anything you say anymore."

"You can trust me—"

Just then, the door opened, admitting affable Mayor Weeks. "Afternoon, folks," he greeted, tapping his generous midsection with a gloved fist. "I'm in need of a little something for my stomach, if it's not too much trouble."

"Dr. Gray can help you," Olivia said curtly, dashing away her tears. With fleet steps and a last glimpse at the man who had broken faith with her, she retrieved her coat from its hook. "I was just leaving."

"Olivia . . . Livvie, please don't go," Ethan appealed. "Please don't leave like this."

"I'm leaving, and you can take your proposal of marriage and . . . and . . ."

Mayor Weeks's eyes grew round. "I could come back later on, if that would be more convenient."

"Now is fine, Mayor," Olivia insisted with a catch in her voice, feeling fresh wetness run from her eyes. It took every bit of energy to keep her face from crumpling as she continued speaking, taking care not to look at Ethan. "Dr. Gray will see to your stomach . . . while I see to mine. You can spread word that I'll be returning to my cabin this afternoon. Anyone wishing to employ my services may find me there."

Quickly, before either man could reply, she opened the door and fled into the chilly March afternoon.

Olivia packed in a haze, jamming her clothing and household items into bags and pillowcases while the scene in Dr. Gray's office played itself over and over in her head. She knew the best thing to do was drop to her knees before the Lord, but she couldn't make herself utter even one word in prayer. She was too angry . . . too hurt. All she could see was that Dr. Gray was trying to prevent her from practicing her healing touch, albeit in a more crafty, underhanded way than before.

In her haste to get her things and be gone, she backed into the small table in Ella's bedchamber, causing the basin to totter dangerously and the hand mirror to crash to the floor.

"Ohh!" she wailed, surveying the mess. "One more thing I didn't need." Bending to pick up the larger pieces of glass, she noticed a small, unmarked book lying partly beneath the table. Picking it up, she leafed through the pages, seeing it was half filled with neat script. Where on earth had it come from? Avoiding the shards of glass as best she could, she knelt and looked beneath the table. Peering upward, she discovered that a fabric pouch had been fastened with tacks to its rough wooden underside.

Too agitated to give much thought to what appeared to be Ella's journal and its hiding place, she returned to her feet and threw the book into the pillowcase she was filling. A loud pounding came from the front door as she was on her way downstairs for the broom. Was it Ethan? She had nothing to say to a man who would secure her agreement to wed while concealing such consequential information.

"Open up, Livvie; it's Marshal Briggs," came a booming voice from the other side of the door. "I know you're in there."

Irvin Briggs. No doubt he would be on Ethan's side of the fence. She stopped at the foot of the stairs, waiting.

"Open the door, Livvie! I'd hate to have to break it down."

Trudging through what used to be Ella's workroom, Olivia unlocked the front door and pulled it open. "What do you want?" she asked in a discourteous tone. "And don't tell me I can't go back to live in my own home. I'm nearly packed, and I'll be getting Pete from the livery and leaving shortly."

"Thanks, don't mind if I do," Briggs said, overlooking her display of incivility. He tipped his hat and stepped in on the rug. "It's a mighty cold afternoon."

"If you're here because of Ethan, you can just turn around and go right back out the way you came in." Olivia thought her tears had been exhausted, yet more welled up while the big lawman closed the door and stamped his feet.

"Aw, Livvie. Come on now. Things aren't really so bad. If it makes you feel any better, the doc's been having a terrible time figurin' out what to do about that letter."

Disbelief stopped her flow of tears. "*You* knew about the letter? What . . . does everyone else in town know too?"

"Well, I figure as postmaster, John Young is aware of its existence," the lawman drawled. "But aside from him, Ethan spoke of its contents to no one but me."

"How could you . . . how could either of you?" Olivia shook her head, feeling doubly betrayed. "Good day, Marshal," she said, turning on her heel.

"Now you hold on there, Miss Olivia," Briggs ordered, his normally good-natured tone sounding both firm and uncertain at once. "You're acting as sullen as a sore-headed dog, and there just isn't a good reason for it. The doc loves you. You love him. He's a good man. You're a good woman. Now, granted, I'll admit he was a bit . . . ah, zealous when he arrived, and stirred up trouble with a big long stick. If he hadn't written to those medical people in Denver, we probably never would have known about their plans to legislate medical practice. But now we know, Livvie, and we can't pretend we don't."

Remaining silent, she turned back to face him.

"Now, nothing's happened yet. There are no laws against you treating folks. But if those Denver doctors get their way, there *will* be a law . . . and because I know about it, I'll have to enforce it."

Olivia felt like her world was crashing to an end. She felt numb all over, unreal. How could her life's work of healing be made suddenly meaningless by a group of lawmakers in Denver? What would she do?

". . . the examination. I don't know what you think about that, but I'd say it's worth a shot."

"What?" Olivia shook her head, having missed most of what the marshal had just said. She was suddenly tired. All she wanted to do was get home and fall into bed.

"I asked you if you were going to take the examination." At her look of confusion, he went on. "You know, the examination by the board? Didn't you know you can go to Denver and . . . uh-oh . . . didn't the doc mention it?"

"What examination, Irvin Briggs?" Olivia's weariness was replaced by outrage. "Your good friend 'the doc' failed to mention anything about it."

"Oh, blast! How did I manage to get in the middle of this mess? I think maybe you'd better talk to him about—"

"What examination?" she repeated, walking over to stand beneath his nose. "With all your righteous talk about upholding the law, I think the very least you owe me is the truth."

He closed his eyes and sighed. "Chances are, you can go to Denver and submit to an examination without an approved degree, Livvie. If you pass, you receive a Colorado medical license."

Doctor Olivia Plummer?

The title produced a scandalous amount of satisfaction inside her, and she nearly laughed aloud at the thought of displaying a valid medical license to Ethan Gray. His assistant, indeed. If she were to pass the examination, she would be his peer.

Yes, but will you be his wife? a place from deep within her heart cried out, causing stabbing grief at the events that had transpired this day. Just an hour earlier, Ethan Gray had declared his love for her and asked for her hand in marriage. *Oh, Livvie, what are you doing?* she asked herself. *What have you done?*

"What are you thinking?" Briggs queried.

She shrugged, seeing no other way to do things. "What choice do I have but to take the examination?"

"You have an offer of marriage on the table. It seems to me that's another choice."

"But you don't understand how he tried to trick me! He was dishonest."

"There was no trickery involved, Livvie. Only a man trying to figure out the best way to ask the woman he loves to marry him. So his tongue gets tied or he doesn't say everything in exactly the right order. Can't you forgive him for that? The mere *idea* of taking a wife is enough to make a fellow feel downright jittery."

For a moment her resolve softened. But then she remembered Ethan's admission of having the letter in his possession for a few weeks, and how he had simply *assumed* she'd lay aside her practice once they were wed. Now that she had a chance to show him they could be on equal footing, she would be a fool not to seize the opportunity.

"I'll have to write to Denver and find out how things are done, but yes, you can count on my taking that examination. I have too much to lose by not taking it."

Briggs stared at her, then replied, "Seems to me you could

lose plenty by taking it, but who am I to tell you what to do in matters of love? However, as your marshal I still have grave concerns about you living by yourself outside of town."

"But you said yourself that you didn't think Donal Connally had anything to do with Ella's death. Remember? You said you figured the killer was long gone from these parts."

"What I mostly remember is that Ella Farwell did not die of natural causes. And if I figure wrong about who may or may not have killed her, another body could wind up as dead as a can of corned beef."

Loud knocking startled both of them. The lawman answered the door, revealing Deputy Johnson. "There's trouble at Kelly's," the younger man said, pressing the marshal. "A big fight about to break out. Kelly sent his boy down to get us, saying it'd be best if we both came." Looking past Briggs, Johnson raised his eyebrows at the pile of articles at the foot of the stairs, then glanced around the room in which Ella Farwell used to work. "What's this? You going somewhere, Miss Olivia?"

"I'm moving back home."

With a questioning glance toward first her, then the marshal, Johnson tipped his hat. "Coming, Briggs?"

"Be right there. Livvie . . ." Words failed the big man, and he sighed. "I won't stop you, but I want you to slow down and do some hard thinking. Understand?"

She nodded, watching the two men take their leave. Briggs wanted her to slow down and think? Well, there would be plenty of time to do both once she got home. *Home.* The word itself stirred the anticipation of building a brisk fire in her stove, of sipping a cup of fragrant tea.

And of writing her own letter to the Colorado Medical Society.

Being back home wasn't anything like Olivia had anticipated. True, her cabin was comfortable and familiar, yet her steps seemed to ring hollow every time she walked across the floor.

She had written a letter to the Colorado Medical Society at once, requesting an examination, and had also written Romy, pouring out her troubles in an eight-page missive.

Briggs stopped by to visit the day after she got home, and she sent the letters with him to post. She didn't want to take the chance of running into Ethan.

Janet had come earlier this week, Briggs having told her what had transpired between Olivia and the doctor. The camaraderie and excitement the two women had shared while preparing Christmas Eve dinner for their men seemed as unbelievable as a flight of fancy to Olivia while she struggled to make polite conversation with her friend. Perhaps sensing it was better to leave Olivia some space, Janet had soon taken her leave, promising her love and prayers.

Olivia had been home more than a week now, and aside from Marshal Briggs's call and Susan's daily before- and after-school visits, only two persons had sought her for healing—both for minor matters. Though she tried not to, she thought of Ethan nearly constantly, wanting him to stay away and yet wishing he would come. With the midmorning sun shining in one of the cabin's two windows, Olivia sat in her rocker with a quilt block on her lap, doing more woolgathering than stitching.

Susan's familiar rap sounded at the door.

"Come in," she called, glancing at the clock. "You're later than usual today."

A bright smile lit the dark-haired girl's face as she stepped inside. "Did you forget it's Saturday? There's no school today. Mmm, what smells so good?"

Despite her burdened spirit, Olivia smiled. Though she hadn't felt much like eating, she could always depend on Susan's appetite. "I've got a dried-apple pie in the oven. I thought you might like a slice after school, but I guess I wasn't thinking. If you want to wait, it should be done in just a few minutes."

"No, thank you—but you could bring it tonight for dessert!" Susan quickly divested herself of her hat, coat, and boots, and skipped over to Olivia's side.

"What's tonight?"

"Pa sent me to ask you to dinner. He wants to thank you for all you've done for us and for all the food you've sent over since Mama took sick and died. He already made Seamus kill a chicken, and the two of them are busy sweeping and dusting. I can tell for sure neither one ever paid attention to how Mama cooked or cleaned. They're so funny to watch." She giggled, then fixed a hopeful gaze on Olivia. "Please say you'll come. We really want you to."

You're Donal Connally's next mark.

Ethan's words rang in her ears, as did Briggs's warning comments about Ella Farwell's killer continuing to be at large. "I-I . . . well," she stammered, not knowing what to do. She pictured Donal and Seamus with dust rags and aprons, going to such lengths to prepare for her. If it was truly out of thankfulness, she would be unmannerly not to accept their invitation.

But what if Ethan was right? Or, worse, if Deputy Dermot Johnson's belief in Connally's guilt was dead-on? She knew that seeing disappointment in Susan's blue eyes would be difficult, but she didn't want to give Donal even the faintest hope that she was open to his affections . . . especially if the man was capable of deadly violence. She shivered, remembering the sight of Ella Farwell's cold, still form.

"Please, Olivia? You made us such a nice Christmas meal, and Mama always taught us to return one favor for another. Please?"

"All right, I'll come," she said after a long silence, wondering at her judgment the instant the words were out of her mouth.

Susan fairly wriggled with excitement as she ran to the door and grabbed her coat. "Good-bye! I'm going to tell Pa you're coming! He'll be so excited! He says you're one fine woman!"

At that, Olivia's heart plummeted. "Wait—," she called weakly. "Susan—"

"I'll come for you this afternoon when we're all ready!

Bye!" the girl said in a rush. Quick as a whirlwind, she was out the door and running toward home.

With this newest problem atop the pile of the old, the remainder of the morning passed slowly for Olivia. She mourned the loss of the easy accessibility she'd had to Ethan's medical volumes, especially in light of the fact that she would most likely be taking the medical licensure examination.

Or was it that she mourned the loss of Ethan himself? His dark eyes . . . his smile. His new openness to God's will. His avowal of love. She remembered her prayer from Ethan's arms after accepting his proposal, of thanking God for providing a man more wonderful than she ever could have imagined. Intelligent, learned, kind.

How could all that have turned sour so quickly?

A sob broke, and she buried her face in her hands. Ethan. She missed him. She still loved him. Why had he assumed she wouldn't want to continue healing folks? Granny Esmond always said it would be a sin to have the healing touch and not make use of it. God had put this ability inside her and Granny and had given her the desire to help people. Why couldn't Ethan understand that?

Why hadn't he told her about the letter right away? And when he did, why didn't he inform her that she could take the examination? If not for Briggs, she might never have learned of her eligibility for a medical license. Was that because Ethan couldn't bear the idea of accepting her on equal footing?

But are you on equal footing? a part of her asked. *Think of his knowledge, Livvie. His medical education. All those subjects about which he could have written the books. Do you really believe you can be his peer?*

No, she acknowledged, she could never be his peer. But part of the reason was because he would never accept her as such. In his eyes, her worth was that of a lowly assistant, a helpmate. What about her skill as a healer? What of her knowledge and relationships with the people of the community?

Though her well-scrubbed cabin needed no further cleaning, she rose from the chair and put the energy of her turbulent emotions into giving her home yet another thorough dusting. What was happening to her life? *Oh, Lord,* she cried from inside, as she had been crying for days. What was his will for her life? In addition to experiencing anger, hurt, and the sting of Ethan's betrayal, she also felt such confusion. Were her feelings wrong? Would God put into her this gift of healing, then ask her not to use it?

As she ran the cloth over the bookshelf near her bed, her eyes lit on the little journal that had fallen from its secret place beneath Ella Farwell's bedroom table. The day she'd returned from Ella's and unpacked her things in a haze, she'd slipped the thin volume between *The National Fourth Reader* and *Illustrated Lives of our Presidents* without giving it another thought. Now she pulled the journal out, curious what its pages might reveal about Ella's life—with respect to Donal Connally.

The fragrance of apples and cinnamon permeated her little dwelling, while outside the warm sun melted what little snow had accumulated on her roof. The steady *drip, drip, drip* was a reminder that spring would soon be here. She was barely aware of these things, however, as she seated herself at the table and began reading.

The first page was dated January 1, 1879.

With this New Year, I resolve to create a record of my life in the West. I have no reason to believe anyone will care about this except for myself, but at least it will help pass time in the evenings. . . .

Olivia read to the bottom of the first page, then the second and the third. The entries were innocuous, telling of Ella's dress-making business and more than hinting at her loneliness.

A deep sigh left Olivia, and she wished she'd tried harder to make friends with the standoffish seamstress. But Ella had always made it clear she had no desire for anything more than a brief hello. A customer needing work done got more conversation out of Ella Farwell than any well-wisher milling about the church steps after an inspiring sermon. Janet's experience with trying to befriend the woman was the same as hers.

Skimming down the next several entries, Olivia's eyes lit with interest on a passage written in the spring of the same year.

April 27

It appears I now have a suitor, though I am not certain because I have not had one before. Donal Connally has been coming around lately. This afternoon he asked to take me for a drive. I did not smell liquor on his breath, though I hear he's scarcely been sober since his wife took sick and died.

That Connally had courted Ella Farwell was not in dispute. Delores Wimbers's hawkish eyes kept track of every such movement about town, disseminating any news as swiftly as prairie winds spread a grass fire.

Reading on, Olivia learned that her neighbor's persistence had been remarkable. Through July of that year he had pursued the dressmaker's affections until, finally, Ella had had enough.

July 5

Last night I told Donal that I should not like to see him any longer. He said he would marry me tomorrow and move me out to his farm. I told him I do not think he cares for me so much as he cares for the idea of all the things I could do for him. He argued and said he had fallen in love with me. But I do not believe him.

He did not take my refusal well. He said many harsh things—I believe he had become intoxicated at the Fourth of July festivities. One thing I know. If I should have a second chance at courtship, it will be in secret. I cannot bear how everyone talks about everything in this town.

July 8

Have I made a dreadful mistake? I am so lonely. I have no friends. I have never desired to marry, but perhaps a man who would

*use me for honest purposes would be better than the life I have made
for myself.*

The next entry was dated September. What had happened
during that two-month period? Olivia wondered, her heart sink-
ing. How many times had she passed by Ella's shop that summer
and seen her at work . . . greeted her at church, unaware of the
dressmaker's heartache and desolation?

September 16
    *D also wishes to keep our seeing each other a secret. He agrees it
is for the best.*

Olivia searched her memory for any recollection of Ella
and Donal picking up their romance where it had left off. To
the best of her remembrance, after Ella had turned Donal
Connally away, he had spent most of his waking hours—and a
few more than that—at Kelly's Saloon. But had the two indeed
begun seeing one another again? Had Connally lied to Marshal
Briggs?

A sick feeling began in the base of her stomach, growing
more pronounced as she continued reading the entries, now
brief and cryptic. She sighed deeply as she read the few sentences
after October 13.

Is this truly love, I wonder? D has found a quiet place for us to meet.

"No," Olivia whispered, realizing it was no doubt at this
place where Ella's child had been conceived. Had Donal
Connally been involved in this secret sin? With sweaty hands,
she turned the page.

November 2
    *Donal felt as though he had to speak to me again the other day.
I told him I am quite content with my life the way it is. The weather
has turned cold—but D keeps me more than warm.*

Olivia was startled by a knock at the door. "Yes?" she called, slapping the journal closed. Belatedly, she realized the Connally dog barked furiously.

"Livvie! It's me, Janet!"

"The door's open," she called, rising to greet her friend.

"Livvie!" Janet burst in, panting, her cheeks suffused with red. "I ran all the way out here to tell you!"

"Goodness, tell me what?" With quick steps, Olivia walked to the door and took her friend's hands in her own. More trouble? More bad news? "What is it?"

A smile with the brilliance of the dawning sun broke out across the schoolteacher's face as she gasped for air. "It's Irvin . . . he's asked me to marry him."

Chapter 14

Ethan had finished lancing and dressing a large boil when Marshal Briggs's booming greeting rang from the front of his office.

"Be just a minute, Briggs," he called, inspecting his handiwork. "Any questions, Mr. Prentice?" he asked, letting the middle-aged rancher's shirt fall back into place. "If not, you can pull up your trousers and be on your way."

"Yeah, I've got a question," Prentice declared, gingerly tucking in his shirt. "Why is it a boil wants to come right where a man's waistband rubs?"

Ethan chuckled. "Sir, you've just asked one of life's great questions. Keep the area clean and dry, and it should heal up fine. If you want to stop in tomorrow after church, I can take a look at things for you."

Prentice nodded, wincing as he buttoned his pants. "Obliged. What do I owe you?"

"How does two bits sound? For everything." Over the past few months, Ethan had reduced his fees to figures that would cause his Boston colleagues' jaws to drop with horror. Olivia had been right: Tristan's economy was feeble. The more he took his lunches at Neff's and spoke with various residents, the more he learned about the area and its people. Knowing what he now did, he was deeply ashamed he'd once told the Leppers they owed him fifteen dollars for Luther's strangulated hernia.

The beefy rancher counted out the correct change. "Sounds more than fair."

Ethan followed his patient out and shook his hand, bidding him farewell. Briggs milled about the big room, his hands jammed in his pockets. Once the door closed, an enormous gust of air left the lawman.

"I just did something, Doc," he said, shaking his head. A second mammoth sigh issued from his lungs.

"Are you hurt? ill?" Ethan asked, puzzled by the marshal's odd behavior. He had grown accustomed to the big man's frequent visits, taking pleasure in their growing friendship. In some ways he likened Irvin Briggs to Nathan Broder, not for any physical resemblance but for the degree of respect and trust he held for each of them.

"Naw, neither. I came to take you to lunch . . . and tell you I just asked Janet Winter to marry me."

"You . . . did?" Ethan studied the lawman, noticing the faint grin twitching at his lips. "I didn't know you were going to do that."

"Well, I sure didn't either. We got to talking about you and Livvie this morning, and what a shame it is how things have turned out." He shrugged, a helpless expression crossing his features. "The next thing I knew, I was proposing—right outside of Young's Mercantile. We're thinking of a summer wedding, after school's out."

"Well—congratulations are in order, my friend!" Ethan exclaimed, extending his hand, truly happy for the couple.

"I hope you aren't . . . well, I don't mean for this to make you feel worse about Olivia than you already do," Briggs replied, his large hand clasping Ethan's. "But I thank you for inspiring me to do what I should have done long ago. Miss Janet's going to make a wonderful wife."

"Yes, she will." Ethan nodded in agreement. "And I wish you every happiness."

"Thank you, Doc. I still have a feeling things are going to work out between you and Livvie."

Ethan forced himself to smile. "I hope you're right. This situation has been . . . difficult. But as I see it, this is my chance to put God to the test." At the marshal's startled expression, he hastened to put into words the thoughts that had been inundating him since Olivia's departure. "I've told you how I've always thought of God, and as you know, we've talked over Pastor Todd's Christmas sermon many times. What I've been thinking is that there's no better opportunity for me to see if Todd was telling the truth about how to know God's will."

"What opportunity? I'm not sure I follow you, Doc."

"The opportunity to trust God. This might sound crazy, but I still have a strong sense that Olivia is going to be my wife. With the way things are right now, I don't know how that's ever going to happen. I don't know; maybe I'm all wet. Since Christmas, I've been praying for wisdom and telling the Lord I want his will to be done, not mine. So right now I believe I'm 'waiting while I keep moving,' or however Todd put it, until things become clear."

Briggs nodded, deep in thought. "Or maybe God does want you to marry Olivia—and she's the one not listening to what he's telling her."

"That's the test I was telling you about. *My* will says to drag Livvie back to town by her heels and talk some sense into her. But if she's truly meant to be my wife, I trust the Lord will clear a way for that to happen."

"I'm a fine one to talk with, the way I've been dodging matrimony, but I rather favor your inclination to haul her back here kicking and screaming. Anybody with eyes in their head can see you two belong together." Cracking his knuckles, the marshal suddenly appeared ill at ease. "Before another day passes, Doc, I have something to tell you that . . . well, may have complicated matters for you just a bit."

"What's that?"

"Well, I never intended to go behind your back about

anything, but it just sort of came up in conversation with Livvie about that examination in Denver. The one she can take to get her medical license . . ."

Ethan sighed.

"Yeah, it's bad, so I may as well just be honest. She was madder'n a peeled rattler when she found out you hadn't told her about the examination, and she's already written to the medical society with her intention of taking the test."

"She'll never pass." Ethan shook his head and sat down in one of the chairs before the window.

"I have to ask, Doc: don't you want her to?"

"Truthfully? No. But not for the reasons she's thinking—or maybe even you're thinking. Olivia's a talented healer, but it's my opinion every licensed physician needs a solid medical education."

"Well, what about her experience? Doesn't that count for something?"

"Of course, but not enough to take the place of a thorough education. For the purposes of this discussion, let's say Livvie *did* know enough to pass the examination—I have to tell you she still wouldn't pass because of her gender."

"Are you saying they don't like lady doctors in Denver?"

"Precisely. I learned that the issue of admitting female physicians to the Colorado Medical Society has been raised— and tabled—more than once."

"You should tell her that."

"Do you think she'd listen to anything I said right now?"

Briggs let out a snort. "No, I don't reckon she would. She's set on believing you were dishonest with her."

Ethan felt a wave of futility sweep over him. How could he ever make Olivia understand that while he appreciated her talents and skills—was in awe of them even—he couldn't condone her practicing independently? It was nothing against *her;* it was because she lacked a solid foundation from a reputable medical school.

Then why don't you give her a medical education?

The thought leapt unbidden into his mind. For some time already he'd tutored her informally in many subjects, the same way Nathan Broder had taught him while they'd worked together. Ethan knew that many fine physicians had been made by the method of apprenticeship, a way beginning to die out because of the number of American medical colleges springing up. While a good many of these institutions were nothing more than shoddily run diploma mills, several superior schools of medicine now existed in the States.

With his Harvard degree, he had no doubt that a few years from now, under his tutelage, Olivia would be suitably qualified for a medical license. However, this arrangement didn't sit right with him. Given Tristan's population, he and Olivia would see only a limited number of patients. Neither did they have access to hospitals, surgery suites, or other physicians. All of these things, as well as a foundation in many different subjects, were necessary to form a good practitioner.

This only left one conclusion: to become the best doctor she could, Livvie needed to attend medical college. Did she even want that? he wondered, or did she want nothing more than to go on practicing the way she had, just as her grandmother before her?

You'll never know unless you ask her.

"What are you thinking, Doc?" Briggs broke in on his thoughts. "You've been sittin' as still as a stone bull."

Planting his hands on his thighs, Ethan resolved afresh to continue on with a hopeful heart. After all, if what Pastor Todd said was true, God would show him the way to go. "I think maybe it's time I paid a call on Miss Olivia. I've kept my distance these last few days, hoping we could talk reasonably once she cooled down. From what you told me, though, she's still red-hot."

"That she is, but let's go have some lunch and mull this over. Maybe between the two of us we can figure somethin' out."

Ethan nodded. "I was just going to close up, anyway. Be glad for your company."

"And my prayers, Doc. I hope you know you've got my prayers."

☙

Romy's wedding announcement had been a stunning thing to read on paper, but Olivia decided it carried not even one-tenth the impact of a starry-eyed bride-to-be announcing her joyful news in person. Janet's countenance shone with such gladness . . . the same gladness, Olivia was sure, with which she had glowed as she'd accepted Ethan Gray's offer of marriage.

"When will the wedding be?" she asked numbly, remembering how she'd flung the handsome doctor's proposal back into his face when she discovered his patronizing assumptions about her . . . his deception, his trickery.

"When school's out." Tristan's schoolteacher whirled around the kitchen area, finally lighting near the table. Taking no notice of Ella's journal, she planted both palms on the wooden surface and gushed, "I can't believe it, Livvie! After all this time—I'm going to be married! I feel like I'm floating on air!"

"I couldn't be happier for you." Olivia tried to smile—and failed.

Janet's bright expression fell. "But you've been happier— much happier. Oh, Livvie, how insensitive of me, coming out here and crowing about my wedding after you and Ethan . . . please forgive me. When Irvin proposed, all I could think of was telling you. Neither of us has been unaware of your matchmaking, you know." Sighing, the diminutive schoolmarm pushed herself upright and clasped her hands before her. "Are you ready to talk about what happened with Ethan yet? All you said the other day was that he'd tried pulling the wool over your eyes."

"That he did."

"Irvin thinks—"

"I know what the marshal thinks. He's already told me."

Did that harsh voice really belong to her? Olivia wondered. She hadn't meant to speak in such a tone.

Janet glanced down at the table, hurt written across her face. Dropping her arms, she traced her index finger along the spine of the journal. Olivia's nervousness about Ella's disturbing writings won out over her desire not to cause her friend further distress, and she reached out and snatched the volume from the table, not knowing what to say.

The schoolteacher's eyes widened at the same time she caught her breath. "Livvie, I wasn't going to—" Her voice quavered. "I'd say it's time to bid you good afternoon. Please know you'll continue to be in my prayers." Hurt, confusion, and tears stood in her blue eyes.

"Janet—please." Remorseful, Olivia followed Janet to the door, humbly asking her forgiveness.

At the threshold, Janet stopped and turned. "Something's happened to you, Olivia Plummer—something not good. I wish I knew how to help you, but right now I don't have the faintest idea. I only know that if I stay, I may say something I regret!"

Wordless, Olivia watched her friend's retreating figure, her emotions as snarled as the strands of Pete's tail. Catching sight of his mistress, the horse whickered hopefully from behind the fence. Shaking her head, Olivia closed the door and walked back to the table, clutching the book to her chest.

Janet was right. Something had happened to her—and his name was Ethan Gray. But if Janet was aware of how the physician had betrayed her, what would make her chide her the way she had? No doubt the good doctor had spread his version of the story as thick as springtime manure and turned her friends against her.

You'd best take to your knees, Livvie.

Granny Esmond's voice echoed through her mind almost as clearly as if the older woman had been sitting at the table. What would her grandmother have made of such a situation? Had the saintly Adeline Esmond ever felt as though prayer was a futile venture? Probably not, Olivia surmised. From as far back as she could remember, Granny Esmond had admonished her to live in the eternal realm rather than in the temporal.

Pulling out the chair, she sat for several minutes, knowing she should pray but not able to make herself utter any words. Finally, she gave up and reopened Ella's journal to the entry where the seamstress had written of Donal speaking to her, followed by the coy reference to how well he kept her warm.

November 7

D has led such an exciting life—and no one but me knows of it. Each time we meet, he tells me more of the extraordinary things he's done with both his brains and his guns. Such exploits! Such a manly man! How can it be that I have known him, yet known him not at all?

Guns? Exploits? Puzzled, Olivia continued reading. What secret, exciting, extraordinary things could the poor farmer possibly have hidden in his background? The next several entries went on in the same infatuated tone until Ella's longing for a more permanent relationship began to surface.

March 19, 1880

I wish D would just take me to the dance, but he says it's for the best that we keep our seeing one another secret. I used to be in accord, but now I am not so sure I like things the way they are. It's hard seeing him about.

Olivia scratched her nose, thinking that none of this made sense. If Connally had wanted to marry the dressmaker the previous summer, why did he now insist on a clandestine relationship? Was it so he could go on spinning his web of falsehoods without fear of discovery? Or was his mind so besotted with drink that he truly believed his fanciful tales? The entries continued, sporadic, until the warm months.

May 28

I told D of our need to wed. He says it is too soon to be sure, but I am certain. His displeasure is great, and I fear my heart is broken. How did this happen? I made careful count of the days. Why did he say he loved me if he did not mean it?

June 14

I have been ailing—some days I have scarcely the energy to baste a seam without wanting to lay my head down and sleep. My stomach is sick morning, noon, and night. Still D hesitates to believe my condition is dire. He has been distant of late.

Olivia's heart went out to the seamstress, but with the next entry, her blood ran cold.

July 12

What am I to do? D tells me he loves me, but wants me to procure a miscarriage. Knowing what I do of O, I do not believe she would participate in this crime. I cannot do the thing to myself, nor do I want it done—I would be properly wed. I shudder to think of the tongues that will soon wag.

She turned the page, but there were no more words written in the journal. Obviously, Ella had not aborted her baby. The image of the tiny boy curled in his mother's womb leapt into Olivia's mind, and she blinked back tears. For all the errors of judgment the dressmaker had made, at least she had safeguarded her child to the best of her ability . . . even to the point of death.

With a shaky sigh, Olivia rose from the table. Not knowing what else to do at the moment, she busied herself heating water for a bath. How could so much be so wrong all at once? Setting out a washcloth, towel, soap, and a tin of fragrant herbs with which to scent the bathwater, she tried digesting the fact that every area of her life stood in shambles.

In her one and only chance for love she had been played false. The problems with Ethan Gray were just too large to be surmounted. And all because of him, her practice and ability to make a living now stood in peril. As of this afternoon, her friendship with Janet was in jeopardy, and on top of that, she'd just learned she could have entertained a killer in her home on Christmas Day.

You'd best take to your knees, Livvie.

How would Granny Esmond have prayed with a situation like this facing her? she wondered with more than a little rancor. The only way Olivia could see out of this thicket of problems was to obtain her medical license. She absolutely *had* to pass the examination in Denver. That was one thing for which she must pray. With an official document in her hand she could stand proudly before Ethan and . . . *and what?* she asked herself.

I love you, Livvie. . . . It hurts me to see you this way. . . . You can trust me. . . .

His gentle entreaties tumbled across her acrimonious thoughts. Love? If he truly loved her, if he cared at all, why hadn't he attempted to see her since she'd left Tristan? Why had only two people sought her healing this entire week? Was he continuing to do the work he had begun his first day in town: maligning her before the people she and her grandmother had treated for years?

After what seemed like forever, the bathwater was ready. Despite its relaxing warmth, she remained tense and edgy while she washed. In light of what she had just read in Ella's journal, how could she go to Donal Connally's this evening? Perhaps Briggs was right about her being in danger out here . . . yet even while she thought this, a part of her railed against believing Connally could have been the man of whom Ella had written.

If not Connally, who else could it be? she wondered. Did there truly exist a mysterious gunman, as Briggs said the farmer had claimed? Her thoughts raced to the Connally children. To turn in Ella's diary to the marshal would mean certain arrest for Donal. What would become of Seamus and Susan if their father was put in jail? hanged?

Deeply troubled, Olivia finished her bath. After dressing

and toweling her hair, she emptied the water, bucket by bucket, until she was able to drag the tub outside the door and dump out the remainder. Her head buzzed with the implications this journal could have—and how many lives it could change.

How was it possible that Donal Connally had pulled off such a double life? To the best of her recollection, his state of consciousness ranged between drunk and asleep during those months of which Ella had written. But now, knowing what she did from the dressmaker's writings, how could she look at Connally and not wonder all sorts of dreadful things?

How could she sit across the table from him tonight?

But if she handed the diary over to Briggs, how could she stand with the children while their father was taken to jail?

No one but you knows of the diary, Livvie.

With that thought, it occurred to her that she didn't have to make an immediate decision about what to do. Months had passed since Ella's death, and nothing else untoward had happened in Tristan. Thanks to Irvin Briggs's insistence that a quiet investigation be conducted, no one except her and Ethan, Marshal Briggs, and Deputy Johnson knew Ella's death was not accidental.

Perhaps the very best thing to do was wait and watch . . . and go to the Connallys' for supper this evening.

After tucking the book back in its place near her bed, she lay down to ponder the seemingly fantastic things Ella Farwell had written of her lover. Sleep must have overtaken her, for Olivia awakened, disoriented, to the sound of the Connally dog's excited barking. The angle of light coming through the southern window was much lower, and she supposed Susan would soon be coming to fetch her.

She jumped at the sound of boot steps on her porch, followed by a knock. Someone needing her assistance? Rising quickly, she called, "Who is it?" while straightening her skirt and attempting to tame her loose, riotous locks. Her saddlebag of supplies was on its hook near the door, ready to be taken at a moment's notice.

She froze, uttering a little gasp, when a familiar voice answered, "It's Ethan, Livvie. Can we talk?"

Peering into the mirror, she was horrified to discover her hair looked every bit as disorderly as she suspected. "Just a minute," she called, frantically raking her hairbrush through the dampish tresses. When the brush slipped through her fingers and clattered to the floor, she realized she was behaving in a ridiculous manner. After what had happened between her and Ethan last week, why should she care what she looked like?

At that, her anger sparked afresh. Leaving her hair unbound, she walked to the door and pulled it open. Despite the hurt and resentment she held for Ethan Gray, the sight of his face still managed to do wild things to her heart—causing her to become even more angry. She noticed his eyes widen slightly as he took in her appearance, her hair.

"May I come in?"

"I don't think so. It wouldn't be seemly."

He nodded, with a sad smile. "I suppose it's too much to ask for you to step out."

She remained silent.

"Livvie." He sighed and lifted his hand in supplication, the whiteness of his scar catching her attention. "Are you still so angry with me? I hoped that by giving you some time alone, you might be ready to discuss our future."

She felt her spine stiffen. "What is there to discuss? When you asked me to marry you, you had already decided what my future was to be."

"I realize it was wrong of me not to tell you about the letter from the Colorado Medical Society as soon as it came, but I didn't know what to say."

Olivia was quiet a moment, remembering what Briggs had unwittingly revealed to her at Ella's. "That may be so, but you were conspicuously silent about the fact that I could be tested for a medical license. Were you even going to tell me about that?"

He shook his head while holding her gaze. "It's not the right way to do things, Livvie."

"In your opinion."

"Yes, in my opinion."

"Well, I don't share your opinion, and I'm going to take the examination."

His chocolate gaze was gentle. "You won't pass."

"Why not? Surely you don't think me completely stupid!"

"Stupid? I don't think you're stupid at all. It's because women—"

"Women! Is that the real issue? You don't think a woman can be a doctor?" The sun shone warm on her face, but its temperature was nothing compared to the burning emotions inside her. "You think us frail and simple and silly and—" Without warning, her voice failed her, and tears clouded her vision.

"Oh, Livvie," came his tender reply, "I don't believe any of those things. I think you're strong and capable and very, very intelligent—" he closed the two steps' distance between them and lifted his hands to her hair—"and so beautiful. You have no idea how lovely you look right now." His hands slid down past her shoulders, and he pulled her into his embrace. "No matter what happens," he murmured, "please know how much I love you."

For a second Olivia gave herself over to the magnificent sensation of being held in his arms. His warmth, his maleness, were irresistible. Why couldn't he understand that she couldn't be someone's subordinate—a lowly assistant—the whole rest of her life?

"Ethan," she said, pulling back, "about the examination. I want a medical license. You have to understand that I *need* a medical license, especially since I won't be able to practice without one."

He sighed. "If you marry me, you won't need to practice. I will support you. I would also spare you the anguish of going through such a grueling process, only to fail."

"Why are you so certain I'm going to fail?" Frustration made her voice high pitched. "You don't understand! I can't just *stop* being a healer. It's *what* I am—it's *who* I am! It's my whole life! And you're trying to r-rob me of it!"

"Come to church with me tomorrow," he urged. "I missed you last Sunday. I'll pack a lunch, and we can take a drive afterward and talk some more."

"See? You won't even talk about the examination."

"Livvie—" At the sound of footsteps behind him, Ethan turned.

"Good afternoon, Miss Olivia," came Donal Connally's greeting. "Are you ready? Good afternoon to you, too, Dr. Gray."

Ethan's face darkened like a bank of clouds preceding a cyclone as he took in the thin man's washed and combed appearance. At the same time the breeze carried the strong aroma of shaving lotion to Olivia's nostrils, she saw the physician's nose twitch.

"Is she ready for what?" the blond man asked, eyes narrowing.

"For supper. I've come to bring her over for supper." After a long pause, Connally sighed and looked at the ground, adding, "Would you care to join us, Doctor?"

"Supper? I don't think so," Ethan replied, staring deep into Olivia's eyes. His jaw tightened. "In fact, I was just leaving."

"Ethan—," Olivia began, watching him turn. Her heart sank. Surely he didn't think Donal Connally was courting her, did he?

If your situations were reversed, how would things look to you, Livvie? In all this time you haven't made one attempt to speak to Ethan, and now when he comes out trying to forge peace, he's interrupted by a man he's already labeled as your would-be suitor.

Ethan was leaving. His shoulders were stiff as he walked down the porch steps and nodded in the farmer's direction. Didn't he know that this supper at the Connallys' meant nothing? She was only going because of Susan. Why didn't he stop and ask her one more time to go to church? to go for a drive and share his picnic lunch?

I still love you, Ethan, her heart cried. *If you ask me again, I'll say yes.*

But even while her heart pleaded with him to stop, her sinful pride welled up within her and held her tongue silent.

Chapter 15

All during supper at the Connallys', Olivia's heart remained
heavy and uneasy. Seamus and Susan were clearly delighted to
have her over, but not half so pleased as their father was. Donal
Connally's hovering manner and solicitude were as cloying as
clotted cream. Olivia was afraid Ethan's perceptions about her
neighbor's motivations had been correct: the widower was
indeed in pursuit of her affections.

Finally, after the pie had been served, she thanked her host
and pleaded fatigue. Each unpleasant event of this long and
disturbing day had taken its toll, and she longed for the consola-
tion of her bed . . . the insensibility of sleep.

Now that the farmer walked her home, his hand guiding
her elbow with more familiarity than was warranted, the disconcerting entries in Ella's journal leapt to the fore of her mind. Was
this man capable of doing the things about which the seamstress
had written? Did he truly have a secret past about which he had
shared details with only Ella? Olivia's earlier plans to watch
Connally closely and garner information had fallen by the
wayside as a result of Ethan's unexpected visit and chilly departure.

"Are you warm enough, Miss Olivia?" the farmer asked for
what had to be the twentieth time this evening. Was she cold?

hot? thirsty? fatigued? Had she had enough to eat? Was her chair comfortable? On and on his questions had gone until she longed to bolt from his presence like a jackrabbit.

"Yes, Mr. Connally," she replied, disguising a shiver of revulsion as she remembered Ella's comment about her lover keeping her warm. Again she tried loosing her elbow from Connally's grip, but his long fingers possessed remarkable tenacity. Thank goodness they were nearly to her cabin, and she would finally be free of him.

"I've enjoyed passing the evening with you, ma'am. Perhaps we can do this more regularly." With an ingratiatory chuckle he added, "As we're neighbors, it would be only neighborly."

"Mr. Connally, I don't believe I'm available—"

The thin man interrupted her protestation. "Oh, but Miss Olivia, I have heard you *are* available. Word is, you refused the doctor's offer of marriage . . . a dispute over education? But that's the trouble with living in a small town. Everyone has their nose in everyone else's business. As I learned with Ella, it's better to keep things hush-hush than out in the open."

He moved closer. "Now, to my way of thinking, a man such as myself might be more to your liking. I never went to school beyond the fifth grade, but even so, there are things about me that would probably surprise you."

"Did you ever tell Ella about these things?" The question was out before she evaluated the wisdom of asking.

"Miss Ella? Sure, I told her some things." They had reached her cabin and paused at the foot of the porch steps. Though she had wrested her elbow from his grip, he remained close. The pungency of his shaving lotion made her draw her breath through her mouth, and her uneasiness gave way to the first few flutters of fright. Why had she been so pigheaded with Ethan? Why had she been so foolish as to leave Tristan in a huff?

Tonight's moon provided only minimal light. A quiet wind rustled the long, dead grasses sticking up through the snow. Though the two of them stood beneath the vastness of the Colorado sky, Connally's presence was suffocating, overwhelming. Good Lord, in what kind of danger had she placed herself? Ethan and Briggs were right: anything could happen to her out here on the prairie.

"Why do you ask about Miss Ella? Did she talk to you?"

Something about the farmer's reply struck further apprehension inside her, and she swallowed, hoping her reply sounded casual. "Oh, no. She always kept to herself. I just know you saw one another for some time. . . ."

"Yeah, I guess that's no secret. Ella was the kind of woman who always expected too much out of life and was disappointed when she didn't get it."

Expected too much? Being wed to the father of your child was expecting too much? The suspicions Olivia hadn't wanted to cultivate were ripening into certainty. Surely Donal Connally was a man filled with incredible evil and guile. He had to be the man of whom Ella had written—there just wasn't anyone else who fit the bill.

She needed to get away from him. Unless she had read something wrong or made a misassumption, there was no choice but to turn the diary over to Marshal Briggs and let the law take its course.

"Thank you again for supper," she said in what she hoped was a confident tone, ascending the first riser. "It's been a long day, and I never know when I might be awakened. Good night, Mr. Connally."

He followed, standing at the base of the stairs. Oh, Lord, what would she do if he didn't leave? Fear made her heart pound and her legs quiver like so much jelly. *Help, Father,* she prayed. *Please make him go!*

"Daddy?" called Susan. A door slammed in the distance. "Daddy! Olivia forgot her pie plate! I've got it!"

A faint, impatient sound issued from Connally, and he stepped back to a seemly distance. "We're already over here," he called in the direction of his daughter's voice. A scant minute later the girl arrived.

"Here you are, Miss Olivia. It sure was good pie. Didn't you think so, Daddy?"

Thankful for her deliverance but sick at heart knowing that what she had to do would leave the Connally children worse off than foundlings, Olivia waited on the stairs as the breathless girl placed the tin in her hands. With another round of good nights, father and daughter returned to their home while Olivia let herself into the cabin, barred the door, and collapsed into her chair.

Tears scalded her cheeks as she wept in the dark. Why had this happened? Why was there such evil in the world? Why had God allowed her to be placed in this terrible position?

Why? Why? *Why?*

Fresh tears flowed as she realized she had to give Ella's diary to Briggs: there was simply no other choice. In light of the dressmaker's writings, the things the farmer had said tonight only demonstrated his guilt.

You'd best take to your knees, Livvie.

Granny Esmond's admonishment penetrated her misery, yet it seemed to Olivia as though something inside her had shriveled and died. She couldn't pray. Aside from her frantic cry to the Lord for help just a short time earlier, how many days had it been since she'd read her Bible? entered into prayer? contemplated what God's will for her might be? Prayer had always been such a vital, central part of her life. How had it dwindled to become something she gave only *thought* to doing . . . and guilty thought at that?

How had she ever considered herself Ethan Gray's spiritual superior, presuming to give him instruction on discerning God's will?

Ethan. His intelligent brown eyes, his avowals of love . . . his marriage proposal, his position on her obtaining medical licensure. She thought about the words he had spoken that day in his office. Hadn't he really asked her to choose between him and her practice of healing?

Between him and the path God had chosen for her?

Then there was Janet's upcoming wedding and the falling-out the two of them had had this morning. How could she have behaved in such a dreadful manner toward her friend, not sharing in Janet's gladness, especially after doing everything in her power to spur on the slow-moving courtship?

Predicaments and problems pressed in on her from every side, too looming—and far too large—to manage. Still, there were no words inside her to pray. What was the matter with her? What kind of person had she become?

The fire in the stove had burned so low it no longer warmed the room. Only a shaft of faint moonlight preserved the room from total darkness. A chill caught her, and she shuddered from head to toe, but she did not know if it had been caused by the cool air or by the coldness inside her. *Oh, Lord,* she began, only to run into a spiritual brick wall. Desolation engulfed her, and she bowed her head and wept for a very long time.

Ethan awakened to the sound of someone pounding on his front door.

"Be right there," he called, pulling on the pair of trousers he kept at the foot of the bed. Quickly he lit the lantern and noted, on his way out of the room, that the clock read two-fifteen. He had been asleep scarcely two hours. The thought of Olivia being in Donal Connally's company had kept him awake much later than usual.

"Doc, are you in there? Open up!"

Briggs. Had something happened to the burly marshal, or had there been some sort of trouble in town? Ethan had learned that Kelly's Saloon spawned its fair share of injuries.

"Been a busy night," the big man said once Ethan had unlocked and opened the door. Deputy Johnson followed him inside. A sooty odor emanated from both lawmen.

"Someone broke into Ella's and turned the shop upside

down." The deputy's stylish forelock hung in a bedraggled manner above his eyes. "Tried setting fire to the place too."

"Thank goodness I happened to be out." Briggs nodded grimly. "Or this whole side of the street could have gone up in flames."

"Are you telling me the fire's out, or are you asking for more help?" Ethan was incredulous at what Briggs and Johnson were telling him. Who would have set fire to Ella Farwell's shop? Why?

"It's out," the marshal went on. "Whoever set it planned for it to burn slow for a good long while."

"Whoever set it." Johnson folded his arms across his chest, a satisfied expression crossing his even features as he glanced first at Briggs, then at Ethan. "You'll never guess who was in town tonight."

Shaking his head, the marshal eyed Ethan. "Donal Connally was over at Kelly's, pouring whiskey down his gullet like there was no tomorrow."

Remembering the farmer's eager, slicked-down appearance at Olivia's, Ethan stiffened. How could she have agreed to take her dinner with the man? A moment later, he was struck by the joint-numbing realization that she might have been in great danger this evening. He had to get out there, make sure she was unharmed. If Connally had touched so much as one hair on her head . . .

Briggs said solemnly, "We charged Connally with settin' the fire and with Ella's murder. Though for the life of me, I can't figure what would have made him tear up her rooms the way he did. Things were layin' everywhere. Drawers pulled completely out, furniture turned over and broken . . ."

"He cried his innocence long and hard," Johnson continued, "but we locked him up anyway. He won't swing from a cottonwood soon enough to suit my liking."

"Don't forget, Deputy, every man's entitled to a fair trial."

"If you'll excuse me, I need to check on Olivia," Ethan said, breaking in on the lawmen, feeling the blood course urgently through his veins. He couldn't rest until he knew she was safe.

"I'm sure she's fine. Janet was out there today." A furrow creased the forehead of the marshal's weary face. "Or yesterday, I guess I mean."

"Well, so was I—just as Connally came to fetch her for dinner."

Briggs's eyebrows rose. "Now *that* I didn't know. It appears, then, I've got a few more questions for the man. I've also got a favor to ask of you, Doc. While you're out seein' to Livvie, will you kill two birds with one stone and ask her if she'll take responsibility for the Connally kids till we get things sorted out? I'll be out to talk to them in the mornin'."

Fifteen minutes later, Ethan turned his horse up the short lane to Olivia's cabin. Aside from a yapping dog in the distance, everything was still. He remembered the hopefulness with which he had made this ride yesterday afternoon, only to return home with those hopes dashed. Livvie couldn't possibly have feelings for Donal Connally, could she?

No, a voice inside him answered as he recalled the way she'd melted into his arms in the doorway yesterday. Granted, she had pulled away and continued arguing her case for needing a medical license, but for a second, he'd felt her response to him. Nor could he imagine any other woman filling his arms as perfectly as she did.

You don't understand . . . I can't just stop being a healer . . . It's what I am . . . It's who I am . . . You're trying to rob me of it. . . .

All evening he'd weighed the things she'd said to him, remembering how he'd felt when the injury to his hand had threatened his future. Uncertainty and worry had gnawed at him nearly every moment, for he didn't know what he would do if he could *not* be a physician. Given what Livvie had said, he knew she couldn't conceive of living life without making use of her healing touch.

Dismounting near the little house, he was startled to hear her call out.

"Who's out there?" Was there a note of fear in her voice? "Who is it?"

"It's me, Ethan." After ascending the porch stairs, he placed his hands on the door as he spoke. "You don't have to open up. I know it's late, but I just came to make sure you're all right. Are you unharmed?"

At the sound of the bolt being drawn back, he took a step away from the portal. "I'm fine," she said, pulling open the door, still dressed in the clothes in which he'd seen her earlier. A lamp burned in the cabin, and behind her, he noticed a book lying open on the table.

She hadn't even been to bed yet. Why?

Her face was drawn, her eyes swollen and swathed in purple shadows, and her normally ramrod-straight posture was as wilted as a week-old bouquet of wildflowers. What had befallen her? How could he have been such a fool to allow her to go off with Connally? As he had done since learning of the farmer's arrest, he continued to kick himself for leaving her the way he had earlier, allowing his temper to get the better of him.

His instincts told him she was upset about more than his position against her acquiring a medical license, but with the lack of harmony between them, he didn't know how best to approach her.

Help me, Lord. I don't know what to do or say . . . and I'm not even sure she'll speak to me.

What was happening to him? More and more frequently, he found himself praying such short, spontaneous prayers. If the situation wasn't so dire, he might have laughed at the fact that he was regularly praying for the "little things" of which Olivia had spoken shortly after they'd begun working together. *God is always delighted to hear from us. It's yet another way in which we can yield our will to be conformed to his.*

In addition to her ability to heal, how had she come by so much spiritual wisdom in her relatively short span of years?

"You've been up reading?" he asked, seizing upon the first thought that came into his mind.

"You could say that."

"Is it a good book?"

"The marshal will no doubt find it interesting. You can take it to him when you leave."

"What do you mean?" Something about the hollowness in Livvie's voice only reinforced that something was very, very wrong. He longed to take her into his arms and give her comfort, but he also sensed it would be wisest to keep his distance.

"It's Ella's diary."

He was silent, encouraging her to go on.

"It was Donal, after all. She wrote about him. I have to get this to Briggs."

"Livvie, Donal Connally is already behind bars. He went to town tonight and tore through Ella's shop, then tried setting fire to the building."

"Oh," was all she said, turning to glance at the book on the table.

Oh? Where was her shock? her dismay? Was she simply at a loss for words, or had something else happened?

"Did Connally do anything to hurt you tonight? Anything at all?"

"No . . . ," she answered, distracted. "But you were right. He told me he wanted to court me."

Both anger and relief coursed through him at that admission. "What is it then? What's wrong?"

Shaking her head, she turned and walked to the table. Holding the book before her as if she could hardly stand touching it, she returned to the doorway and placed the slim volume in his hands. "Just take this to Briggs."

He accepted the journal without a glance, focusing his attention instead on her wan features. "Livvie, I'm very concerned about you. May I come in and make you some tea? help you get settled?" What he ached to do was gather her into his arms and hold her until every bit of her pain was salved by his love. "You have my word that I'll observe all rules of propriety."

"No." She shook her head, not meeting his gaze. "No, I don't think so."

"Please . . . will you tell me what the matter is? If it helps, I confess to experiencing more than a little jealousy this afternoon. I hope you might forgive me for the way I behaved when Connally came for you."

"That doesn't matter," she said woodenly.

"You don't think so? We both know I acted like I didn't have the sense God gave a prairie dog." He raised his eyebrows, hoping a little levity might break through the brittle walls she'd erected.

Still no response. He shivered, standing outside in the cold.

"Tell me what does matter then," he went on. "Tell me what's in your heart, Livvie."

"You don't listen to me." Her words were so soft he had to strain to hear them.

"I listen to you, honey. I hear everything you say."

"Then why wouldn't you talk about the examination yesterday?" Her gray eyes swung up and focused on him. "What made you want to talk about going on a picnic when I had just finished telling you the most important things about myself?"

"I heard every word you said. If you recall, I asked you to go on a drive with me after church so we could continue talking." He sighed and rubbed his jaw. "We disagree about this examination, Livvie. I'm not unsympathetic to your perspective, but I don't hold with haphazard methods of medical licensure. There's a proper way for things to be done. I've been doing some thinking, and I want to ask you about—"

"Ethan, what you're asking is for me to make a choice," she interrupted, her voice gaining strength. "You want me to choose between you and what God's will for my life is. If you love me, how can you put me in such a position?"

"You think I'm asking you to choose against God's will?" He was incredulous. "I don't believe I'm asking you anything of the sort."

"Oh yes you are, by telling me I can't practice."

"Livvie, I'm not the one forbidding your practice. A group of *lawmakers* is now considering this legislation. If it passes, the state of Colorado—not Ethan Gray—will say you cannot practice."

"Then I don't understand why you're set on withholding from me the only means by which I may legally continue treating patients. I believe I can pass the examination, yet you don't think I should even try. God put this healing touch inside me, Ethan. What would you have me do? Marry you and let it lie fallow? How would that give any honor or glory to the Lord?"

"Have you considered that perhaps God has other plans for you now?" he asked gently. "Have you asked him lately?"

At that, her spine stiffened. "So now you presume to know God's will for my life?"

"No. You're right; that is a great presumption. But what I do know, Livvie, is that I love you and want to spend the rest of my life with you. Perhaps I was mistaken, but I thought you felt the same way about me."

Lowering her head, she shielded her eyes from him.

He pressed, wanting—no, needing—her to declare her true feelings. "Olivia, do you love me? If you don't, tell me, and I'll leave you in peace. But if you do, please take heart. With the Lord's help, we can overcome every obstacle."

"It's not as simple as all that, Dr. Gray." She raised her head, revealing cheeks wet with tears. "Unless you're telling me I have your blessing to sit for the examination. Is that what you're saying?"

He bit back a sigh of exasperation. Not only had she not answered him, she persisted in her determination to acquire a medical license without the proper education. He felt his patience slip a few notches. "Are you saying your love for me is conditional?"

"It seems yours is for me."

"How so?"

"All is well and good as long as I serve as your assistant, but I don't think you can stand the idea of my being your peer."

"But that's not at all what I—"

"Then, Doctor, we continue to be at an impasse. Good night." After a brief pause, she added stiffly, "Thank you for coming to check on me."

Despite his rekindled anger and frustration, her thanks jolted his memory. "Briggs asked if you would see to Susan and Seamus. He'll be out in the morning to talk to you and the children."

Ethan continued standing on her porch in disbelief long after she nodded and closed the door. How had he managed things so poorly? Why did she have to be so unreasonable? *Now what, Father?* he asked, walking slowly back to his horse. The journal in his hands seemed to be made of lead.

Why won't she accept my love? I would make her my wife and cherish her all the days of our lives. I believe in her healing gifts to the degree that I would establish her in a medical college. I've contacted the Pinkerton Detective Agency to search for her friend Elena. And yet she's so angry with me that she won't allow me to tell her about either of those things. What else can I do?

Swinging into the saddle, he realized he could do nothing—nothing at all. What happened now was up to God . . . and Olivia.

The remainder of the night passed fitfully for Olivia. What sleep she got was shallow and fitful, plagued by disturbing thoughts and dreams. Donal Connally's cologne-scented face leering into hers . . . her cabin burning . . . Susan weeping and weeping.

At six she arose and splashed water on her face. How could she face Seamus and Susan with the news of their father's arrest for the murder of Ella Farwell, especially after sharing supper in their home just last night? What would she say? What sort of comfort could she possibly offer them?

Her questions about Ella must have spurred Donal's suspicions. Had he known the dressmaker kept a diary? Is that why he had gone to town after walking her home, tearing apart Ella's shop and setting it afire? Or did he know of further evidence inside Ella's residence that he hadn't wanted anyone to discover?

Would he have killed her, too, for knowing the truth?

But what further indications of his involvement could there have been? she reasoned. It still seemed impossible to believe that the weak-willed farmer could have done anything so heinous. And after the spinster's death, Briggs and Johnson had thoroughly searched the shop and rooms. Surely they would have found anything suspicious.

They missed the diary, though, didn't they?

Amidst these troubling thoughts was interwoven the memory of the early morning scene with Ethan. Why couldn't he accept the idea of her being a licensed physician? Why the inflexible insistence on academic accomplishment? Over and over she replayed his words and their interaction, wondering how things might have turned out if she had allowed him in . . . allowed him to make her a cup of tea.

Why couldn't she just have admitted she loved him? She did. In fact, she loved him so much it hurt. Throwing her cloak over her dress, she stepped out into the chilly morning and started toward the Connallys'. Dawn had not yet broken, but the eastern sky was beginning to show light. Why, she wondered, after so many years of peaceful living, had life become so difficult?

The Connally dog set to yapping before she had gotten ten yards from her cabin. The sound of a lone horseman coming up the road carried to her ears, and she was unable to control the leaping of her heart at the hope that it was Ethan.

She paused, squinting, trying to make out the rider. Briggs? Ethan had said the marshal would be out in the morning. She retraced her steps and began down the lane beside her cabin, while the rider passed the Connallys' drive and continued toward hers.

Was it Ethan?

Her heart sank when she was able to make out the rider:

Dermot Johnson. Briggs was probably still occupied with Connally's affairs and had sent the deputy in his place.

"Morning, Deputy," she called, raising her hand in greeting.

"Morning, Miss Olivia. Can you get your bag? Luther Lepper's in a bad way again. Terrible pain."

"You should call for Dr. Gray. Luther may need surgery this time, and I can't do that."

"Mabel insisted she wanted you to come, Miss Olivia. I'd better take you over there."

"What about the Connally children? They don't even know about their father yet. I was just on my way over—"

"I'm sure Briggs will take care of it. He'll be along shortly to talk to them."

Torn with indecision, Olivia sighed. Perhaps she could quickly evaluate Luther's condition and convince Mabel it would be best for Ethan to see him. Quickly she fetched her bag and allowed Johnson to pull her up on the back of his horse. The sooner she saw Luther and was back, the sooner she could get to the Connallys'.

With a shake of his reins and a quiet *haw*, they were off.

Chapter 16

Olivia had the first inkling that something was wrong when, two miles from town, the deputy left the track and veered toward the west. The sun had risen, its brightness warm on her back. "Where are you going, Deputy?" she called out as soon as she noticed the change of direction. "The Lepper farm is north of here."

He made an unintelligible reply and spurred his horse to greater speed. Clutching his coat to keep her balance, she repeated her question while alarm streaked up her breastbone. What was he doing? Where was he taking her?

"Deputy Johnson! I insist you stop this horse and tell me where you're taking me," she shouted in the most commanding tone she could muster. "If you have another purpose in detaining me this morning, you owe me an explanation."

"You insist, do you? Ella was always insisting on this or that, but she learned the hard way that I don't let a woman tell me anything."

Learned the hard way? Ella?

Lord have mercy, could the *D* in the dressmaker's journal have stood for *Dermot* Johnson?

Her worst fears were confirmed when he turned his head, revealing a face of leering malevolence. In the space of her next heartbeat, she knew Luther Lepper was not ill and that Donal

Connally had not killed Ella Farwell. Deputy Marshal Dermot Johnson had been the dressmaker's secret lover . . . and it had been at his hands that she'd met her death. The disturbing entries in Ella's diary jelled in her mind, making perfect sense.

"Stop! Take me home!" she screamed, beating her fist against his back. The horse was in a full gallop, its stride eating up enormous chunks of ground. Ignoring her, Johnson now steered the mount due west in his course away from Tristan. What was she going to do? How could she escape?

Looking one way, then the other, her eyes connected with nothing but grassland. Fear made her sick, desperate. Not a soul knew where she was or what was happening, and she realized there was no one to see her, no one to hear her, no one to help her.

Never forget, the Lord sees you, Livvie.

Another of Granny Esmond's admonitions leapt into her mind, bringing with it a small flicker of courage. The Lord saw. *What do I do, Father?* she implored. *I don't know what to do. Please forgive me. Please deliver me.*

Whether it was the response of the Holy Spirit or her own instincts, one word flashed across her mind: *Jump!* Immediately she glanced down at the earth, her vitals shrinking at the sight of the ground hurtling by.

I can't jump. I'll be killed. She nearly sobbed aloud, her fingers grasping the deputy's coat even tighter.

What are you doing, Livvie? another part of her reasoned. *Let go of this man—he's evil! He killed Ella, and chances are, he's going to kill you, too. Let go!*

Not allowing herself further time to contemplate what she was about to do, she opened her hands and leaned hard to the right, hoping to avoid the black horse's churning hooves. *That wasn't so bad,* she thought, closing her eyes, feeling as though she were floating.

A split second later she struck the ground. Something cracked—a sickening sound—while she tumbled end over end across the frozen prairie. Disorientation gave way to wings of blackness well before her body came to rest against a snowy hillock.

❧

A despondent mood had settled over Ethan by the time he prepared for church. Lathering his face, he recalled the events of the night. A lantern had burned in the window of the law office on his way back into town after seeing Olivia, but neither the marshal nor the deputy had been in when he'd stopped to give the dressmaker's diary to Briggs. After a long, hard night, both men were probably in bed, exhausted.

Their prisoner had also lain in slumber on the bench in his cell. For a span of some minutes, Ethan had watched the rawboned man sleep off his drink. Connally's snoring shook the rafters of the small building, and the aftereffects of his binge had turned the air in the building rank. Ethan fought the urge to awaken the farmer and ask some questions of his own, knowing it wasn't his place to do so.

The desire was even stronger once he sat in Briggs's chair and read through the dressmaker's diary. None of it made sense. Why had Connally wanted to keep his courtship with Ella secret the second time around? And if he had at one time begged the seamstress to marry him, what would make him later turn his back on her delicate condition and her desire to wed? One journal entry had spoken of his wanting an abortion procured. Ethan couldn't help but think that by suffocating Ella Farwell, Connally had indeed accomplished the nefarious thing he desired.

Leaving the journal on Briggs's desk, he'd returned home and passed the remainder of the night in troubled sleeplessness. The thought of Olivia spending the evening in the man's company made his blood run both hot and cold. He prayed but failed to receive any peace or comfort from the act.

After shaving and dressing, he snatched a stale biscuit from the kitchen on his way out the door. The bright morning sunshine was warm on his face, hinting of the coming spring and utterly unsuited to his mood. He hoped Deacon Carlisle would offer some words of wisdom from the pulpit, for after last night, his hopes for working matters out with Olivia were fading fast. Lost deep in his thoughts, Ethan didn't notice Marshal Briggs until the lawman was close enough to reach out and touch him.

"Say, Doc, do you know where Livvie's at?" the burly man asked, concern etched on his features. "I was out to her place awhile ago and couldn't find hide nor hair of her."

"No," Ethan answered slowly, remembering her bleak manner and the dismal tone of the conversation they'd shared. "After I left the jail last night, I rode out and talked with her; probably around three. She agreed to look after the Connally children. Did you check with them?"

Briggs shook his head. "She hasn't been there, and those two could sure use her right now. I had to tell them that their father was arrested on suspicion of killin' Ella Farwell . . . and . . . well, I suppose there just isn't any good way to deliver that kind of news. The boy's doin' his best to take it like a man, but the girl is in a bad way."

Ethan's heart went out to Susan and Seamus while the marshal continued, his face looking older by ten years, "Janet's on her way out to do what she can, but frankly, Doc, I'm worried about Livvie. Both me and Janet think she's been more than a little off since this business about the Colorado Medical Society came up."

Ethan sighed. "She's got it in her head that she's going to take that examination, and there's nothing I can say to dissuade her. I think finding Ella's diary upset her greatly too."

"Ella's diary?" Briggs barked, incredulous. "What in the blue blazes do you mean, 'Ella's diary'? How long has Livvie had that? What does it say?"

Ethan shrugged. "I don't know when or where she found it; she just asked me to give it to you. I hope you don't mind, but I read through it this morning before leaving it on your desk. Truthfully, it didn't make much sense to me."

"I just came from my office. I didn't see any diary."

"It's there. Maybe you piled some papers or another book on it."

"I'm tellin' you, Doc, it's not there. If it was there, I would have seen it."

Ethan rubbed his jaw, puzzled. "Well, this can be settled easily enough. Let's walk down to your office and have a look on your desk."

A minute later the two men stood on the wide-planked floor of the law office, gazing at the marshal's desktop.

"I left it right there," Ethan said, perplexed, pointing to the now-bare surface. "Like I said, I sat in your chair and read through the entries, then put the book on your desk so you'd find it first thing."

"Well, it wasn't here when I got here."

"The deputy had a book this morning," Donal Connally croaked, leaning up on one elbow. He peered at them through bleary eyes, his hair sticking out wildly from his head. "I saw him looking at a book, and then he left."

"What time was that?"

"I don't know . . . it wasn't light outside yet."

Briggs walked over to the bars and peered inside at his prisoner. "You were so drunk last night, Connally, that you couldn't have hit the ground with your hat in three tries. In fact, you were so drunk that you're probably *still* drunk. Based on that, can you give me one good reason why I should believe anythin' you're tellin' me right now?"

"I swear to you, Marshal, I had nothing to do with Ella's—" The farmer's voice rose in pitch, desperate, then broke. "Y-you have to b-believe me, Briggs. I swear it on my children." His weeping was harsh and loud, interspersed with fragments of discourse.

"After that Fourth of July . . . w-we only talked a few times . . . said she wasn't interested in me." Shoulders shaking,

Connally bowed his head. After a long pause, he went on. "She said she was seeing a real man . . . wouldn't tell me who. She made fun of me. I got mad . . . but I ain't lying . . . I didn't kill her."

"Or beget a child on her?" Briggs's voice was sharp, his expression hawkish.

"Never!" Connally gaped at the two men. "I never did more'n try to kiss her!"

Ethan watched the marshal digest this information. After a moment, the big man turned and began pacing, his footfalls striking sharp and loud on the floor. "Where is Johnson, anyway?" he asked in obvious irritation. "And what did that blasted diary of Ella's have to say?"

"I read it, Briggs. Remember?" Ethan supplied, feeling the lawman's attention clap on him with the force of a magnet striking steel. "She wrote about Connally, that he asked her to marry him on that Fourth of July. She turned him down and said if she was ever to be courted again, she would do it in secret to avoid being the object of gossip."

"And that was it?"

"No, a few months later she started up with talk about being in love and keeping everything secret. Toward winter, she wrote that Donal came to see her and . . ." It was true, Ethan thought, that he'd been tired when he'd read the journal, but something about the latter entries still bothered him.

Ella had written of her lover's exploits, his exciting life, his guns. *How can it be that I have known him, yet not known him at all?* Later she wrote of disliking the secrecy of their relationship and how difficult it was to see him about. If Connally had worn his heart on his sleeve for wanting to marry her months earlier, why had he later insisted on a covert affair and an abortion as to avoid wedlock? Something wasn't adding up.

"Finish your sentence, Doc." Briggs was impatient. "Donal came to see her and what?"

"She said Donal came to see her," Ethan answered slowly, remembering something that had seemed odd. "She was excited about the love affair then but grew more disillusioned with the way things were . . . particularly when she became pregnant."

"It wasn't me!" came Connally's desperate voice from his cell on the other side of the room. "It couldn't have been! She had to be writing about somebody else."

Writing about somebody else?

At those words, something clicked inside Ethan's brain, and he hastened to the bars confining Donal Connally. "Did you say you saw the deputy looking at that book?"

The farmer nodded, fixing bloodshot, gratitude-filled eyes upon him. "He didn't know I was awake. He looked at the book awhile, then left."

Ethan swung his head back to the marshal. "And the deputy's name is *Dermot* Johnson?"

Briggs nodded.

"Several times Ella used only the initial *D* in her entries."

"Just what are you sayin', Doc?" The marshal's face drew into a scowl.

"I'm saying I wonder if she could have been writing about two different men. When she started the diary, she used Connally's given name without exception. Later, after the Fourth of July, she referred to him by name only once." Ethan gained confidence as he spoke his thoughts, finally realizing what had troubled him about the later entries. "She used the letter *D* for everything else. What if she was writing about Dermot Johnson? Think about it, Briggs. It fits."

"It would fit if he weren't my deputy, duty- and honor-bound to uphold the law." The big man kicked his foot in disgust and let a foul word slip.

At his next thought, Ethan's blood chilled. "What if he's got Olivia right now? If he came in here this morning and found the diary, he must suspect she found it."

For his size, Briggs moved with surprising agility. "Saddle up, Doc," he ordered, ignoring Connally's pleas to be freed as he pulled open the door. "Let's go check Livvie's place one more time."

༈

In her years of teaching experience Janet had encountered troubled children of all sorts, but none so disconsolate as Susan Connally. The young girl lay prostrate across her bed, weeping as though her life had come to an end. Nothing Janet did or said seemed to make any difference.

Seamus had jammed his hat on his head and stalked outdoors when she'd arrived, his face stiff with unshed tears. She ached for him, as well. What greater blow could these poor children have suffered than this? she wondered, her own eyes filling with moisture. Not even the news of their father's death would have been so difficult.

Donal Connally had killed Ella Farwell.

If she was still reeling from the revelation of Irvin's terse words, what must be going through their young minds? After the years of suffering and hardship the pair had already endured, what would it be like to be told your father was a murderer? She tried imagining the shame, the disgrace . . . and found she couldn't even conceive of something so dreadful.

Kneeling next to the bed, she mothered the young woman as best she could, murmuring words of love and sympathy and hope. But Susan sobbed on, oblivious to Janet's ministrations and gentle touch. Susan's soft, dark hair was damp from perspiration, as was her back, and Janet began to feel alarm at the girl's uncontrollable distress.

As Janet became aware of a dog's frenzied barking, she heard the sounds of horses and boot steps and men's voices. The door shuddered in response to forceful knocking, and she excused herself from the bedside to see who was there.

"Open up, Janet. It's me."

"Irvin!" she cried with relief, pulling open the door and flying into his strong arms. He hugged her tight before releasing her. Her beloved's face was worn, exhausted.

"Has Livvie been here?" he asked, looking beyond her into

the meager quarters. Spying the weeping girl upon her bed, his expression softened into sorrow.

Glancing past Irvin to Dr. Gray, Janet shook her head. "I wish she had."

"So do we," the physician answered grimly, causing her to look with alarm between the two men. Something was very, very wrong.

"Livvie's horse is at her place, but she isn't," the marshal spoke as though he were thinking out loud. "Her drive is a mess with the snowmelt and people comin' and goin' yesterday, but it appears there may be some new tracks out there. Connally has been behind bars since the middle of the night, and the doc spoke with Olivia well after we locked him up."

Baffled, Janet looked at Ethan for enlightenment, but Briggs continued speaking. "This whole thing stinks to high heaven. And now the diary we knew nothin' of is missin'—and so is Dermot Johnson."

"Irvin, I'm not following you. What are you saying?"

"I'm sayin'—"

"Our dog barked something awful this morning, real early," Susan said from behind her. Turning, Janet took in the girl's swollen, blotchy face, watching as she took a shuddering breath. "He usually barks like that when someone comes for Miss Olivia."

"Did you see anything? Who was out there?" Briggs grilled.

"I don't know; I didn't get up and see." Taking another trembling gulp of air as she sought shelter beneath Janet's arm, Susan ventured, "Are you saying my pa *didn't* kill Miss Farwell?"

Hunkering down so he was at eye level with the girl, Briggs replied, "I don't know quite what I'm sayin' right now, honey. But I promise you this: as soon as I figure things out, you'll be the first one I come talk to."

"If I did anything wrong, I-I'm sorry," she pleaded, her eyes spilling with fresh tears.

"You didn't do anything wrong, Susan," Ethan quickly replied, stepping forward and ruffling her hair. "Not one thing."

"Yes, I did," she wailed, her thin shoulders shaking. "Miss Olivia belongs with you, but I hoped . . . I hoped . . . she would love my pa so she could come and live with us. That was a sin. It was wrong. Even though you're mad at each other, I know you're the one she really loves."

Janet noticed Ethan swallow hard before answering. "Wishing for Olivia to marry your father isn't a sin, sweetheart. Why, if I were of your age and circumstance, I would wish for the very same thing. She's a wonderful woman, and we all love her dearly."

Janet encircled her arms around the lank girl and squeezed hard while trying to discern what lay deep in the marshal's gaze. "Do you believe Olivia is with Deputy Johnson?" she asked.

His mouth tightened. "Seems to be lookin' that way."

"Where are they?" she asked, her heart pounding in fear for her friend's safety and welfare.

"Your guess is as good as mine. Our best bet is to go back and try to make sense of those tracks as quick as we can. Ready, Doc?" Before he turned to leave, he added, "A little prayer would go a long way."

"You'll get more than a little, Irvin," Janet vowed, squeezing Susan.

"I'm coming with you," Seamus announced from behind the men. "If finding Deputy Johnson makes my father innocent of what you said he did, then you can't stop me from looking for him."

Briggs started to object, his words of protest fading on his lips. "I reckon I can't stop you, son," he conceded, extending his hand to the tall youth. "And besides that, I'd be grateful for your help. We're going to need to interrupt Sunday services and get us some more manpower. Get your horse."

With Susan's warm body against her, Janet commenced praying as the men departed, realizing that as the marshal's wife, she was going to be giving large amounts of her time to this very pursuit.

Chapter 17

Cold. Pain. The smell of earth and mildew.

Confused, Olivia tried rolling to her side and opening her eyes, only to cry out in agony at those small movements. Her head, her arm, her entire body throbbed with liquid fire. The side of her face felt raw, searing.

"So you decided to wake up, did you? It's got to be nearing noon."

The man's voice was surly, cruel. Who would speak to her in such a manner? Where was she? The surface beneath her was unyielding, excruciating in its hardness. What had happened?

"That was a mighty stupid stunt you pulled back there."

The voice faded away, and all was silent. Once again she tried opening her eyes, this time without moving any other part of her body. Mottled darkness materialized above her, illuminated by dim light coming from somewhere beyond the end of her feet.

Had she closed her eyes again? Why was her bed so hard and uncomfortable? Was she sick with the fever? A noise startled her, followed by the shock of slushy wet coldness slapping her across the face. Her reflexive movements caused unbearable pain to course through every part of her body while her screams were swallowed by the murky surroundings.

"Time to wake up, Miss O-livia," the voice snarled. "Thanks to you, I can't idle around here all day. I can't even go back for my things."

That voice. To whom did it belong? By slow degrees, the pain receded, and she tried focusing on the man's rapid-fire rantings.

"Oh, yes. Looks like you got yourself a mess of problems there. I don't know what you were thinking by jumping off the back of my horse. Did you think I wouldn't notice? Where did you think you were going to go? You didn't really believe you weren't going to bust half your bones, did you? I should have let you lay and been done with you."

With every bit of effort she possessed, she opened her lids and looked up into the face of her assailant.

Dermot Johnson.

Oh, my, she remembered.

His expression was without pity. "You do realize you wouldn't be in this predicament if you hadn't found the diary."

"You . . . killed . . . Ella."

His smile was slow and mean. "Yes, ma'am, I did. Right here in this soddy. Then I put her back in her buggy and fired a shot. Her horse did the rest."

"Why?" she rasped, craving water to quench the terrible dryness of her mouth, yet knowing her stomach would reject anything she swallowed.

"Why? Now, that's a fair question," he mused. "I might not have even meant to. I've wondered about that a few times. But she just wouldn't stop with talk of the baby and getting married. Besides, she knew too much about me."

"Who . . . are you?"

"I suppose it makes no difference what I tell you." He shrugged, then touched the brim of his hat. "Lannie Faulk is the name, at least in Kansas and Arkansas. So far it's horse stealing, grand larceny, bank robbery, and murder all to my credit. Oh, and I suppose I can't forget the bigamy."

Poor Ella, Olivia thought.

She knew she should be frightened for herself, but at this moment she felt sorrow for the dressmaker more than anything else. How had she gotten tangled up with such a horrible man? What's more, how had Johnson—no, *Faulk*—ever passed himself off as a law-abiding citizen, such that the marshal would appoint him deputy?

The pain in her right arm told her that something was indeed broken. From head to toe every joint throbbed, and her spine felt as though it had been used as a whip. Each breath she drew was an exercise in suffering. From the feel of her face, she surmised she'd abraded the entire right side in her tumble from Faulk's speeding horse.

Her eyes had adjusted sufficiently to the dismal surroundings for her to realize she was lying on the floor of a small soddy. Next to her was the frame of a rusted iron bed, its mattress stinking of mold and rot. For all her affliction, she was glad she lay on the dirt rather than on that filthy, defiled surface.

The toe of his boot nudged her rib, causing her to cry out. "I bet you're wondering where your God is now, aren't you? Little Miss O-livia, so sure of her Jesus," he taunted.

In her spirit, Olivia cried out to the Lord for deliverance, realizing there was no one and nothing to prevent Faulk from snuffing out her life the way he had Ella's . . . and God knew how many others. This very day, she could die.

Was she ready?

Oh, Jesus, please forgive my sins and my stubbornness. I believe in you and trust in the saving power of your name, even if this very day you should demand my life. . . . Our Father which art in heaven, hallowed be thy name—

"Doesn't it say something in the Scriptures about a fellow giving his life for another?" Faulk interrupted her prayer and scratched his cheek as he quoted, "'Greater love hath no man than this, that a man lay down his life for his friends.' What do you know? I still remember my Sunday school lessons."

The boot dug into her ribs again. "Just think of the love you'll be showing today. Jesus ought to be mighty pleased that you're laying your life down for that wastrel Connally and his two brats."

Olivia closed her eyes while the deputy went on.

"No, Briggs and Gray aren't half-wits. They know Ella didn't die by accident, and they're going to suspect foul play if you turn up dead. With Connally behind bars, they're going to know *he* didn't do it. And then there's the matter of the diary."

Hearing a rustling sound, Olivia opened her eyes. Faulk had reached inside his coat and was withdrawing Ella's journal. He laughed quietly as he knelt beside her. "She told me she kept this, but she swore she never used my name. If nothing else, she was true to her word. It even appeared as though she was writing about Connally the whole time. That's what you thought, wasn't it?"

Olivia managed a slight nod.

"I could tell, because you never would have come with me, otherwise." Faulk's face clouded over. "I was happier than a flea on a dog when he showed up in town last night, pouring cheap whiskey down his throat like there was no tomorrow. It was the perfect time to frame him. So I went over to Ella's and pulled the place apart—I found that cloth packet tacked underneath her table, by the way—and started a little fire. After the fire was out, it was easy enough to convince Briggs that Connally was behind it, so we went over to Kelly's and arrested him."

He dropped the book on her chest. "And then this turns up. I didn't count on Ella's diary coming in the same night, nor can I take any chances on someone figuring out she was writing about me. So once again, I'm on the run. It's been a good three years in Tristan though."

He ran his knuckle up the left side of Olivia's face, causing her insides to quake with revulsion. "You know, I always thought you were a pretty little thing. You're still sweet on the doctor, aren't you?"

Olivia didn't answer, but inwardly she cried, *Oh, Ethan, I'm sorry! Oh, Father God, what have I done? I love him so much, and I may never have the chance to tell him again.*

She lay as still as she could, trying not to move as Faulk bent toward her, his forelock dangling. Surely he wasn't going to *kiss* her, was he? Panic rose within her, and her instincts took over. She tried to rise, to push him away, to flee, but agony of intolerable proportions consumed her, overwhelmed her, and forced her back into the land of darkness.

"We've been looking a couple of hours now, Briggs, and we're no closer to finding Miss Olivia than we are a needle in a haystack. With this slush out here, it's no wonder we haven't found any kind of trail." Tristan's barber, Jay Payne, gestured toward the unending vista of flatland. In the warm sun, the snow was melting rapidly.

Five of the seven search parties had reassembled on the edge of town, and the men were tossing out various strategies and ideas for locating Dermot Johnson as if they were pitching so many horseshoes. Ethan sat numbly on his horse, trying not to think about what might be happening—or what had already happened—to Olivia. His beloved.

Father, Livvie is in your hands. Please protect her. Please help us find her.

His prayers seemed weak, disjointed, futile. Part of him wanted to lash out at Ella Farwell for her disingenuous representation of Donal Connally—and Dermot Johnson—yet he knew his feelings were irrational. The dressmaker was dead.

And, maybe, so was Olivia.

Oh, Lord, his spirit groaned, *lead us to her. Save her. Spare her life.* He remembered his first few meetings with her, his acrimony toward the unassuming woman he'd presumed ignorant and illiterate. How wrong he'd been on both counts! There was nothing the matter with Olivia Plummer's mind, and her faith in Christ was both well founded and mature.

He remembered the way she'd proved her mettle by

expertly stitching his hand, then later performing the majority of Ella's postmortem examination.

Ella's postmortem examination.

A sudden thought made him shift in the saddle and interrupt Mayor Weeks's scheme for splitting up and searching anew. "Where was Ella's body found?" he asked, drawing the attention of the assembled men.

"A ways west and north of here." Briggs's reply was affirmed by four of the six townsmen he'd sworn in for the inquisition.

"Ella's diary made reference to a meeting place," Ethan went on. "It's just a thought, but it might stand to reason that she was killed near where her body lay."

Murmurs of assent began rippling through the group, cut short by Jeb Grosset's excited voice.

"Out by my farm, close to where I found Ella's body, are a couple of soddies that were abandoned years back. The one is so overgrown you'd never know it was there unless you stumbled right into it. Ella's body wasn't far from there . . . but of course, until this morning, I had no idea someone'd done her in. Do you suppose—"

"Right now, that's as good a lead as any." Briggs's expression was shrewd as he lifted his reins. In addition to his pistol belt, a rifle and holster were attached to his saddle. "Let's go find out."

En masse, nearly a dozen men kicked their horses and rode hard toward the northwest.

Ethan found that having an objective sharpened his mind and lent fresh hope to his sagging spirits. At least now they had a definite place to search. This sense of purpose seemed to have filtered into the other members of the party as well, for no words were spoken as they sped toward the deserted soddy. With Briggs and Grosset leading the way, one mile had quickly passed, then two, three.

How could the sky be such an impossible shade of blue on such a day as this? Ethan wondered, taking in the incongruous glory of the tableau. The sun was so warm that he sweated beneath his hat and coat . . . or was that caused, instead, by his grave concern for Olivia?

Suddenly Briggs lifted his right hand high into the air and pulled his horse to a halt. When everyone had stopped and gathered around, he fired off his instructions. "We're getting close. I'm going to position three of you out of sight, in case anything goes wrong. Ingersoll, Connally, Mulgrew—that means you."

Seamus Connally's features manifested his great displeasure at not being included in the front lines, but he nodded stiffly, indicating he would abide by the marshal's words.

"The rest of you, listen up. We're goin' to come up on the back of the soddy. It's cut into the side of a hill, so if Johnson's not watchin' for us, he's not goin' to know we're comin' until we're on top of him. With the element of surprise, odds of apprehendin' him are good." With a glance at each man's face, Briggs added, "Let me make myself clear. *Apprehension* is what we're aimin' for. I want your word; no one fires a shot unless it's on my order."

Jim Snow, the man who had brought his dog in to be doctored, made a face and muttered something to Herb Greenfield, the undertaker. The rest of the men quietly murmured their assent.

"I'm goin' to station a couple of you on your bellies aways in front of the door to cover me when I go down there."

"Let me go," Ethan protested without thinking.

"Not unless you've suddenly sprouted a star on your vest," Briggs retorted in a voice that brooked no argument. "I'm marshal of this town, and this is my responsibility. *Johnson* is my responsibility."

Ten short minutes later, everyone was in place. A sense of unreality settled over Ethan while he waited in the melting snow next to John Young. *Can this really be happening?* Was he truly standing on Colorado soil about to become embroiled in what might very well become a shoot-out, with the life of the woman he loved at stake? He started when the owner of the mercantile handed him one of his pistols.

"I've never had reason to shoot a man." The kindly proprietor's face was drawn into lines of tension as he whispered, "And I hope to God I never do. May he be with us all. I want you to know I've been praying for Olivia to come through this without so much as one lovely hair out of place, Dr. Gray. I've got a hankering to eat a great big slice of your wedding cake and dandle your children on my knee."

Young's words were nearly Ethan's undoing. In the midst of the search, he had laid aside his hopes of reconciliation with Livvie for the mere wish of finding her safe, unharmed. The storekeeper's remarks, however, reawakened the grinding fear that she was already gone . . . that he might soon be standing at her graveside, knowing there was no hope of ever making her his bride.

What would he do? Though love was the last thing he'd ever expected to find in his move west, he couldn't imagine life without Olivia Plummer's sweet smile and wonderful voice. And her hands. How he loved watching their sure, graceful movements.

"There he goes," Young said under his breath, drawing Ethan's attention to Briggs's broad back as the lawman stepped out from the group and advanced bravely, both guns drawn. Several yards ahead of him, the ground dropped away into a gully.

Slowly, quietly, Ethan and the remaining men edged toward the gulch as the marshal sidestepped down the hill and disappeared from sight. In the silence, Ethan's heart pounded double-time, then seemed to stop as a series of gunshots rang out. Without thought for his own safety, he ran forward and negotiated the steep downward slope in two long hops.

Briggs was on the ground.

Chaos ruled as the townsmen swarmed in from their positions, several of them rushing to their fallen leader. Protruding from the soddy's doorless entrance were two legs, splayed in careless fashion. In a half-dozen long steps, Ethan reached the doorway and ducked inside, stepping over the inert form of Dermot Johnson.

Please, God, let her be here.

He cursed his momentary blindness in the soddy's unlit interior, nearly losing his balance as he stumbled over a second pair of feet. *Olivia!* He was only dimly aware of the voices behind him, of Johnson being dragged from the dank dugout. His only thought was of the woman who lay before him.

Olivia!

Dropping to his knees beside her, he was horrified at her condition. Abraded, filthy, inanimate. Was he too late? Like Ella Farwell, had she already passed from life to death in this squalid, wretched place? A sob wracked his chest as he enfolded her limp hand in his own and lowered his ear to her chest.

Oh, Father, what will I do without her? I don't think I can go on.

Through the thickness of her cloak he heard nothing. Dimly, he was aware of someone kneeling beside him.

Please, Lord, he prayed. *Let her live.*

Instinctively, his fingers curled over her hand in search of the radial groove in her wrist, seeking any spark of life that might beat within her. At first, he wasn't sure he felt anything, but a second later he was certain he discerned a weak, slow pulse.

Joy flooded his soul. She lived.

Olivia was *alive*.

Whatever might happen, it was enough to know she lived. "Thank you," he whispered, feeling a burning tear trace its way down his cheek. Turning, he looked into Seamus Connally's frightened gaze. Young, Weeks, Mulgrew, and Payne stood in a huddle at Olivia's feet, their faces lined with worry.

"She's alive," he said, his voice breaking.

"Praise God." John Young unashamedly wiped his eyes and blew his nose with his handkerchief. "How is she?"

"I can't tell. We need to get her outside so I can determine the extent of her injuries."

"Does that mean . . . ?" young Connally began, searching Olivia's bloodied face.

"I don't know what it means yet, son," Ethan spoke, breathing hard. "But I do know it makes your father a free man. I hope you'll accept my apology for believing he was capable of such a crime."

Seamus nodded. His palm was large and his grip firm, Ethan noticed, as he shook the hand the youth offered. For more than two years already this adolescent had done the work of an adult, shouldering the burden of supporting his family. Despite the adversities he'd seen in his young life, he was well on his way to becoming a good man.

"Marshal's been shot in the belly," Jay Payne announced somberly, "but he's alive."

"Johnson's down, too. Shot." Portly Mayor Weeks ran his hand through his thinning hair. "Lord above, what kind of snake were we harboring in this town?"

"Help me move Olivia outside," Ethan directed, his mind beginning to process how he might best manage the injuries of three severely wounded persons. He had nothing with him with which to render aid. "Connally, I'll need someone to ride back to town and get my bag. You'll find it just inside the door. We'll need a few wagons, too, to bring back the wounded."

"We'll take care of that, Doc," Weeks supplied. "And I'll gather some of the womenfolk to help you tend to Miss Olivia and the marshal."

Ethan was heartened to hear a soft moan issue from Olivia as he, Young, and Payne carried her outdoors. Several of the men had shed their coats and spread them on the ground, fashioning a makeshift pallet near the marshal on which to lay her. Jeb Grosset and Jim Snow ministered to Briggs, who Ethan noted was conscious.

Dermot Johnson had been dragged several feet from the soddy, a good ways from where the marshal lay. As Hawley and Greenfield stood over him, Ethan briefly wondered if the undertaker stared down at his next patron.

Olivia's eyelids fluttered, then her face contorted in a mask of pain. Dropping to his knees, Ethan sought the Lord and began the long and arduous tasks set out before him.

Chapter 18

Olivia was aware of a touch on her forehead, smoothing back and stroking her hair. It felt so pleasant, so soothing. Granny Esmond? No . . . Granny was gone, wasn't she?

Who then?

Where was she?

Why couldn't she open her eyes?

Her lids were so heavy she could not lift them. Belatedly she realized her arm hurt, her side hurt, her back hurt. Every part of her body hurt. But at the same time, it didn't seem to matter. She was warm and comfortable and snug in what felt like a feather-bed sandwich.

Straddling wakefulness and sleep, she decided it would be nicest of all to burrow back down into the soft tunnel of slumber. This bed didn't feel or smell like her bed at home, but it was a nice bed . . . a pleasant bed. She sighed.

"Olivia, dear, are you awake? Shall I call for the doctor? Do you need more morphine?"

Morphine? The doctor?

The words disturbed her and pulled her away from that delicious, drowsy comfort. Who was speaking? If she didn't know better, she would have guessed it sounded like . . . Delores Wimbers.

"Olivia, can you hear me? If you understand what I'm saying, open your eyes. Gracious, child, you've worried ten years off my life!" The gentle touch moved to her shoulder and squeezed lightly. "Come on, dear. Wake up."

With as much effort as she could muster, Olivia opened one eye and focused blearily on Tristan's busiest body. Sitting in a chair next to the bed, the matron looked more disheveled than a well-worn scatter rug. A lamp burned on the table behind her, highlighting the multitude of hairs that had escaped their normally neat confines and created a gray halo about the older woman's head.

"Ohh," she breathed, noticing the cracked eyelid, a weary smile creasing her face. "Thank goodness. You've been in this bed nearly thirty-six hours now."

"Where . . . am I?" Olivia's tongue was thick. The right side of her face was so tight it felt as though it might crack.

"You're safe, dear. You're at my home, and Dr. Gray has been at your side every minute he's not with the marshal. He'll be so glad to see you've come around."

"What happened?" she croaked, not understanding why she was lying in Delores Wimbers's bed. Why would a doctor be at her side? And what did she mean about the marshal? Everything seemed fuzzy, unreal.

Delores began talking, but her words ran together and didn't make sense. Olivia tried opening both eyes to pay closer attention but found it impossible to keep even the one open. Of their own volition, her upper and lower lids converged, and she was back in that warm, soft, comfortable place where there were no voices or pain or trouble.

A tugging feeling brought her to consciousness. *Ouch!* Her arm. Strong hands beneath her lifted and pulled and resettled her from her back to her side. A male voice said something, followed by a woman's higher-pitched reply.

"The fact that Livvie conversed with you last night is a hopeful sign, Mrs. Wimbers." The rumbling sounds went on, suddenly focusing into clarity. "The initial periods of agitation seem to have passed, and I'd expect longer periods of wakefulness from her today. Bear in mind the blow to her head was quite severe. We'll hold the morphine for now and see if we can get her to wake up."

"What about her arm?"

"The bone is set and immobilized. I suspect a fractured rib or two, as well. She was conscious for a short while before the men returned with the wagons. If what she told me can be believed, she threw herself off the back of Johnson's horse at full gallop. Her injuries are certainly consistent with that sort of activity."

"The poor lamb. In the clutches of that . . . that . . . " Delores Wimbers sputtered as she searched for words.

"Yes, I know. But Dermot Johnson is beyond hurting anyone else ever again. If he hadn't been mortally wounded, I fear I wouldn't have had much success in preventing his neck from being stretched on the spot."

Ethan!

Oh, Ethan. Olivia tried licking her lips to speak, but her mouth was as dry as dust. His words had triggered a cascade of fragmented memories. Johnson . . . the dirty soddy . . . his horrifying confession. A sob racked her chest as she remembered the pain and terror of her captivity.

"Olivia . . . my sweet Olivia." Ethan's touch was tender on her shoulder, her cheek. "You've been injured, but you'll mend. I promise."

"Faulk," she managed to whisper.

"Fault? Whose fault was this?"

Olivia opened her eyes to see Ethan's face just inches above her own. At his elbow, Delores Wimbers jockeyed for position. Tears glistened on her fleshy cheeks.

"This was all Dermot Johnson's fault, Livvie," Ethan spoke softly. "He was Ella's killer, not Connally."

Not *fault.* Faulk. Lannie Faulk. Why wouldn't her tongue form the words?

"No" was all she was able to utter. She tried shaking her

head, only to discover what pain such a slight motion set off. She groaned and closed her eyes. Perspiration moistened her forehead while nausea threatened, intimidated, then receded. She heard the sound of water, followed by the blessed coolness of a damp cloth across her forehead.

"The most important thing for you right now is rest, Livvie," Ethan said soothingly. "Johnson's wounds were mortal—he's dead. Briggs has had a time of it, but I think he'll pull through. He's got a strong constitution . . . not to mention a bride-to-be who's determined to have her groom. Now go back to sleep, dear one. There will be plenty of time for explanations and talk later on."

Was it the power of suggestion contained in his words, or had an overwhelming languor just coincidentally overtaken her? Like a stone through water she sank back into the arms of slumber, all thoughts of Lannie Faulk and Ella Farwell whisked from her mind. Her last recollection was the image of Ethan's face . . . growing farther and farther and farther away.

"How's she doing today, Doc? You said she was awake most of the day yesterday."

The marshal readjusted himself in the chair at his bedside, his face revealing his discomfort. Instead of his usual trousers, shirt, and leather vest, a loose nightshirt and socks were his only clothing. His lower legs stuck out from the gown and, despite his infirmity, revealed a pair of calves surprisingly knotted with muscle.

"First things first," Ethan replied, assessing the pallor of his patient's complexion. "How are *you?* This is only your second time sitting in that chair, and I don't relish the thought of picking you up off the floor should you decide to faint." He was heartened by the offended expression that crossed Briggs's face.

"Faint? Like some dainty little woman? It's a good thing

you're standing as far away as you are, Doc; otherwise you'd find out just how far from fainting I am."

Ethan laughed and pulled up the other chair. He sat and straddled it so he faced its ladder back. He folded his arms across the top rung and rested his chin upon one fist. "It's good to see you full of vinegar again, Marshal. Jay Payne's coming over later this morning to give you a shave and a haircut. Miss Janet's going to change her mind about marrying you if we don't do something with your appearance."

Briggs rubbed his palm across his cheek, then through the disheveled locks of hair atop his head. He chuckled ruefully. "I reckon you're right."

"And in answer to your question, Olivia is beginning to heal nicely from her injuries. She faded in and out of consciousness most of Tuesday and Wednesday, but yesterday she was able to recall much of what had happened on Sunday."

"What about her face?"

"I don't believe there will be any scarring. The whole right side was scraped raw, but none of it very deep. Her arm will be out of commission until the bone heals, and those ribs will no doubt give her some trouble, but it's my opinion she'll make a full recovery. Just as you will."

The big man nodded, seeming to search for words. "When that bullet hit me, I thought I was done for. I . . . I owe you my life, Doc."

Ethan smiled ruefully as he remembered the hours of prayer and anguish he'd spent caring for his beloved Olivia and the man whom he'd come to regard as his best friend. Both patients had been challenging. Olivia's comatose state and periods of agitation had been deeply concerning, and Briggs had required surgery to extract the bullet from his abdomen. Thankfully, none of his vital organs had been damaged. If the marshal's course of healing was not complicated by infection, he ought to be fit in a month's time.

Ethan pointed upward. "I think we both know to whom you owe your life."

"I suppose you're right. But having a surgeon on hand

didn't hurt matters, either." The lawman sighed. "What I don't understand is how I could have been so completely hoodwinked by Johnson . . . I mean, Faulk. He did tell Livvie the truth about his past, by the way. Hawley wired Arkansas yesterday and got the whole sorry story."

Ethan shook his head, remembering his last look at the deputy as he'd confirmed Greenfield's supposition and pronounced him dead. It was hard to say which of the two shots to his chest had taken his life, just as it was impossible to know for certain who had fired those shots. Ethan had felt no small amount of relief at the criminal's death, for he'd not known how he could have dispassionately rendered care to a man who had just tried to kill the two people most dear to him.

"His references looked good," Briggs went on, "and he seemed to know what he was doing. I don't know, Doc. I've been over it in my head a thousand times since I've been lying here, and I can't come up with a single time during the past three years that Dermot Johnson didn't seem to be anything but a law-abiding citizen." He cracked his knuckles and concluded angrily, "Aside from the fact that he had a whole secret life I knew nothing about."

"Given your line of work, is there any doubt in your mind that there are men in the world without a conscience?"

"No . . . but I like to think I can spot them."

"Psychopathy is a severe disorder, marked by egocentric and antisocial behavior. Unfortunately, many psychopathics are also extremely intelligent people—cunning and clever. Don't you remember how cool Faulk was right after Ella's postmortem examination? He stood next to Olivia and looked at his baby with no emotion whatsoever."

"Those are the kinds of things that can make me mad enough to swallow a horned toad backward."

A silence passed while each man was wrapped in his own thoughts. Finally, Briggs shifted his feet and spoke. "I've been wanting to ask you, Doc, if Livvie's softened any about that medical license business since she's been hurt."

Ethan sighed, feeling the weight of that particular burden settling once again on his shoulders. "We haven't discussed it."

"Doesn't she know how much you love her—that you risked your life to save her?" In his outrage, the marshal let a colorful word slip, promptly chasing it with a sheepish apology. "I guess I just don't understand how a woman's mind is put together. One thing I know is that Olivia Plummer loves you, Doc. I'd stake my life on it. But I'm as confused as you are by the fuss she's put up about taking that examination. I've never known her to act so stubborn about anything."

"I guess there's only one thing to do then."

"What's that?"

"Keep on praying."

Briggs chuckled, his eyes warm with vicarious emotion. "Amen, brother, but only if you'll return the favor when I get myself into hot water with the future missus."

Olivia sat in the wide padded chair near Mrs. Wimbers's bedroom window. On the other side of the lace curtains, melting snow dripped steadily from the overhanging eaves. The sun shone warmly down from a broad blue sky, but she had lived in Colorado long enough to know the weather this time of year was fickle.

More than a week had passed since . . . since what? Since the accident? Since her foolish decision to get on the back of a horse with Ella Farwell's murderer? Since her brush with death? She stared down at her splinted arm. Had it been sheer lunacy to throw herself off Lannie Faulk's speeding horse, or had her injured state spared her from much worse things at his hands?

Who could know? Who could make sense of any of this?

Despite the kindness and generosity Mrs. Wimbers had shown by taking her in and caring for her night and day for all this time, it was a bit of a relief to have the hovering matron out of the house for a spell. Satisfied that her charge had done well during the time she'd been at church yesterday, the widow had just put on her hat and gloves and set out for the mercantile, promising to be back in a short while.

Knowing Mrs. Wimbers's propensity to talk, Olivia had no doubt her self-appointed caretaker could easily be gone two hours. Heaven knew there was plenty to talk about in Tristan these days.

She sighed and shifted in the chair. Time was beginning to take care of the worst of her injuries, but she wasn't comfortable in any position for long. In addition to the pain of her broken bones and bruises, the scabs on her face had set to itching terribly. Her head ached frequently, and periods of dizziness would descend from time to time. Every day Ethan assured her that everything would continue to improve, and that he doubted she would bear any permanent marks upon her face. She had managed only a glimpse of herself in Mrs. Wimbers's silvered hand mirror before laying it down, unable to examine her appearance any further.

Reluctantly, her thoughts turned to Ethan and the strain he had endured since the day of the shooting. The widow had told her time and again of the townsmen's tireless search for her, and of Briggs's bravery in confronting Faulk head-on. If Ethan hadn't been there with his surgical skills, would she or the marshal have survived? A sick, anxious feeling started in the pit of her stomach every time she thought of what she had put the people of this town through. Briggs taking a bullet. Ethan running himself ragged. All because of her.

A knock at the bedroom door startled her from her reverie. "Who is it?" she called, awkwardly tugging the blanket further toward her chest with her left hand.

"It's Ethan. May I come in?"

She caught her breath as he entered, looking tired yet handsome and irresistible all at once. Her heart pounded as he brushed a kiss against her uninjured cheek and took a seat on the foot of the bed, facing her.

"I just ran into Mrs. Wimbers at the mercantile. She said you were sitting up and that it might be a good time to visit."

Oh, why was it so difficult to look at him? He had shown her nothing but kindness, devotion, and love during her confinement . . . and all this in spite of the discord between them. He was a good man, much better than she deserved. Yet regarding the issue of her medical practice, he was inflexible. How could they ever get past that?

Could they ever get past that?

"Livvie," he said gently, "don't feel as though you have to hide your face from me. Even if it were to scar—and my professional opinion goes against that—I can't think of any more beautiful woman on this earth. When I thought I might lose you, I . . . I . . . " He shook his head.

What was happening? Where was the safe boundary of the medical questions he normally asked regarding her aches and pains and overall condition? The small talk about the weather and the melting snow? Answering tears burned in her eyes as he went on.

"I hope you're strong enough to hear these things today because I don't think I'm strong enough to go on another day without saying them to you. I thought I was, but I'm not." Kneeling before her, he took her uninjured hand and pressed a kiss against her fingers. His expression was earnest, his eyes deep pools of emotion. "This set of circumstances hasn't changed the way I feel about you, except to make me realize that I love you more deeply than I ever imagined. I still want to be your husband, Livvie, as soon as you'll have me. I'll marry you today, tomorrow, next Thursday . . . whenever you wish. After all that's happened, I hope we can finally lay aside the differences that have divided us. Life is too short . . . and far too precious."

"And you'll go on healing . . . and I won't." At her grudging, whispered words, she felt his hand stiffen around hers. Agony clawed at her chest, worse than any of the physical pains she had endured. What was the matter with her? She loved Ethan Gray beyond all reasoning, yet she could not accept the fact that if she married him, she would no longer be free to use her healing touch. Even if she didn't marry him, without a medical license the pending state legislation might soon reduce her livelihood and income to nothing. She could pass the examination; she was sure of it. Why wouldn't he let her at least try?

"Livvie, I had hoped . . . ," he began again, then withdrew his hand from its place over hers and carefully arranged his fingers over his knee. "Let me ask you one question: Does having a medical license matter more to you than I do?"

"Of course not," she burst out. "It's just . . . just . . ."

"Just what? I'm trying to understand, I really am."

Oh, Lord, what was the matter with her? What was this terrible thing that stuck inside her and prevented her from accepting the gift of this man's love? When she had been at the mercy of Lannie Faulk, she had despaired of ever seeing Ethan's face again . . . of ever being able to tell him she loved him.

"I do love you, Ethan," she said through hot tears, feeling as though a stranger were speaking the words. "But I also don't know how I can walk away from a gift and calling the Lord gave me. You're asking me to make a choice I just can't make."

"Livvie, the governor signed the bill into law on March 14. In some manner of speaking, perhaps the Lord has already spoken. As believers, we're bound to follow the laws of the land."

"Which I can follow *if* I have my medical license." Frustration burned inside her as their eyes locked.

For a long moment they stared at one another. "I'm beginning to think, Olivia Plummer," he said bluntly, "that for all your Christ-loving ways, you have a rebellious streak a mile wide."

A rebellious streak a mile wide? She wasn't rebellious. How could he say such a thing? She was speechless as he sighed deeply and stood. Reaching inside his coat, he withdrew a pair of envelopes—one large, one small—and extended both toward her. "John Young gave me your mail to give to you."

At his expression, she took the envelopes and immediately

recognized Romy's handwriting on the smaller of the two. The
larger packet was postmarked Denver, addressed to "O. Plummer"
in a crisp, masculine hand with which she was not familiar. Could
it be . . . ?

Awkwardly she attempted to tear open the flap, using her
left hand and what little of the exposed fingertips of her right
that she could.

"Here. Allow me." With his pocketknife, Ethan slit open
the envelope and unfolded the letter. He walked to the window
after placing it in her hands, presenting her with his back as he
stared outdoors.

The elation she had expected to feel at reading the words
before her did not occur. The first short paragraph acknowledged
receipt of her letter and informed her of the State Board of Medical Examiners, which had been newly established in anticipation
of the adoption of the upcoming legislature. The second invited
her to report to Denver in a month's time to submit to the
board's examination questions.

Now what?

She glanced at Ethan, then back at the paper in her hand.
Rereading its words, she wondered at her lack of joy. Where was
her excitement, her happiness? Wasn't this examination the
answer to her prayers? the perfect solution to all her problems?

Ethan remained silent at the window, his taut shoulders
revealing his displeasure. He wasn't happy, she knew, but surely
he must understand the desire to heal. It blazed within him, too.

Would he help her?

Some of the most wonderful times she had passed with
Ethan were the long hours in his office during which he had
tested and quizzed and cross-examined her on a wide variety of
subjects. Between his tutoring and the study she had made of his
library of textbooks, she had learned an incredible amount of
information. Surely it was enough with which to pass the examination and be granted a medical license.

The fingers of her splinted hand were puffy and stiff.
Would she be required to write down her answers? she

wondered. In her weakened state, would she even be physically able to take the test? *Father,* she prayed, *is this your will for me? Is this the way you would have me go?*

But even before she finished praying and certainly long before she had discerned any sort of reply, she set the letter in her lap and said Ethan's name softly.

Half turning, he asked, "Will you be going to Denver?"

"I have to," she replied, feeling her voice choke. "I have to try, Ethan."

"You don't, you know."

"Yes, I do." The thought of using her tears as leverage was repugnant to her, yet at the same time she felt the wetness escape her eyes and trail down her cheeks, she saw indecision flicker across Ethan's profile. Maybe this was the time to try explaining to him that after years of being on her own, the idea of being utterly dependent was both foreign and frightening. Before she could form her thoughts, he turned and reclaimed his seat on the end of the bed.

"Livvie, your being licensed in this manner goes against my better judgment for all the reasons we've already covered. You know a great deal about the human body, and I believe that your instinct for treatment is truly a gift from above, but there is much you don't know. I'm understating the facts to say that even after my matriculation, there's still much *I* don't know. Have you thought about how you'll feel when your patients suffer because of the gaps in your knowledge?"

Niggling doubts assailed both her will and her logic, but she pressed on. "I can learn. You've taught me so much already, and I'll keep studying. I can be a good doctor; I know I can."

"I know you would make a good doctor. An excellent doctor. It's just that—" his smile was slow and sad—"tell me what happens if you should fail the examination."

"If I fail?" Wiping her eyes as unobtrusively as possible, she squared her chin. "If I fail, I'll accept my lot, but I hardly think I'm going to fail. I have a whole month to study . . . if you'll share your books with me," she added coyly.

He didn't smile. In fact, the blood seemed to drain from his face. "Am I your lot then, Olivia?"

"Oh . . . Ethan . . . I didn't mean it that way. I do love you, I truly do. When you first asked me to marry you, I was delirious with joy."

"A rather short-lived joy."

"Because you were talking like I'd never use my healing touch again."

Some of the tension seemed to leave him at that. Sighing, he stroked his jaw. "Being a doctor means that much to you?"

She nodded, feeling fresh tears form. "Healing people was all I ever wanted to do, Ethan, just like my granny. It's my calling, just as it was hers. But now . . . if I can't even trim a hangnail without breaking the law . . . oh, what's the use?"

"I see you will not be dissuaded from your course." Abruptly he rose and handed her his handkerchief. "I'm going to check on Briggs. When I come back, I'll bring you some books. But I want you to know I don't like this, Olivia, and I'll tell you again that I don't believe you're going to pass."

"It would be a sin not to try."

He did not reply to that but asked only if he could assist her with anything before he left. In the silent wake of his departure, she realized that neither had he said anything more about marriage, leaving her to wonder if she had just traded a husband for a career.

Chapter 19

Briggs was asleep. After a few minutes of observing his friend in repose, Ethan was satisfied at the lawman's color and rate of breathing. Good. Plenty of rest would go a long way toward the amount of mending his body had to do.

Leaving the room, he eyed the sofa he'd moved out to the reception area . . . and on which he'd gotten the brief amounts of sleep he'd allotted himself during the past week. With the marshal's condition as touch and go as it had initially been, he'd insisted Briggs be moved down the hall to his bedchamber after his surgery had been complete. Delores Wimbers had taken Olivia into her home, despite his initial misgivings, and had done a splendid job of caring for her.

Olivia.

He walked to the bookshelf and selected a few of his medical textbooks. As he turned toward the door to take her the volumes, he stopped, deep in thought. Retracing his initial steps, he walked back to the other side of the office, toward his desk, and took a seat. *Father*, he prayed, bowing his head, *you know what I think about any person obtaining a medical license by the route Olivia intends to travel. It's wrong, and it's what I've been fighting against ever since I became a physician. But at the same time, she has such a desire to help and heal . . . and is extraordinarily gifted. Please guide me—and her. I submit this entire situation to your hands.*

After a thoughtful *amen,* he opened the top drawer of his desk and withdrew a sheet of writing paper.

Dear Sirs, he began, tapping his heel against the floor as he gave thought to how he might best proceed. Settling on the proper wording, he moved the pen in decisive strokes across the paper while, unconsciously, he drew resolve from the milky white scar on the back of his hand.

For Olivia, the next weeks passed with alarming speed. Eighteen days after her narrow escape from Lannie Faulk, she was back home at her cabin in spite of Delores Wimbers's vociferous misgivings. Ethan had supported her wish to go home, however, and after a tearful farewell, the matron had waved until the doctor's team had drawn the carriage a full quarter mile away.

Pushing aside Henry Gray's *Descriptive and Surgical Anatomy,* she reflected on the benevolence she had received from the garrulous widow. After spending more than two weeks in Mrs. Wimbers's home, Olivia decided that her patroness wasn't so much a long-winded gossip as she was just a lonely, middle-aged woman, eager to lavish her love and attention on anyone who would receive it. During the small hours one night when Olivia hadn't been able to sleep, the widow had sat at her bedside and held her hand. Mostly, she'd been quiet, just offering her presence, but she had also confided that it meant a great deal to her to care for Olivia, for her life's keenest sorrow was never having borne children.

The widow had been a frequent visitor to Olivia's cabin, bearing gifts of deliciously prepared foods. Janet also stopped several times a week to check on her, all vestiges of their disharmony forgotten. Olivia noticed, however, her friend scrupulously avoided conversation having anything to do with wedding plans, Ethan Gray, or the upcoming medical licensure examination.

As usual, Susan Connally tended the animals and did odd jobs around the house for her. After Donal's brief incarceration, he was home and sober and still making efforts toward filling his own shoes and those of his late wife. The girl seemed to have bounced back quickly from her family's latest ordeal. Every bit as chatty as usual, she had no compunction about bringing up Ethan's name in front of Olivia—frequently.

Ethan came once a day, if not twice, monitoring her convalescence and bringing her study items from his collection as needed. He did not quiz her in the way he previously had, but he answered her questions and clarified the complicated concepts with which she struggled. His manner was almost . . . reserved. No, she amended, that wasn't entirely true. He was kind and solicitous, and when their eyes met, his gaze was warm upon her. And still, her heart never failed to flutter when that happened. A fragile peace existed between them, but something was not right. Since the day she had received the invitation to take the examination in Denver, the tension between them had continued to grow, only now it lurked beneath romantic yearnings, pleasant superficialities, and the shadow of her brush with death.

Ethan's noticeable silence on the subject of the future had not escaped her attention. The air needed to be cleared, she knew it did, but it would have to wait until she returned from Colorado's capital city. Since that day at Mrs. Wimbers's, he had not raised any discussion of her practice . . . their practice . . . or what kind of relationship they would share once she completed the examination. After all his talk of marriage, this sudden reticence left her with an uneasy feeling.

Then sunshine broke through the gathering clouds and lit up the shadowy corners of the cabin. Pondering the glad change in her home's atmosphere, she longed for as dramatic a spiritual illumination to flood her soul. Lately her prayers seemed to be as stale as old bread. Was it just because she rushed through her time with the Lord in her quest to study, or was there another reason?

Glancing back down at an artist's rendering of a spinal ganglion, she sighed. There was so much yet to learn, and the examination was only three days away. At some point, she would just have to close the books and say *enough*. She had dreaded making the trip to Denver with her ribs as sore as they'd been, but in the past few days they'd improved dramatically, along with her allover soreness. And as Ethan had promised, the abrasions on her face had healed commendably, leaving behind new, fresh-pink skin.

She wriggled the fingers of her right hand, which were now far less restricted in the new splint the physician had fashioned a few days earlier. It would come off in two weeks' time, he had promised, for the bone seemed to be setting well. After learning how to write in a passable manner with her left hand, she was finally able to hold the pen awkwardly in her right. How much of the test would be written she did not know, but at least she would be able to draft her answers.

A shiver of anticipation . . . dread? . . . fear? . . . went through her every time she thought of sitting for the examination. Ethan had said the examiners were all men. What would they think of a humble prairie woman seeking a medical license? Would they treat her fairly?

The Connally dog began yapping, signaling a traveler. Her heart quickened at the thought of Ethan coming to see her. Today he had promised to bring her his latest medical journal, which featured articles about such diverse topics as animal parasites and diseases of the myocardium. He had warned her that the examiners could question her about any conceivable subject, and to be as widely read as possible to be prepared.

A few minutes later, she heard the familiar sounds of his carriage outside the cabin. After three short knocks, he let himself in and said hello. She responded in kind but remained seated at the table. As laborious as her movements had been, he had insisted she stay put rather than get up and answer the door.

"Ah, spinal ganglia," he commented after he'd walked to the table and leaned over her shoulder. "An absorbing subject." With a soft thump, his newest copy of the *Boston Medical and Surgical Journal* joined the stacks of medical literature covering her table. "Are you hungry?"

"A little," she responded, acutely aware of his proximity. For a moment she closed her eyes and simply enjoyed the nearness of his presence. Unbidden, the memory of their Christmas Eve hayride came back to her, causing a sharp, sweet pain that had nothing to do with her injuries.

"What sumptuous delights has Mrs. Wimbers brought you now?"

She forced her thoughts back to the present. "Sliced ham, scalloped potatoes, and a whole raisin-spice cake dripping with almond frosting."

"Yes, indeed, I see the cake. I'm going to have to get my suits let out if I keep eating the way I have been." He chuckled as he moved around the table and took the other chair. More seriously, he inquired, "How's the arm this afternoon? Is your new splint holding up?"

"It's much better, thank you."

"The marshal's been poking around his office today."

"What about the deputy the county sheriff sent to help?"

"Briggs is itching to get back to work and wants to send the fellow packing, but I don't want him that active for another week or two. I told him the deputy stays for now, so he isn't very happy with me."

"Will someone fill Johnson's—Faulk's—position?"

Ethan nodded. "It's being advertised. Hopefully it will be filled soon by a much better man."

Raising her injured arm, Olivia replied wryly, "We could hardly do worse."

Ethan idly flipped the pages of the journal he'd brought. "I've been wanting to ask you something, Livvie."

"Yes?" A nervous quiver ran through her. After his long silence, was he once again going to bring up . . . marriage? She swallowed. With all that was on her mind, she could hardly think about that right now.

". . . willing to accompany you to Denver," he was saying. Again she had to redirect her thoughts to the present. "That doesn't mean I condone the course you've chosen, but I have concerns about your physical condition."

"I'm fine, Ethan," she demurred. "Doing better every day."

"Nonetheless, I would like to be there with you. You'll be all alone in a strange city. What happens if you relapse or fall ill?"

She forced light laughter. "In the company of nearly a dozen medical examiners? I daresay they should be able to put their heads together and manage any situation that might arise. And Denver is not completely foreign to me. I've been there once before."

He said nothing but continued gazing at her with an unfathomable expression. What was he thinking? Were her actions destroying any tender emotion he held for her?

"Ethan," she appealed, "I've recovered sufficiently to travel. With the differences in our convictions, I think this is something I best do alone. When I come home, we can . . . well . . . " She knew she no longer dared presume anything about what might happen when she came back to Tristan.

Slowly Ethan pushed back his chair and rose. "I bid you farewell and good travel then, Olivia. If you should need anything before you depart, you know where I can be found."

When the latch clicked behind him, Olivia stared first at the stack of books and then at the door. The uneasy feeling mushroomed as she heard his team depart, and she nearly ran outside to call him back. Blinking away tears, she resumed her study of spinal ganglia, turning the page with shaking fingers.

Chapter 20

Olivia traveled by stage to LaSalle, then completed her journey by rail. The day seemed to take forever, yet at the same time she felt as though the Colorado Central coach arrived in the bustling city of Denver all too soon. In the gathering shadows of dusk, she was boarded onto a hack by the gregarious conductor, who instructed the driver to take her to The Wentworth on Arapahoe Street.

"It's a pleasant hotel with a central location, miss. Not far from where you want to be tomorrow. Most of the fancier places are taking two dollars a night, but you can stay at The Wentworth for a dollar. Just a friendly tip for the fairest of today's passengers," he added with a wink as he stowed her valise beside her. "Best wishes to you, now." Tipping his hat, he waved farewell as the driver shook the reins.

Almost immediately her attention was captured by the sights and sounds and myriad activities of Denver, Colorado. The city had grown remarkably in the three years since she'd visited, not even appearing to be the same place. And the people! They were everywhere—driving, riding, walking—seeming to have tripled in number in those three years.

As it had the entire journey, nervousness competed with her excitement. She had been instructed to report for her examination tomorrow afternoon at one o'clock. She glanced down at her hands, the right lightly sheathed by its splint and wrapping. The very next day at this time, she might well bear the title of *Doctor* Olivia Plummer, legally sanctioned by the General Assembly of the state of Colorado to ply her hands in the healing trade. As it did every time she thought of that, a little thrill shot through her.

Had Granny Esmond ever dreamed of such a thing? she wondered. Becoming a doctor? If this legislation had passed during Granny's time, what would the older woman have done? The new Medical Practice Act called for a fine of fifty to three hundred dollars, or up to thirty days' imprisonment—or both—for *each and every offense* of an unqualified person practicing medicine or surgery in the state of Colorado. When Olivia had learned the particulars of the new enactment, she'd dared not treat anyone.

Neither would Granny have broken the law. Surely her grandmother would have seen obtaining her medical license as the only course open to Olivia. She sighed. What a blessing it had been to have access to Ethan's medical books and journals. Because of that, she had a great advantage over many other lay healers.

The vehicle rounded a corner, causing her valise to shift against her. "Almost there," the driver called from his seat ahead of her, while her thoughts turned to Ethan.

The blond physician had worn an inscrutable expression as he'd seen her off. Briggs and Janet had also been there to bid her farewell, along with what seemed like half the townspeople. Just before she'd boarded the stage, Delores Wimbers had enveloped Olivia in a maternal hug and told her how proud she was of her.

If the people of Tristan were happy and excited for her . . . why couldn't Ethan be? Why was he so against her becoming a doctor?

"Here you are, miss," the driver announced. "I'll get your bag for you."

The conductor's advice had been good. The Wentworth

appeared to be a respectable establishment. A FAMILY HOTEL, the lettering beneath its title advertised. The paint was fresh, and cheerful curtains adorned the many-paned windows.

She was relieved to note the building's interior matched up with its exterior, and she was soon registered and settled into a clean, simply furnished room. Mr. Banks, the proprietor, had informed her supper would be served in the downstairs dining room for another forty minutes, but once she reached her room, she didn't know if she could eat anything or not. The more she thought about the examination . . . Ethan . . . the examination . . . Ethan . . . the more goosey her stomach became.

Deciding against food, she opened her valise and hung the dress she had packed for tomorrow. After shaking out the worst of the wrinkles, she hoped the rest would be gone by morning. At the bottom of the bag lay Ethan's copy of *Man and Medicine* and Granny Esmond's Bible. Maybe another skimming of *Man and Medicine*'s more complicated chapters would ease the anxiety she was experiencing and help her feel more prepared to stand before the board of examiners.

Reaching past her grandmother's Bible, she picked up the heavy medical text and began reading.

Morning came too quickly. As it turned out, Olivia hadn't been able to put down the book until nearly two o'clock, and even then she hadn't felt any more confident than when she'd started reading hours earlier. What sleep she'd gotten had been troubled, causing her to feel tired and headachy when she awakened.

After washing and dressing, she went downstairs and forced herself to eat a sturdy meal of flapjacks, eggs, and sausage. It would have to last through the day, until after she completed the examination. Following breakfast, Mr. Banks gave her directions to the address where the medical examiners wished her to report. From The Wentworth, it was a walk of less than two miles, and he assured her it could be easily made through good neighborhoods.

With some spare time on her hands, Olivia returned to her room, a terrible restlessness upon her. While she paced about, she saw a wrinkle in the bedspread near the pillow and spent a full five minutes straightening the covering so its plaid pattern was in exact alignment with the right angles of the bed. Next she noticed a few bits of lint on the rug and bent to retrieve them.

Standing back up, she sighed as she walked to the wastebasket. What was she doing frittering away her time in such a manner? Guilt washed over her as she realized just how little time she had been spending in prayer. She glanced out the window at the beautiful April morning. When was the last time she had praised the Lord for the beauty of his creation? How had she allowed her quest for medical licensure to override all else in her life?

Her gaze fell on Granny's Bible. Seating herself in the chair near the window, she read several psalms, feeling a long-forgotten sense of peace steal over her. All her life she had known that nothing was more important than the Lord. Teary-eyed, she wondered how, during these past months, she could have lost sight of that central truth.

Oh, Father, she prayed, bowing her head. *I have allowed so many things to come between us. This morning I'm aware of my sin. It grieves my heart deeply to realize how I have offended you. Please have mercy on me, and forgive me for all the many ways I have not put you first in my life. Truly, my sin is pride, and I beseech you to restore a humble heart within me.*

A tear, then two, dripped onto her lap as she continued. *The only thing on my mind has been this examination . . . and becoming a doctor. Without a medical license I can't treat anyone, and I've always believed you put me on earth to heal people. Have I been wrong? Please help me to pass this examination.* Pausing, she wiped her eyes and sniffed while words from Pastor Todd's Christmas Eve sermon wafted through her mind.

Do you believe *the Lord has a plan for your life? . . . Do you*

delight to do his will—or do you want your own? . . . Ask for wisdom!
. . . Abandon yourself to the will of God!

The will of God.

How long had it been since she had said, *"Thy* will be done"? Ever since she'd learned about the new medical legislation, she'd had her own goal in mind: becoming a doctor. Along the way, had she ever asked God if being a physician was his plan for her . . . or had she merely assumed it was?

And what damage had her stubbornness done to her relationship with Ethan? He'd professed his love and asked for her hand in marriage—more than once. And each time she'd been argumentative, contentious, unyielding. She wouldn't blame him if he never wished to speak with her again, much less practice in the same town.

With the force of a summer squall, sorrow and grief inundated her. As she sank from the chair to the floor, sobs racked her chest while tears of remorse flowed unchecked from her eyes. What a fool she'd been! God, ever loving and faithful, had provided a prospective husband more wonderful than she could have ever imagined, yet she had spurned both the Lord and Ethan to follow her own selfish plans.

Please have mercy on me, a sinner, she prayed, overwhelmed by the magnitude of her realizations. Finally, with the worst of her misery spent, she arose shakily to blow her nose and wash her face. A quarter hour later, her appearance had been restored to nearly what it had been. Looking closely, one might be able to discern she had been weeping from the puffiness of her eyelids, but she hoped the brisk walk to the examination would put a natural flush in her cheeks and disguise the effects of her tears.

She leaned closer to the mirror. Dove gray eyes stared back at her, reflecting uncertainty. What should she do? With her awareness of her sin, should she even sit for the examination? She had taken no time whatsoever to discern what God's plan might be for her life. What if he didn't want her to become a physician?

"As long as I'm here, Father," she said, pushing herself

away from the mirror and pacing once again about the small room, "I may as well go take the test. But the outcome is in your hands. Whether or not I become a doctor is up to you. Thy will be done, not mine."

At her surrender, a burden in her heart seemed to lift, and the importance that the examination had held in her life all these past weeks faded away. If she didn't pass . . . well, God would provide for her somehow. He always had.

After spending thirty minutes longer immersed in the Scriptures, she set aside the Bible and prepared to depart. Before leaving the room, she double-checked her handbag and found the ten-dollar examination fee still safe and sound in the bottom. Without payment in advance, she could not even take the test.

Mr. Banks waved to her as she passed through the lobby, wishing her a pleasant walk. The springtime sun was warm on her face, and the directions he'd given her easy to follow. With each step she took, she felt more peace at having relinquished her fate to the Lord. Of greater concern was patching things up with Ethan. How terribly she'd behaved. Did there remain any possibility of sharing a future with him?

Glancing about, she saw that a staggering number of grand establishments had sprung up since her last visit to the city. Stone structures of many stories scaled skyward, dominating the mind and the eye. Mr. Banks had told her of the five-story Windsor Hotel, with its elevators and gaslights—and even a swimming pool! She shook her head as she walked on, thinking how very different the city was from the country.

Finally, she arrived at the two-story brick building bearing the address specified in her letter. As she ascended three stairs to its wooden gingerbread porch, she was able to read the elaborate gold lettering on the glass of the elaborately carved front door: Essery Clemens, M.D.

She was here. She was really going to do it.

Inhaling deeply, she entered the building to the tinkling of a bell. A faintly medicinal smell hung in the air, mingled with the scent of lemon oil. Before her, a shiny wooden staircase led upward, its open side flanked by a scrolling balustrade. The hall-way leading to the rear of the structure terminated ten feet beyond at a closed door. From overhead, she heard the rumble of male voices, the creaking of the floor, the scrape of a chair. Against her will, her heart pounded in her chest.

"Good afternoon. May I help you?" a pleasant female voice asked.

To the left of the foyer was a reception area, made glad by a trio of lace-curtained bay windows. Into this bright room Olivia walked, marveling at the affluence of its carpeting and appoint-ments.

"Are you here to see the doctor about your hand?" At a sumptuous desk sat a young woman of perhaps twenty years, a sympathetic expression crossing her pleasant features. "I'm very sorry. Dr. Clemens is hosting a meeting of the Board of Medical Examiners this afternoon and cannot be disturbed." She turned the page of the ledger before her. "If you are able to return tomorrow morning at ten-thirty, he can see you then."

"Oh, no. Thank you, anyway. I'm here to . . ." Swallowing, Olivia wondered where the moisture in her mouth had gone. The young woman eyed her with curiosity, tapping a prettily manicured finger against the open appointment book.

"My name is Olivia Plummer," she said, "and I'm here to be examined for a medical license."

Round blue eyes grew even rounder. "Oh . . . my. Certainly. There are to be three of you today, but I thought your name was *Oliver* Plummer. Well . . . but . . . not that it matters." Flashing an uneasy smile, she gestured toward the bank of chairs. "Please be seated. When the other two examinees arrive, I'll announce you together."

Before Olivia had taken her seat, the bell tinkled as a pair of men in their twenties, seemingly well acquainted, stepped through the door and entered the office.

"Misters Bryant and Metcalf?" the young woman sang out, springing up from her chair like a bird flitting from its perch.

At their affirmative responses, she excused herself with a

hurried, "I'll tell the doctors you're here," and climbed the stairs in a flurry of quick-clicking heels. The men eyed each other and shrugged, and Olivia noticed the shorter man's lips twitching beneath his mustache.

Catching sight of her, the same man lifted his hat and greeted her with a pleasant "Good day."

Smiling politely, she dropped her gaze to her lap.

"I suppose we could take a seat, Ralph," he said to his companion. "Perhaps as we leave, I shall address you as 'Dr. Metcalf,' and you can call me 'Dr. Bryant.'"

Did the same flutters of anxiety plague the men as they did her? she wondered as they chuckled between themselves. They appeared relaxed and nonchalant as they sat on the green velveteen sofa perpendicular to the line of chairs and stretched out their legs.

Remember, Livvie, the outcome of this afternoon is in the Lord's hands. His will is to be done today. Calm yourself.

Scarcely a minute later, the young woman *tap, tap, tapped* back down the stairs with such haste that Olivia worried she might stumble and hurt herself. But she appeared around the corner unharmed, holding a sheet of paper, her cheeks flushed with exertion.

"I'll collect your fees before you go up. It will be ten dollars apiece," she said with a quick glance at Olivia, then at the men, then at the paper, as she resumed her position at her desk. She seemed flustered as she continued reading from the page, her words flowing as fast as a high creek in the spring. "The first portion of your test is written and will cover anatomy, physiology, chemistry, pathology, surgery, obstetrics, and the practice of medicine in general. Once you are finished with that, you will be examined orally, one at a time. Upon successful completion of both portions of the test, you will be issued a certificate that will entitle you to all the rights and privileges of practicing medicine in the state of Colorado." Her cheeks were quite pink by the time she'd finished.

"Here's my fee," Olivia said quietly, walking to the desk

and handing over ten hard-earned dollars. The young woman took the money and began scribbling a receipt.

"By George, Ralph, this lady is going to take the examination with us today," the shorter man, Bryant, exclaimed from behind her. "What's your name, miss? Where are you from? We came up from Colorado Springs a few days ago."

"I'm Olivia Plummer, from Tristan," she replied, turning her head. At his quizzical expression, she added, "Northeast of here."

"Ah. Never been there, but all the same, I wish you good luck. My name is Matthew Bryant, and this here is Ralph Metcalf. My goodness, how it inspires me to meet my first female doctor. Truly, there is a wide-open place for the gentle hand of a woman in the healing practice of medicine."

"I'm not a doctor yet, Mr. Bryant."

"And neither are we. A situation we hope soon to amend."

Nodding in agreement, she turned back when the young woman announced, "Everything is in order. You may proceed up the stairs, Miss Plummer. Make a left when you reach the top, then enter the first door on your right." Lowering her voice as she handed her the receipt, she added, "I'm sorry. They weren't expecting a woman. . . ." An anxious smile curved her lips as she finally met Olivia's gaze. "I hope you do well."

Even though Olivia's heart sank at those words, she replied, "Thank you. I'm sure everything will turn out just fine." Squaring her shoulders, she passed back through the waiting room and began up the staircase, her nervousness increasing with each riser she climbed.

She never should have come. The board hadn't been expecting a woman. Just before Donal Connally had come to fetch her for supper that ill-fated evening, Ethan had tried to tell her something about the Colorado Medical Society and females, but she hadn't listened. She'd merely assumed him guilty of bigotry when he'd flatly informed her she wouldn't pass the examination. Now, however, this young woman's response to her gender gave Olivia reason to think Ethan might have indeed possessed valuable information about the outcome of the test.

Oh, Lord, she prayed, her steps growing slower, *once again I put the fate of this afternoon in your hands. Though I cannot imagine how it will be to live without treating folks, I trust that you have the perfect plan in mind for me. I yield myself to your will.*

With those words of relinquishment ringing in her mind, she finished climbing the stairs. Several male voices could be heard speaking from behind the shiny walnut door she had been instructed to enter. As she raised her hand to knock, she closed her eyes and whispered aloud, "Thy will be done."

Three hours later, while Doctors Metcalf and Bryant fraternized with their new peers, Olivia exited the same door she had entered and trudged back down the lustrous stairs with tears in her eyes, exhausted . . . defeated.

She hadn't passed.

Some of the written questions had been difficult, but she thought she had done passably well on that portion of the examination. When it came time for the oral questions, things had gone downhill straightaway. Though approximately half of the examiners had been carefully neutral, the remainder were openly hostile toward her, challenging and ridiculing her replies.

She swallowed hard, remembering one question in particular. Even though she hadn't known the answer and had said so honestly, her inquisitor had taken the opportunity to shame her for daring to show herself . . . and wasting his time. If only she could get out the door below before the dam of tears burst.

As she strode across the foyer, she was dismayed to hear the young woman from the desk call to her. Without looking, she took another step, intent on escaping the unpleasantness of this place as quickly as possible. She hoped the woman would forgive her for pretending not to hear.

"Miss Plummer," the woman called again, "please wait. Someone is here for you."

Someone was . . . *what?*

Turning her head, Olivia was stunned to see Ethan rise from one of the padded chairs in the waiting area. Garbed in a fine black suit, he was every bit as elegantly dressed as the gentlemen upstairs . . . and so handsome that her heart hurt. Raising his eyebrows, he opened his arms as he walked toward her, his expression suffused with tenderness.

"Oh, Ethan," she cried, flying to the shelter of his strong arms. "You were right. I failed. Can . . . you . . . ever . . . forgive me?" Dissolving into tears, she wept as he comforted her. "I . . . was ready to fail . . . but I didn't know I'd feel so . . . bad . . . about it," she sobbed into his chest. "I told the Lord . . . that . . . his will be done, but those . . . men upstairs just didn't . . . like me."

"Shh, Livvie," he whispered into her hair. "It's all right. I love you, my dearest."

"How can you? I've been so . . . horrid . . . to you."

A rumbling chuckle filled her ear. "Yes, you have. But I've also seen your persistence, and how much your healing touch means to you."

"I can't do it anymore, Ethan. I have to give it up. The new law says I can be fined or sent to jail for practicing medicine without a certificate," she said, turning her face toward his. "I had no business trying to get my medical license. I'm not a doctor. Oh, why couldn't I have listened to you?"

He pressed a kiss against her forehead. "All is forgiven, my love, but I have an important question for you." Holding her at arm's length, he looked deeply into her eyes. "Do you *want* to be a doctor, Livvie?"

Crying again, she nodded. "I want to say no, Ethan, but it isn't the truth. I do want to be a doctor and practice medicine. I expect that with time, it will be easier to accept—" she swallowed—"whatever the Lord has planned for me."

One side of his mouth quirked upward. "Well, my dear,

expecting such a reply, I have taken the liberty of registering you at the University of Michigan's school of medicine. There they welcome female students, and my recommendation of your skills has apparently made them quite pleased to receive you."

At her gasp, he held up a finger. "There is, however, one catch."

Nodding, she waited for him to go on. Ethan had enrolled her in *college?* Halfway across the country? What could he tell her that was more outrageous than that?

"If you're willing, you'll begin your classes in the fall." She saw his chest rise and fall as he breathed deeply. His brown eyes searched her face. "I have entered you, however, as Olivia *Gray* . . . if that is acceptable to you."

Olivia *Gray?* After all these months of trouble, he still wanted to marry her?

"Yes," she whispered through her tears, fastening her arms around his neck. "Oh yes, Ethan, I will marry you . . . today, tomorrow, or next Thursday—whenever you say. I love you, my dearest, and I shall love you until the day I die."

Love, a husband, and now a fresh chance to use her healing touch within the confines of the law. Nothing on earth could measure up to the treasures she'd just been given. As Ethan's lips sought hers, Olivia was humbled by the immensity of God's forgiveness and generosity.

Epilogue

May 21, 1881
Dearest Romy,

I must beg your forgiveness for the many weeks that have passed since my last letter. No doubt YOU are wondering what has become of ME.

We have experienced a bit of trouble ourselves here in Tristan, and as it turns out, our deputy marshal was wanted in two states for all sorts of hideous crimes. Most sadly, he was responsible for the murder of our dressmaker. I believe I wrote you about Ella Farwell's death last autumn. What I couldn't tell you then was that we discovered evidence of foul play during her postmortem examination. He made an attempt on my life as well, but I'm still here to tell the tale. Due to the bravery of the men of this town, he is not.

My lovely friend, I have much more to tell you! (Are you safely seated?) I am not a doctor, but I, too, am now a wife. You recall Ethan Gray, the new physician of whom I had written? As I informed you, our initial and thoroughly mutual distaste for one another yielded most remarkably during the Christmas season. Then I believe I wrote you of our troubles over my determination to have a Colorado medical license at any cost. Though Ethan denies it, I fear my rebellious heart nearly cost me his love.

Two weeks ago we shared our wedding day with Marshal Briggs and Janet Winter. She once joked of us having a double wedding, but neither of us dreamed such a thing would come to pass. I shall miss them both dreadfully, for the doctor and I will be moving to Ann Arbor, Michigan, during the summer. I am to attend medical college, Romy. Can you conceive of such a thing? I cannot, and I will soon be packing.

Miracle of miracles, Ethan has found a fellow physician to take *over his position while we are away. Also, as I write this, track is being laid for a railroad spur to Tristan. Such progress—and convenience.*

If Mr. Landis is anything at all like Dr. Gray, then the Lord has been very good to us both. Do you remember how we used to pore over the Song of Solomon? I wonder if Elena is wed—and if so, what her husband is like? I know nothing of our long-lost friend, but I recently learned that Ethan has hired a Pinkerton agent to search for her. Just because he loves me, he said.

Now I must close, for my husband will be wanting his dinner soon. Tonight I believe I shall make him a kiss pudding.

Yours lovingly,

Olivia

Recipe

Kiss Pudding

Boil one quart sweet milk in custard kettle. Stir into it four heaping tablespoons sugar and four tablespoons cornstarch, dissolved in a little cold water or milk and added to the well-beaten and strained yolks of four eggs. Have the whites of eggs beaten to a stiff froth with a teacup of pulverized sugar and one teaspoon essence of vanilla. Spread on top of pudding, set in a quick oven, and brown. Take out, sprinkle with grated coconut, and set dish away in a cool place. Serve cold after three or four hours. The sweet liquor which settles to the bottom in cooling serves as a sauce. —Mrs. W. E. Baxter

—From *Buckeye Cookery and Practical Housekeeping* (Minnesota Historical Society Press, 1988). First published in 1880 by Buckeye Publishing Company.

A Note from the Author

Dear Reader,

When I proposed the Abounding Love series to Tyndale's HeartQuest team, I alluded to the fact that I am well qualified to write about rebellion, the series theme I had chosen. After all, I lived the first thirty-some-odd years of my life doing things my own way. (Anyone who knows me is saying, "She sure did!" and nodding right about now.) I lived to break rules, find loopholes, and challenge authority.

Rebellion is an ugly word. Olivia was both shocked and stung when Ethan told her she had a "rebellious streak a mile wide." She wasn't rebellious . . . was she? After all, she only wanted to continue her virtuous practice of healing people. Even if the law changed, she didn't think it was fair that *she* would have to make some changes herself or, heaven forbid, lay aside her healing touch.

Though Livvie's sin of rebellion came more from her heart attitude than her lifestyle, she finally realized she was rebelling against the Lord himself. Do we always realize this? I know I don't always follow this concept through to its rather painful conclusion, but the truth is, no matter whether we defy rules, laws, situations, parents, or authorities, the end result is the same: our opposition is ultimately against God.

I invite you to come along as I explore the theme of rebellion more deeply in *Romy's Walk* and *Elena's Song*, books 2 and 3 of the Abounding Love series. In these stories, Olivia's friends struggle with some very challenging and complex issues of their own. Next you'll meet Romy (pronounced with a short *o*), a schoolteacher in Washington Territory, whose life-threatening accident shatters her comfortable convictions and imposes upon her a lifelong handicap . . . as well as a marriage for which she hadn't bargained. And finally, you'll meet the long-lost and mysterious Elena, a life-scarred woman who has been on the run from the Lord for years.

Amidst their struggles, however—just as amidst our own— let us remember that even though we may have to suffer the consequences of our rebellion, there is no sin beyond forgiveness, and that our Lord is indeed "abounding in love and forgiving sin and rebellion" (Numbers 14:18, NIV).

Your sister in this journey of life and faith,
Peggy Stoks

About the Author

Peggy Stoks lives in Minnesota with her husband and three daughters. She has been a registered nurse for nearly twenty years but recently resigned her hospital nursing position to be a stay-at-home wife and mom, and to cope with the logistical challenges of getting her daughters to their various school, church, and athletic activities. A homebody at heart, she loves to cook and bake, and especially enjoys making jams and jellies when the fruits are in season. Peggy also enjoys reading, gardening, swimming, tackling home-improvement and decorating projects, and getting outdoors to walk through the nearby woods as often as she can. She has published two novels as well as numerous magazine articles in the general market. *Olivia's Touch* is her first full-length HeartQuest novel. Her novellas appear in the HeartQuest anthologies *A Victorian Christmas Cottage, A Victorian Christmas Quilt, A Victorian Christmas Tea,* and *Reunited.* Look for Peggy's newest novella, "Wishful Thinking," in *A Prairie Christmas,* coming in time for Christmas 2000.

Peggy welcomes letters written to her at P.O. Box 333, Circle Pines, MN 55014.

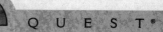

Current HeartQuest Releases

- *A Bouquet of Love*, Ginny Aiken, Ranee McCollum, Jeri Odell, and Debra White Smith
- *Dream Vacation*, Ginny Aiken, Jeri Odell, and Elizabeth White
- *Faith*, Lori Copeland
- *Finders Keepers*, Catherine Palmer
- *Freedom's Promise*, Dianna Crawford
- *Hope*, Lori Copeland
- *June*, Lori Copeland
- *Magnolia*, Ginny Aiken
- *Olivia's Touch*, Peggy Stoks
- *Prairie Fire*, Catherine Palmer
- *Prairie Rose*, Catherine Palmer
- *Prairie Storm*, Catherine Palmer
- *Reunited*, Judy Baer, Jeri Odell, Jan Duffy, and Peggy Stoks
- *The Treasure of Timbuktu*, Catherine Palmer
- *The Treasure of Zanzibar*, Catherine Palmer
- *A Victorian Christmas Cottage*, Catherine Palmer, Debra White Smith, Jeri Odell, and Peggy Stoks
- *A Victorian Christmas Quilt*, Catherine Palmer, Debra White Smith, Ginny Aiken, and Peggy Stoks
- *A Victorian Christmas Tea*, Catherine Palmer, Dianna Crawford, Peggy Stoks, and Katherine Chute
- *With This Ring*, Lori Copeland, Dianna Crawford, Ginny Aiken, and Catherine Palmer

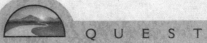

Coming Soon

- *Freedom's Hope*, Dianna Crawford—Summer 2000
- *Awakening Mercy*, Angela Benson—Summer 2000
- *Lark*, Ginny Aiken—Fall 2000

- *A Prairie Christmas*, Catherine Palmer, Peggy Stoks, and Elizabeth White—Fall 2000
- *Glory*, Lori Copeland—Fall 2000

Other Great Tyndale House Fiction

- *As Sure As the Dawn*, Francine Rivers
- *Ashes and Lace*, B. J. Hoff
- *The Atonement Child*, Francine Rivers
- *The Captive Voice*, B. J. Hoff
- *Cloth of Heaven*, B. J. Hoff
- *Dark River Legacy*, B. J. Hoff
- *An Echo in the Darkness*, Francine Rivers
- *The Embers of Hope*, Sally Laity & Dianna Crawford
- *The Fires of Freedom*, Sally Laity & Dianna Crawford
- *The Gathering Dawn*, Sally Laity & Dianna Crawford
- *Home Fires Burning*, Penelope J. Stokes
- *Jewels for a Crown*, Lawana Blackwell
- *The Last Sin Eater*, Francine Rivers
- *Leota's Garden*, Francine Rivers
- *Like a River Glorious*, Lawana Blackwell
- *Measures of Grace*, Lawana Blackwell
- *Remembering You*, Penelope J. Stokes
- *Song of a Soul*, Lawana Blackwell
- *Storm at Daybreak*, B. J. Hoff
- *The Scarlet Thread*, Francine Rivers
- *The Tangled Web*, B. J. Hoff
- *The Tempering Blaze*, Sally Laity & Dianna Crawford
- *Till We Meet Again*, Penelope J. Stokes
- *The Torch of Triumph*, Sally Laity & Dianna Crawford
- *Unveiled*, Francine Rivers
- *A Voice in the Wind*, Francine Rivers
- *Vow of Silence*, B. J. Hoff

HeartQuest Books by Peggy Stoks

Wishful Thinking—Betsy Wilcox's heart has betrayed her. She believes herself to be long past the fluttering hearts that beset the very young. But her new neighbor, an exuberant and winsome widower, makes her feel like a girl again. Only when she faces the threat of losing him forever does Betsy realize the depth of her love for this dear, godly man. This novella by Peggy Stoks appears in the anthology *A Prairie Christmas* (Available Fall 2000).

The Beauty of the Season—A determined suitor risks everything to help a vulnerable young woman overcome her wounded past. This novella by Peggy Stoks appears in the anthology *A Victorian Christmas Cottage*.

The Sound of the Water—A sports hero, intent on serving God and making things right with his first love, returns to his hometown and the girl he left behind. But will Holly's disillusionment with God forever be a barrier between them? This novella by Peggy Stoks appears in the anthology *Reunited*.

Crosses and Losses—On Christmas Eve in snowy St. Paul, Minnesota, a cherished Crosses and Losses quilt opens the door of healing and love for a grieving young couple. This novella by Peggy Stoks appears in the anthology *A Victorian Christmas Quilt*.

Tea for Marie—In rural Minnesota, love springs unexpectedly from the ashes of disaster. This novella by Peggy Stoks appears in the anthology *A Victorian Christmas Tea*.